Happy reading
Barb.

Love Wendy
xx

Looking Towards the Tamar
More Tales of Devonshire Life

Also by Ted Sherrell:

Looking Towards the Tamar

More Tales of Devonshire Life

Ted Sherrell

UNITED WRITERS
Cornwall

UNITED WRITERS PUBLICATIONS LTD
Ailsa, Castle Gate, Penzance, Cornwall.

British Library Cataloguing in Publication Data:
A catalogue record for this book is
available from the British Library.

ISBN 9781852001513

Printed in Great Britain by
United Writers Publications Ltd
Cornwall.

To Ann,
my lovely, loyal and wise wife
and
to my vibrant, generous and ever supportive family.

Contents

I

Looking Towards the Tamar

The old Gent sat alone, feeling the warm May sunshine on his face; how many times he had perched in this spot during his 89 years he knew not – it was hundreds, possibly even thousands. And he never tired of it, even though so much had changed – and, generally, for the worse. There were still craft on the Tamar, mind you – many; for this part of the river had become a popular spot for leisure activities – folk 'messing about in boats'. They were mainly yachts, varying greatly in size – some large, sophisticated and clearly expensive; also, though, there were motor cruisers and a few speed boats, the roar of which, at full throttle, could be heard inland on both the Cornish side and on the verdant terrain of his own beloved Devon. He had no great problem with such craft dominating the river – it brought life to its waters, and some benefits to the local economy; yet he could not help but pine for the old days, those when he was a boy – indeed, a young man as well.

In those days the river was a commercial highway supplying the southern part of West Devon – especially the Peninsula – with so much of the raw material vital to a burgeoning horticultural industry, as well as other things necessary to the everyday well being of the three thousand, or so, who lived on the hilly terrain which lay between the Tamar and the Tavy. Probably the golden era of such incessant commerce lay before he was born – before the coming of the railways in the early part of the twentieth century. Much produce, though, travelled the river right up until the 1940s.

Indeed, he could remember as a lad – and as a young man, before being called up for army service – going with his mother on the steamer to Plymouth, usually of a Saturday, when they took produce grown on their small-holding to sell in Devonport Market. That resilient lady had continued to do so right up until the time when the market was no more, obliterated, like so much of the city, by the Luftwaffe. They could be eventful journeys those, down the Tamar, under the Brunel Railway Bridge, and then past part of the massive sprawl – and the array of mighty warships – of the biggest dockyard in Europe. For the steamer ran in virtually all weathers, only really severe gales bringing cancellation of the service; he had been sea-sick a few times on days when the river was in ferment, though not often enough to deter him from the journeys; his Mother, on the other hand, was never sick, having the constitution and 'sea legs' of a master mariner.

Mind you, it was not only the turbulent waters which could make him feel queasy – the vile smell from the barges laden with 'dock dung' did likewise. These craft carried their malodorous cargo from the docks of Plymouth to the quays of West Devon and East Cornwall – a slurry-like substance dredged from the river bed to keep the passage clear for large craft, merchant and military. Once unloaded, horse drawn carts and wagons would transport it, almost always uphill to the market gardens of the Tamar Valley where it was spread, by hand, over the land. Despite its odour and disgusting appearance, it had two qualities – it was cheap and it fed the demanding, ever hungry soil which needed regular sustenance if it was to produce the manifold range of fruit, flowers and vegetables that since the nineteenth century days of tin, copper and arsenic mining, had become the principal industry on both sides of the river. Back breaking work it was, too, spreading the glutinous mixture; but then, wresting a living from the hilly, often very steep land of the valley was constantly tough and unforgiving. Men and women did it, though, year in, year out during a large part of his youth and early adulthood – an era lived under the dark shadows cast by the depression.

From those often stony and shallow soiled acres came forth quite magnificent crops which matured in a reasonably constant sequence from March to October. Daffodils were the first, usually to be found on the more sheltered, south-facing gardens from early March, and going on until the harvesting of the 'double white', propagated in the valley – in early May. During that time the valley would be ablaze with colour – mainly yellows of different hue, and white, glorious to see, fragrant to the nose – yet, to the grower, not a welcome sight; for it meant that flowers were blooming at such a pace that pickers could not keep up; thus a large part of a valuable crop would be lost. This, usually, was the product of a warm spring, so growers liked to see a March and April of, at best, average temperatures, with regular showers to encourage steady growth.

'The Yellow Peril', as his father always called daffodils, would give way to the digging of early potatoes, usually grown in the steep ground running down towards the two rivers – thus sheltered from cold winds from the north; the problem, though, was that most of the harvesting, indeed, of the planting, also, had to be done by hand – hard, exacting work, brutal to both back and hand. So much of it, though – so much of all the planting and harvesting of many of their crops – was done by women. A large number of the men living in the area worked full time upon the land, as either owner or hired hand, whilst their wives, mothers, sisters, daughters would generally work part time and would be known – why, he did not know – as 'strappers'. They would not be required during the cold, wet winter months, but for nine months of the year they gave of their labour either as much, or as little as they wished; for sure, it was their harvest time as well, the chance to augment family incomes and put by money for Christmas and the 'rainy days'.

An unstated agreement existed between grower and worker, each interdependent on the other, all with a common purpose. Thus the community spirit was high and mutual respect flourished, as did tolerance and understanding in a way which had

11

ceased to exist in the modern age – or so the old man felt. No, it was all different now, he mused, feeling the awakening of a south west breeze upon his face.

All now was silence, save for the sound of an outboard motor on the river, or that of a passing car. Back then, though, throughout the valley – especially in the summer when the soft fruit was picked – there would be the low murmur of chatter amongst the pickers interspersed with peals of laughter, or the odd shout or call; and all around would be life, with some folk kneeling plucking strawberries, others standing gathering raspberries, black and redcurrants, or – having drawn the 'short straw' – trying to avoid the savage spikes to pick off succulent gooseberries. And the amounts gathered were awesome, keeping busy – during the 15 to 20 years following the Second World War – a fleet of vans, tractors and trailers, even horses and carts, transporting the fruit, most hours of long working days, to the local railway station to be ferried around the country. Some years, when the June sun shone too much and too warmly, the fruit – especially the copious strawberry acreage – would ripen faster than human fingers could pluck them from the plant, a situation which did not need to be articulated, as a pungent, somewhat sickly sweet aroma would permeate the air. He had not experienced such an odour for over forty years, but he could recall it clearly as he sat there in the sunshine.

Sadly it was a story with an unhappy ending, it all ceasing with vicious rapidity; for in the middle sixties, the never to be forgotten – and, by many, never to be forgiven – Dr Beeching, carrying out the wishes of a blinkered Government, had wielded his notorious 'axe' and chopped off the railway line which led north from the Peninsula to the great cities of Britain. The bulk of the horticultural industry of the Tamar Valley, which had sustained thousands of folk in West Devon and East Cornwall for three or four generations, came to an end within just a handful of years, the means of transporting the valuable, but perishable crops in bulk, denied to the growers.

Some sold up altogether and moved south to Plymouth or into the village, or north to Tavistock – a few out of the area altogether

– their houses and holdings being bought, in the majority of cases by folk from outside the district to whom the attraction was the beauty of the valley, the river and the opportunity to 'mess about in boats' to their hearts' content. He, though, had not sold out – he had been born on the small-holding, as had his father before him, and had no intention of selling – at least not until bad health, or old age, made him. And he well knew that even if he had wished to sell, he would not have been allowed – his Lorna would have seen to that. She also had been born on the Peninsula and that was where she intended to stay.

They had been fortunate to a degree in that their two children, Martin and Alice, had already left home to pursue their lives before the collapse of the industry, making their commitments, financially, fewer and lighter. So they had soldiered on, with he continuing to work his holding part-time; growing crops of fruit, vegetables and potatoes which he knew he could sell locally, whilst renting out over half of their land to a nearby farmer who turned it to grass and ran livestock on it. Also, he had managed to obtain a job with the local Parish Council as part time Groundsman, and General Caretaker of the local football and cricket pitches, and children's play area. It amounted to roughly two days a week, was steady, regular money and had even carried a small pension. Lorna, meanwhile, a woman of relentless energy, played her part by getting the post of Secretary to the local primary school – a dozen hours a week, and most of the school holidays off. This way they had lived their lives without any real worries in terms of finance, and still resided in the house where lay the roots of his family for so long.

All about them had been changing; of course, they were aware of that – but they ignored it as best they could. It was then, though, that their forays to this lovely eyrie overlooking the Tamar became ever more frequent. For there they felt peace, and the sense of eternity and perpetuity; Yes, the craft had changed and the activities out there on the water, but the river itself was unchanging as it meandered its stately and ever wider way towards Plymouth Sound and the open sea; and the countryside bordering it, whilst lacking the market gardens of old – thus, much of the colour – and the bustle of their cultivation, were still mercifully free of houses. The only buildings, save for that of the occasional farm house, being ruined mine stacks and pump-houses, relics of an even more distant age. How long this would remain the situation was impossible to say, but the short term, at least, was taken care of by the designation by officials of rare wisdom that the Tamar Valley be classed as an area of outstanding natural beauty – a guarantee that little development would be allowed there until such a time when, cynicism suggested, the pursuit of profit would sweep aside the integrity of the Valley's official status. His beloved Lorna had lived just long enough to have seen the preservation order put into place, she dying just three months later from a severe stroke. The suddenness of it shocked him immensely, whilst her loss had created a void in his life which would never be filled. He was close to Martin and Alice, and to their families, the four grandchildren being of great comfort to him. But he was, nonetheless, lonely without his lovely Lorna, his lifetime partner, and thought of her constantly, never more intensely than when he sat on this seat gazing south towards their river.

Here, though, it was more than just thinking of Lorna – no, here he felt close to her; he could feel her sitting there beside him, imagine her hand in his; he could feel some comfort, could relive to some extent the fifty plus years they spent together – rich, fulfilling times.

The sun felt so warm on his face, the breeze almost like a caress of his thinning hair; he felt so peaceful, the river down there in front of him, his dear Lorna by his side – life felt good, worthwhile, fulfilling. He felt a hand on his shoulder; he must have dozed off – Lorna was trying to awaken him. His eyes flickered in the bright sunshine, then opened wide; he looked up at the lady gazing down upon him – a pretty face, but not Lorna's. A puzzled expression flitted across his face – an unspoken question which was answered by the nurse who stood over him. "It's me, Mr Benson – Lisa. You know me, don't you? I help to take care of you." He slowly nodded his head, then a few seconds later, confirmed he did know her.

"I'm sorry, Lisa – of course – of course it's you; yes, of course, I know who you are now. It's just that clearly I've been dozing; I thought I was sitting on our favourite place, up above the Tamar gazing down upon it – with Lorna beside me. I dreamt we were holding hands – we always held hands, you know, when we sat there; always."

"I'm sure you did, Mr Benson – and I think it's lovely that you did; it's so romantic and gives me such a warm feeling. And when you doze off, you nearly always dream you and Lorna are up there on that seat, gazing down on the river; when I saw the expression on your face just now, I thought that you were there. I'm only sorry I had to wake you, but it's time to take you in now – it's teatime; and it's pasties tonight, cook's home-made ones too. I know you like those."

"Yes – yes, she makes a good pasty. My Lorna did, you know – she made a wonderful one, full of meat, potato, onions and turnip; my Mother as well – she made a lovely pasty."

"I know, you've told me before. Anyway, it's time to go in; I'll bring you out here again tomorrow if the weather's nice – you'll enjoy that, won't you?"

As the old man nodded his agreement, the nurse grasped the handles of the wheelchair, turned him around from his panoramic view of Dartmoor, and pushed him slowly towards the large building looming before them, then, once inside, towards the residents' dining room of the Moorland Nursing and Residential Home, his abode for the past two years.

II
The Rat

Jimmy Jordan was adamant, his Jack Russell, Maisie, had the sweetest of natures – except on those quite frequent occasions when she was chasing, and catching, rats. The only reason she had bitten the lad was because he had tried to pet her whilst she was eating the succulent heap of Kennomeat that filled her bowl.

"She would have thought he was after her dinner – naturally enough. I mean, Phil, you'd be none too happy if somebody came petting you when you were in the middle of your grub, would you?" stated he in somewhat aggrieved tones.

PC Phil Martin took the words at face value; "Well, I reckon it would depend on who was doing the petting," he replied in his dry, understated way. "And I have to say that even if I wasn't keen, I'd not bite their hand."

"Well, no, 'course you wouldn't. But you're human – she's a dog, and biting folk is the only way she can defend herself, and protect that which she thinks is hers. Anyway, the boy shouldn't have been there – he was trespassing. I never gave him permission to come into my garden. Yes – trespassing, that's what he was doing. I could have him for that – have him in court."

The village constable shrugged his shoulders – "Well, possibly I suppose. But he was only there because he had kicked his football over the hedge into your garden, so he had to come and retrieve it. There was little else he could have done."

"There was something else he could have done," rasped the elderly widower. "He, and those other little devils he was playing with, could have played on the football pitch – that's what it's for. And it's only half a mile away – less than that, probably. No, they can't be bothered – too idle to walk just a little distance. So instead they play in the road and cause nothing but aggravation to law abiding folk like me. My Maisie was eating her dinner outside my front door as she always did in good weather – always has, ever since she was a pup, which is a long time ago now; she was minding her own business, but he wasn't – he came in to collect his football, without permission. That's bad enough, but then he also starts to interfere with my dog – so she bit him; it's totally his own fault."

"Come on Jimmy – he's a ten year old lad who just wanted to make friends with your dog – but clearly your Maisie didn't want to make friends with him. To be fair, she was eating and he was trespassing in that he came onto your property without permission, but the law could still class your dog as being dangerous even though she was on her owner's property. Whatever, his mother wants to prosecute so my hands are tied, I'm afraid."

"She's the woman who runs the Post Office Stores, isn't she?"

"Yes, that's right – Mrs Conway."

"Only been here a dog's watch – no more than twelve months," snorted Jordan. "I don't like her – not in the slightest; I only ever go in there once a week to collect my pension. For shopping I use my bus pass and go to Tavistock – a lot cheaper it is, too."

"Yes, yes, I don't doubt it is," agreed the constable. "Anyway, she wants to take you to court, so I've got to interview you formally and get a statement; then I've got to forward it to the Crown Prosecution Service Officers in Plymouth – and they'll make a decision as to whether or not they take it any further."

"Do you think they will?" came the question, the tone betraying considerable anxiety – even alarm. Jimmy Jordan was not used to being in trouble with the law.

The policeman's expression was one of dismay; "I fear they will, Jimmy – it's rare they do not proceed with cases such as this.

Public opinion tends to demand that owners of dogs that bite are brought to court."

"Well, what will happen then – what will happen to my Maisie?" The question was asked in a tone of urgency, and no small measure of fear. Widowed for five years, with no offspring, to the elderly man his eight year old terrier was his only family.

"Well, if the magistrates find against you, you'll probably be fined and, regarding Maisie, they can order she be muzzled and kept on a lead when out and about – and that will include your own garden. The worst that they can order is that she be put down . . ."

"Put Down," cried the elderly man. "Put Down, just for giving the lad a bit of a nip – and that's all it was. It scarcely broke the skin."

"Come on, Jimmy, it was a fair bit more than a nip – the boy had to have ten stitches in his hand. Still," added he, hastily, "it's unlikely they'll order she be put down, seeing as it's a first reported attack." He regretted having mentioned the unlikely scenario that the destruction of the dog could be ordered, as it had convulsed the features of the old gent into an expression little short of terror. "But, technically, they could – that's all I'm saying." The policeman paused, but seeing the worry etched upon the face of a man whom he liked, and had done for several years, he continued to pour balm on the wounds. "It's very, very unlikely that such a thing will be ordered. I mean, not only was it the first time Maisie has been in any trouble, it's also that it took place on your property, and the boy was there without your permission. As I said, you'll probably be fined – a smallish one – and be ordered to keep the dog under control. Nothing to worry about, Jimmy – absolutely nothing at all."

"That's easy for you to say, boy – you'll find, as you get older, you'll worry more, and a lot more, too; and I've nobody to share it with now that I've lost my Emma. We shared everything, we did. How I miss her – every hour of every day, I do."

"Yes, yes, I'm sure you do," replied the constable in a most sympathetic tone. Silence reigned for a few seconds as he made some notes on his pad; he glanced up at the somewhat distressed pensioner – "Tell you what I'll do Jimmy, I'll go round to the Post Office and have a chat with the boy's mother and see if she would be willing to drop the charges. If she did so, then it's highly unlikely the CPS will proceed to prosecute it; you would hear no more about it. All that would happen is that the attack would be put in the records in case Maisie did it again."

Jordan's alarmed expression eased a touch. "Would you do that, boy – would you really? It would be such a weight off my mind if the charge was to be dropped. I'd appreciate it more than I can say."

"You're more than welcome, Jimmy. I'm sure it was an isolated incident and, anyway, the lad was certainly partly to blame."

"Yes, yes, he was. Maisie is as good as gold; it's just that her reflexes are so fast, even though she's knocking on a bit now. Something happens to surprise her, and she pounces right away. That's why she's such a good ratter; in fact, she's more than just good – she's the best I've ever seen – perhaps the best ever known in this parish. As you may know, I spend a lot of time down at the farms close to the Tamar; get an awful lot of rats, they do, as always happens if you live close to a river. It's a constant problem for the farmers – so much so, in fact, that they pay me for every rat Maisie catches; that keeps me in beer, boy. She's got a nose like no other dog I've ever known – and I've known a brave few; and once she scents one, it's rare they ever escape from her. Marvellous dog, boy, marvellous; she's the best friend I've got. I can't let anything happen to her – it would break my heart. So if you could talk this lady into forgetting about the bite to her lad's hand, I'll be in your debt forever."

"Well, as I said just now, I'll do what I can, Jimmy. I can't promise, obviously, but I can at least try. And I'll do it now – a case of striking whilst the iron's hot." The policeman moved away towards the road and his car. "When I've got some news, you'll be the first to hear it," said he, as a parting comment aimed in the direction of the stressed older man. Within a few seconds PC Martin was driving off in the direction of the village – and the Post Office.

Jimmy Jordan had not expected to see the police officer again that day; he surmised that even if he was able to have a word with the post mistress, his duties would probably stop him returning for a day or two. He was wrong; for in less than half an hour, Phil Martin was walking down his path again, just as the cottager was coming around the corner of the house from the back garden, having just picked a few ripe tomatoes from his small greenhouse. There was little need for the elderly gent to ask how the interview with Mrs Conway had been – the glum expression on the officer's face said it all.

"She's going ahead with it, isn't she, boy – the prosecution, that is. It's obvious to me, the way you're looking."

The policeman nodded. "I'm afraid so, Jimmy. I tried to get her to change her mind, but with no joy. Unfortunately, she seems to be the sort of woman who, once she makes her mind up, sticks with it come hell or high water. She says she feels that the safety of children in the village is at stake, and that she sees the prosecution as a way of ensuring that safety."

"That's nonsense – Maisie isn't a threat to kids, or to anybody else for that manner. As I said to you earlier, she only bit the lad because she thought he was after her dinner." He spoke the words in anguished tones, tears of stress and futility appearing about his eyes – his dear little canine friend and companion was being threatened and he did not know how he could protect her.

"Well, I understand what you're saying, Jimmy, and I've got much sympathy with you as I'm sure you're aware. But if she wants to prosecute, then clearly there's nothing I can do about it. Mind you, it could be that the CPS might not proceed with it, but I'm afraid it's unlikely. You'll have to prepare yourself for a court appearance I'm afraid. I expect you'll hear from the court within the next week or so regarding when you have to appear and such like. In the meantime, I would strongly advise you to get hold a of a solicitor; it'll cost you a few bob, of course, but it could be money well invested. You need somebody speaking for you – and Maisie – in court, a professional who knows the loopholes. Julia Wallace, in Tavistock, is very good. I'll give you her phone number." He reached into an inside pocket of his tunic, produced a small notebook, consulted it, then wrote down a name and number on his notepad; ripping it off, he handed it to the downcast dog owner. "There's her name and number, Jimmy – phone her, the sooner the better. I reckon she'll be able to help you. Promise me you'll do that."

There was a tone of concerned insistence in the officer's voice, which was typical of the man. A Devon man born and bred, he had been stationed in the parish for almost ten years, and had considerable affection for it and for many of the folk that lived there; also, he was a man with a strong sense of justice, and in this instance felt that Jimmy Jordan was in danger of suffering the opposite, with his best friend, Maisie, being on the wrong end of a law which could at times be draconian.

The old fellow nodded – "Yes, all right Phil – I'll do what you suggest; and thank you for your help and concern, it's more appreciated than you may realise."

"Welcome, Jimmy," replied the policeman. With that, he turned, walked down the garden path to his car, waved, got in, and drove off towards the village police station – and his lunch.

Jordan slumped down onto the somewhat rickety seat just outside the front door, then called his faithful friend over to him and gently stroked her as he sat contemplating the future. To say his spirits were low would be an understatement – he felt despairing; he could see no happy ending to the situation he was in. Even if the Magistrates were lenient, his Maisie would cease to enjoy the freedom of action and movement she had enjoyed all her life; the thought of her perpetually muzzled, or on a lead – or both – was nightmarish to him. What sort of life would that be for a creature that had generally been free to roam as she wished as long as her owner was nearby. It didn't bear thinking about. Curse the woman – it was all her fault; she was making a drama out of a trivial incident. He was sorry the lad had been bitten, and he had no problem in apologising for it, even though it was the boy's own fault, he being somewhere – namely on private property – where he had no right to be. But to pursue it through the courts was an act of vindictiveness which was totally excessive. He had not liked her, right from the first day she had come to the village and taken over the Post Office, feeling always that she had a most patronising manner towards good Devonshire folk like himself. Indeed, he had on several occasions thought about switching to Tavistock Post Office regarding collection of his pension, even though it meant he would have to take the bus the six miles to the town every week to collect it. But then, he mused to himself, he already went to the Market Town at least once a week to buy the bulk of his provisions; and also it wouldn't cost him anything, his bus pass would see to that.

Yes, that's what he would do – and take the necessary action, urgently. He had to go to the Post Office to collect his money the following day, so whilst there he would collect the necessary form regarding transferring his pension to Tavistock. He knew a couple of people who had done this in recent months – largely because they didn't like the Post Mistress – and, as far as he was aware, it had only taken a couple of weeks for the transfer to be activated. So, with a bit of luck, the following day would be one of the last in which he had to stand in front of, in his eyes, the despicable Mrs Conway, and receive from her hands the rather meagre pension for which he had worked for over fifty years.

The thought cheered him a little; and within ten minutes an idea came to him which lifted his spirits further. He continued to sit there in his front garden, allowing the idea to circulate within his head. The more he contemplated it, the more he realised that it was by no means guaranteed that it would work; there was, though, no real reason why it would not. For sure, it was worth a go – certainly, he had nothing to lose and so much to gain.

A born worrier, he had spent most of his life worried about something or other – often matters of supreme triviality – and as he got older, he became ever worse. If his Emma was still alive, he would not be as bad, for she had always had the ability to be able to cajole him into a positive frame of mind; and when that did not work then she would activate the core of toughness that lay within her and say, in a voice which brooked no dissent, "Don't be so silly, Jimmy – snap out of it. There is absolutely nothing to worry about" – or words to that effect; it was rare that her influence failed to be effective. As it was, despite PC Martin's confident assertion that there was no way his Maisie would be put down, he still feared the worse. There was, after all, no way of knowing just how 'black' a prosecutor would paint his little dog; he or she could make Maisie sound like the 'Hound of the Baskervilles' – truly a savage brute that attacked young children. No, he had to do something to prevent it all coming to court – something to try to persuade the vengeance seeking Mrs Conway to drop the charges.

He looked down at his little canine friend lying patiently at his feet. He stroked her head gently, then spoke to her as he would a person. "I've got to go out in a minute, Maisie; I've things to do – important things. I don't know if they'll work, but I've got to try. I can't risk losing you, maid, can I? Something has to be done – and I'm going to do it. But this time you can't come with me – sorry about that. So I'll put you in the kitchen, and give you a nice bone I got from the butcher's yesterday." With that he got to his feet in sprightly fashion – as did Maisie – and walked in through the front doorway and through to the kitchen. He took the promised bone from the fridge, gave it to his doting friend in her bed in the corner of the room, patted her, said, "I shouldn't be too long, maid, I hope," locked the back door, then went out the front, locking that behind him. He went around the side of the house to his shed in the corner, rummaged around in it for a couple of minutes, found what he wanted, then carrying it in somewhat furtive fashion, went out of his front gate and set off in the direction of the Tamar, which lay about a mile away down a long, unrelenting hill.

The following morning found Jimmy, with Maisie on a lead, walking quite briskly towards the middle of the village heading for the Post Office to collect his pension. On arriving, he saw that there was quite a queue for the Post Office counter, whilst the grocery section was also busy – Mrs Conway had a good business, and one she ran herself, there being, for reasons unknown, no Mr Conway. She did most of the Post Office work herself, and employed a couple of local ladies to staff the shop side, although both of these were able to undertake the often quite complicated work involved with the postal side of things if their

Employer was not available. That did not apply this day, however, the highly efficient owner dispensing stamps, postal orders, pensions and performing all the manifold and myriad tasks which came the way of a village post mistress. A woman of some forty years, she was quite good looking but there was somehow, in Jimmy's eyes, a lack of charm and grace about her which, in his view, meant she was not a 'lady' – unlike his Emma who had very much been one.

Jimmy took his place in the queue, with Maisie sitting quietly at his feet, and waited patiently for his turn at the counter. There were still some five people in front of him when the terror began – a happening heralded by a piercing scream. It came from Mrs Roberts, a youngish, rather plump lady – wife of the local butcher – who had no sooner picked up her family allowance, than she had felt something running over her foot, had looked down and seen a rat – a very large member of the species – scurrying away towards the greengrocery section. Her screams became stereophonic as other female customers espied the rodent, and their shrill cries were augmented by the shouts of a couple of the male customers who, whilst trying not to look too alarmed, were nonetheless beating a hasty retreat towards the door.

Jimmy Jordan was quick to react; he had with him an expert in vermin control, so he rapidly bent down, let a quivering Maisie off her lead, shouted a sharp "Get him, maid!" and saw the little dog hurtle across the floor in the direction of the rat which was clearly, but unsuccessfully, seeking an avenue of escape. Once Maisie was on its trail, there would assuredly be no way out for the hapless beast. Within seconds, the Jack Russell's strong jaws had locked themselves around it, and it was being squeezed and shaken to a rapid death. Jimmy ran across to his brown and white warrior, grabbed her collar and led her outside.

"Well done, maid – that showed them, didn't it, that showed them what you can do." He looked closely at the rat still clamped within the little dog's jaws; clearly it was dead. "Let go, Maisie," said he, gently. "He's well and truly done for. You've done a marvellous job." With that he leant over and slowly, but firmly, prised the creature from Maisie's uncompromising jaws. He reached into his pocket for a bag in which to put the corpse but, somewhat to his surprise, couldn't find one. There was, though, a litter-bin just to the right of the door to the shop, so he walked over to it, pulled a piece of newspaper from it, wrapped up the dead beast, and tossed it in to await collection by the bin men the following day. Re-attaching the heroine of the hour to her lead, he went back into the Post Office to collect his pension.

He was greeted with warmth and enthusiasm by those customers who had not made good their escape at the time of the 'incident', and by the two ladies who were behind the grocery counters. The customers remaining in the Post Office queue insisted that Jimmy went to the head of it – "The very least we can do, Mr Jordan," said Mrs Barnard, the vicar's wife. "You, and your lovely little dog, have saved the day. I shudder to think what would have happened if you'd not been here. It doesn't bear thinking about – such horrible things, rats."

"Thank you, Mrs Barnard," said he. "She's a marvellous dog, Maisie; I've had dogs all my life, but I've never had one – or seen one for that matter – that was in her league when it comes to catching rats." As he said the words, he moved to the grill and confronted a somewhat sheepish looking post mistress. Maisie, meantime, on the end of her longish lead, receiving pats and praise from all around.

"I expect it's your pension you've come for, Mr Jordan, is that right?" Her tone was as brisk as ever, but there was a softness to it which was not customary – and, as she spoke, she avoided looking directly at him. This was one highly embarrassed woman, Jimmy mused to himself – a factor which caused him immense satisfaction. He pulled his pension book from his pocket, pushed it beneath the grill and within thirty seconds was receiving the amount due to him.

"Thank you, Mrs Conway," said he in his ever courteous way.

"You're welcome, Mr Jordan," came the reply, the tone again soft – almost friendly. Still she did not look him in the eye, but did wish him a polite "Good morning" – which was reciprocated.

Praise for his Maisie still ringing in his ears, he left the premises and proceeded homewards, a spring in his step once more. It had been, he felt, a good morning's work – especially by his Jack Russell. "I think you've earned a special treat, maid," he said cheerily to his companion as they entered the kitchen. With that, he went to the fridge, pulled out a large pork pie, cut it in half, put one part on a plate for himself, and, after cutting it into smallish pieces, the other portion into Maisie's feed bowl. It being very much to her taste, it quickly disappeared.

Jimmy spent the afternoon, Maisie at his feet, sitting outside in the warm sunshine, firstly reading the paper, then dozing. His reverie was broken by the sound of a car door shutting. He glanced at his watch and saw, to his surprise, that it was almost six o'clock. He also espied the tall figure of PC Martin strolling down the path towards him.

"Afternoon, Jimmy," said the constable in his affable fashion. "Sorry to wake you up – it looked like you were asleep when I came through the gate."

"No – no – no," he retorted, hastily. "I was only resting my eyes a bit – it's lovely here in the sunshine, although it'll soon dip now."

"Well, Jimmy, you'll be glad I've awoken you when you hear the news I've got."

"Oh, what's that boy? The way you put it, it sounds like it could be good news." He tried to keep his tone level and normal as he said the words, but in reality was seized by a nervous apprehension, one which made him mentally offer a prayer to God that the news the policeman was about to give, was that which he desired so desperately.

"It is good news – the best. I had a phone call from Mrs Conway at the Post Office this afternoon; she asked me to call as soon as I was able, which was about an hour ago – and I've just come from there now. It seems that your Maisie saved the day this morning – caught and killed a rat of all things in the Post Office. Not that Mrs Conway told me – it was the ladies who work there; they told me as soon as I walked into the place. It would appear that she's a heroine in their eyes."

"But obviously not in Mrs Conway's eyes," retorted the dog

owner, worry once more apparent in his tone. "I thought she might at least be appreciative of what the little dog did. I mean that rat terrified the people in the shop. More than that, she could have been reported to the public health people – after all, it's a poor show having rats run around a food store."

"Quite right, Jimmy – and I'm sure that in her way, she is grateful; she's not, though, the sort of woman who'll be seen to climb down at all. What she has done, however, is to withdraw all charges regarding Maisie biting her lad. So you'll hear no more about it. Maisie, hopefully, will have many more good ratting years ahead of her."

"Yes – yes, I hope so. She loves it." He glanced at the policeman and smiled broadly. "Thanks, Phil – it's the best news I've had in years. I'm deeply grateful to you – so's Maisie, of course, although I don't suppose she knows it."

PC Martin shook his head. "You've nothing to thank me for, Jimmy. It was Maisie's fearless killing of the rat that did the trick," he said grinning broadly. "There was no way that even Mrs Conway, who I wouldn't judge to be a particularly forgiving woman, could proceed with the prosecution of the dog that had averted total panic in her store, and kept the environmental health officer at bay as well – and she knew it, although there is little chance she would ever admit as much."

"No, I suppose not. But you've been on my side all the way through this, boy, and I appreciate it. I mean, you even gave me the phone number and address of a solicitor. I'll not forget it."

"Well, it's over and done with now. Anyway, Jimmy, I'm away home for my tea – it's been a long day, one way and another." He half turned to go on his way, but stopped and looked again in the direction of Jordan. "By the way, have you still got a ferret?"

The older man looked surprised. "Well – yes; Tiger – had him for years, as you know. He's in his run in the back garden. Why?"

"It's just that I've not seen you with him for a while. Have you taken him out today?" The question was asked, Jimmy felt, as one from a police officer, rather than somebody just interested.

"No – I've not taken him out for two or three weeks. I usually only take him when I'm going rabbiting, and I've not done that since last month. I might go out next week, though – Farmer Collins down at Crossways tells me that he's having problems with them eating his kale just as it's beginning to sprout, so he wants me to see if I can catch a few."

PC Martin's face registered surprise. "Well, that's odd then, Jimmy; 'cause a bit earlier, when I was at the Post Office, I saw a well known bag peeping out from under a stand holding greetings cards. Somebody had dropped it, and somehow it had skidded on the smooth floor and ended up there. I recognised it right away – I've seen you carrying this many times over the years, always, as far as I'm aware, with your ferret in?" With that, he produced from his pocket, like a conjurer from a hat, a blue bag made of thickish material, with a white splash on the side where, many years before, emulsion paint had been spilled. "It is yours, Jimmy, isn't it." The Officer made it a statement rather than a question.

"Yes." The reply was terse, the tone tense; the business had taken a turn which he had not anticipated, even though he was well aware that he had missed his ferret bag.

"So the puzzle is, why did you have that bag with you at the Post Office today when, by your own admission, you didn't have the ferret in it – and it had to have been dropped today because they sweep and tidy up each evening and so would definitely have picked it up if it had been dropped, say, yesterday. I mean, Jimmy, what would be the point of carrying it around empty?" The officer paused momentarily, but seeing that there was going to be no answer to his question, he continued. "And another thing that puzzles me is something I saw yesterday afternoon. I was driving along by the river towards Alf Mason's place – he reckons he's had half a dozen sheep rustled – when who should I see walking through the gateway to Farmer Collin's house but yourself. Nothing unusual about that, of course, as I know you regularly go there to catch rabbits and rats. But clearly you were not going rabbiting as you didn't have your ferret with you – and I don't see that you were going there to kill rats, either, because you didn't have Maisie with you. Rather, you were carrying a small rat trap – being a country lad, I know what they look like –

which suggests to me that you were there not to *kill* a rat, but to catch one. And knowing your skills in decimating rats – and rabbits as well, for that matter – I'm sure it wouldn't have taken you long to get a lodger for your trap." He paused briefly to see what effect his words were having upon the pensioner, but could glean no clue from the man's deadpan expression, something which Jimmy had always found it relatively easy to adopt. "So, as I was driving over here, I did a bit of thinking. Now, I've never had ambitions in the force to be a detective; that's partly because I don't like the hours they have to work, but mainly the reason is that I know full well I don't have the deductive powers necessary. I'm a reasonably good local community copper, and that's all I want to be. But Jimmy, it doesn't take Sherlock Holmes to work out what happened in the Post Office this morning. The first question to ask is, what was a big rat doing there in the first place, it being a most pleasant, sunny day – not the sort of day when it would be looking for shelter. Nor would it have come from within either – that shop is always spotless, beautifully kept. And is it not a remarkable coincidence that in the shop, on a lead held by yourself, there just happened to be the best rat catcher in the parish, Maisie? And is it not also strange that before the rat's appearance, I just happened to see you carrying a trap – something I didn't even know that you owned, as I've never seen you carrying one before; and then, once again, very odd that after the rat was caught by your dog, I happened to find your ferret bag in the shop – even though you've not taken the ferret out anywhere for weeks. No, Jimmy, it doesn't need a squad of officers from CID to work it out really, does it; no, it's just a matter of putting two and two together and making – well, I think my maths are good enough to calculate that, although I could be wrong; I mean, it could be five."

He grinned broadly. "Whatever, I don't know that anything could be proved even if somebody wanted to. And it's not illegal to catch a rat in a trap such as you've got; nor for that matter to carry it in a bag – after all, the material is soft and it can breathe all right. But, anyway, there would have to be a confession of sorts for any sort of charge to be brought and that, as I see it, could only be breaching the peace – and I'm led to believe that it certainly did that, with the ladies screaming, and the men scarpering. But, as I say, there would have to be a confession – and I hold out no hopes of that happening."

The policeman paused, glanced at his watch, then looked again at Jimmy Jordan. "As I said just now, before I went off on my – theory – it's time I was away home for my tea. So I'll be seeing you, Jimmy – but not in court." He bent over and patted the little Jack Russell on the head then straightened up and gazed at her master. "Have a good evening, Jimmy. Mind you, I've a feeling you will – and also that you'll sleep well tonight." With that he turned on his heels, strode rapidly to the garden gate and to his car, pausing briefly to wave at the pensioner, before climbing into the driver's seat – noting the old man returning the wave – and then driving off.

Jimmy sat down on the garden seat, then looked down at his faithful companion, she coming to lay at his feet. "Do you know, Maisie, it seems to have been a while since we had some really decent sport," said he softly. "Tell you what we'll do, tomorrow we'll go down to Farmer Collins' place and catch a few more rats; he'll be happy, I will – and I'm sure you will, as well. What do you say to that?"

Maisie said nothing, but she did wag her tail – and with enthusiasm.

III

The Baler

Harry Walton mopped his brow then returned his handkerchief to a trouser pocket. He glanced up in hostile fashion at the midday sun beating down upon him, picked up the grease gun and continued with the laborious task of applying the lubricant to the working parts of his veteran baler. He had never liked the heat but as he grew older he found he detested it. And today it was baking – 'hot as the hods of hell' – as he had said to his Janet when he had gone in for a cup of coffee a couple of hours earlier. Mind you, he was no fan of the cold either, but he had always found that cold weather didn't get on his nerves – or affect his mood – the way the blazing sun always did; also, a fellow could wrap up against the cold but there was little which could be done to neutralise a searing sun.

The upper eighties was the weather forecast and the farmer had no doubts such a prediction was going to prove accurate. Also promised, for the next day, was rain, and plenty of it; whilst Harry had no major faith in the Met Office, he felt that the forecast would prove accurate for the simple reason that his barometer – in which he had great trust – was predicting the same. Hence the reason he had spent a goodly part of the morning 'rowing up' four acres of first class hay and would spent most of a blistering afternoon baling it; he did not look forward to it but if this fine field of future forage was going to be saved to feed hungry stock in the winter, then it had to be done. Still, it could wait until he had a spot of lunch and cooled down with a cup of tea, and a couple of cans of lager from the fridge.

He continued to apply grease to a baler so ancient that he had not been able to get spares for it for several years. Fortunately though, about ten years previously, he had bought another machine of the same make – and similar vintage – at a farm sale for just a few pounds, and had been able to 'cannibalise' it ever since. He glanced at his watch – nearly lunchtime. Another five minutes and he would be done greasing around and checking over the implement that had baled his hay for more than thirty years.

The job done, he returned the grease gun to the tool box attached to the baler, then turned and walked towards the house. There was no reason why the old machine should not fulfil its function that afternoon, but there were a couple of parts – one in particular – which he would need to replace in the very near future, of that he was sure.

Harry entered the kitchen, washed his hands at the sink, took a couple of cans of lager from the fridge, then sauntered out into the garden where Janet was laying lunch upon the picnic table situated under a huge cherry tree, its thick green canopy providing delicious shade from the rampant sun. He slumped down into a somewhat decrepit canvas chair, and thanked his wife for the cup of tea she placed before him. Harry opened the can he held then poured the contents into the glass thoughtfully provided; in hot weather, one of his habits was to drink copious amounts of beer and tea with every meal – and often in between. Suddenly he felt relaxed and gazed contentedly outwards and downwards at the Tamar snaking in unhurried fashion towards Plymouth, then peered through an increasing heat haze to take in the verdant fields on the Cornish side of the river. It was assuredly a marvellous day for contemplating and doing little else, as he intimated to Janet with the simple statement – "I wish I could sit here for the rest of the day." No sooner had the words passed his lips than he realised his mistake – too late; Janet had taken her cue.

"Well, you could if you would only retire, Harry," she admonished. "You're seventy later in the year – and I'm not far behind you. We could take life so much easier. As I said before, we would not have to leave here, 'cause we could sell off the grass each spring. There's always a fair demand for that."

"Well, well – we have cut back a fair bit on what we do, maid," he muttered somewhat lamely. "There's nowhere near the work there used to be, especially now we've got rid of the milking herd. All we've got these days are a few store bullocks – and some sheep of course; but there's only real work involved with those come lambing time, and we've got the barley crop, of course – but again, there's a large part of the year when that needs little or no attention. So – well, there's nothing here now that we cannot handle, is there? Anyway, as I've said before, we're too young to retire."

Janet was about to give a sharp reply to her stubborn, 'pig-headed' husband, when the relative peace was shattered by the roar of a tractor engine. They both turned their heads towards the short drive from the road to the house, and saw a huge red machine thundering – far too quickly – towards the yard.

"Oh no," cried Janet in exasperated tones. "It's Toby Telford; that's all we need."

"Come to borrow something for certain," opined her husband, annoyance in his voice. His plans for a quiet, leisurely lunch before he baled the hay had been shattered. And it was not as if it was remotely a welcome visitor. Not that there was anything disagreeable or unpleasant about the fellow; the opposite, in fact. For Toby Telford was a genial, courteous, friendly man, whilst his wife Marie was a charming lady. Hailing from the Midlands, they had arrived in the parish almost four years previously; and they brought money with them. Both successful business people, there seemed to be no problem in paying for the better things in life; each had a top of the range car, plus there was a Range Rover, a sizeable boat was moored down on the Tamar and they appeared usually to have two to three foreign holidays each year; and they sent their two teenage sons to public school. Also, there was a goodly portion of the builders in West Devon gainfully employed, with them having the farmhouse renovated and two of the old granite barns converted to holiday lets. However, as farmers they were hopeless. In fairness to Telford, he made no claim to be anything other, admitting when they bought the place that he and Marie knew nothing about farming but had always wanted to own land. Sadly, the pair of them had seemed to have learned precious little during their occupancy of the 100 or so acres of rich Devon land, the farm – not in the best of states when they had bought it – now looking very tired and sad indeed. This was largely due to the fact that whilst they enjoyed owning land, they had no great desire to work it. They ran half a dozen fine horses which they used for hunting, they grew about thirty acres of corn, had a dozen or so bullocks cropping the grass, and made hay – much of which they sold.

The basic maintenance of the place, however – hedge trimming, maintenance of gates, repair of Devon hedges that were always prone to erosion by the frost and the area's annual rainfall, and so forth – was addressed in very erratic fashion, if at all. One of the major problems regarding the running and upkeep of the place was the reluctance of the Telfords to invest in basic farm machinery – strange in a couple who were clearly well off and, generally, free with their money. They had inherited a few battered and out of date implements – none of which were really up to the job – but had failed to invest in any new machinery, except for the magnificent 'beast' of a tractor which had transported the rookie farmer to the Walton's well kept farm that hot day. This equipment deficit meant that whenever a farm task needed the use of reasonably modern gear Telford either hired an agricultural contractor, or borrowed the implement from a neighbour if he decided to do the job himself; and often that man had been Harry Walton. Not that the veteran local farmer minded helping anybody out in a crisis or an emergency, but he had long since become a touch annoyed at the newcomer's all too regular requests for the loan of well maintained, usually valuable implements. Over the past three years, Telford had borrowed a hedge trimmer, harrow, a plough and the veteran baler that was poised for action that afternoon – and more than once. It got worse, though, for on occasions the equipment would be returned in inferior condition to that when it had been borrowed. Apologies were often forthcoming from the fellow, although no defect was ever his fault – rather, it was bad luck or some such thing; and even more irksome to Harry Walton, no offer was made to pay for any necessary repairs. And every time Harry suggested – Janet as well – that he purchase his own implements, Telford invariably replied that he intended to, but had not got around to it. From conversations with other farmers in the parish who had lent to the man, Harry found that this was his stock answer to all – and that damage to implements, without offer of compensation, was an all too frequent event.

The visitor jumped down from the tractor then, espying the Waltons in the garden, walked rapidly – indeed almost ran – in their direction.

"Good afternoon, Toby," said Janet politely, if not warmly, as the fellow approached the picnic table. Her husband followed suit.

"Hello, Janet, Harry. Sorry to disturb you at your lunch like this."

"That's all right," the lady replied. "We've not started yet; can I offer you a cup of tea?"

"Or lager?" enquired Harry. He, like his wife, believed totally in preserving basic courtesy, but again, like Janet, hoped the offer would be refused.

They were not to be disappointed.

"No – no, thank you. It is tempting – certainly a lager on a day such as this, and it is most kind of you, but I really do have to get on. The situation is that I've got some hay down – twelve acres, could be more. Lovely hay it is too – I could eat it myself. The problem is baling it. Jack Langman the contractor came round this morning and swept it into rows for me and I assumed that he would bale it as well. But having finished that job, he calmly told me that he cannot bale it because he had promised to bale somebody else's this afternoon whose hay he had swept into rows yesterday evening. He did apologise and did admit he should have thought to mention it when I phoned this morning. And he had the gall to tell me how good a crop it is and how ideal it will be for the horses come winter – they only eat the very best hay, as no doubt you know; poorish, dusty, hay does them no good at all." He paused briefly as Harry nodded to indicate that he was well aware that anything other than good hay was highly unsuitable for horses. He mused to himself that he had probably forgotten more about the equine species than Toby had ever learned, he having worked heavy horses as a teenager upon the steep acres of his farm when he was learning his craft from his father.

"Well, anyway," continued the visitor, "I am singularly unimpressed by the way he has treated me, and I doubt if I will ever use him again. Still, the problem now is that I've got this hay to bale and no means of doing it – and they give rain for tomorrow, which will ruin a crop of such high quality."

"You're right – they do give rain," agreed the farmer, "and I fancy I believe them this time – my barometer agrees with them, and that little beauty is rarely wrong. Gone back hell-gallop these past 24 hours; rain for certain, and there could be a brave bit of it and all."

"Yes, precisely – so you see the predicament I'm in, Harry. I need to bale it now, this afternoon, so I've come to throw myself upon your mercy and ask if I can borrow yours – I see it out in the yard. If it's all right with you, I can just take it off your tractor and attach it to mine. I'll have it back to you this evening – if that's all right with you?"

A touch taken back by the man's presumption, it was a few seconds before Harry replied. When he did, he came directly to the point.

"Sorry boy, it can't be done; I need it myself. I've four acres to bale this afternoon – rowed it up this morning. Soon as I've had my lunch I'll be at it."

Telford, for a few seconds, looked almost as if he was going to burst into tears.

"Well that really puts me in a fix," said he. "I must bale it today – it's probably the best hay I've ever made; it would break my heart to see it ruined."

The words were in keeping with the pained expression upon his face. Quickly, though, it was replaced by a look of positive intent.

"Would it be possible to borrow the baler after you've finished with it? You said you've only four acres to bale; I wouldn't think that would take you all that long. Could I borrow it when you've finished?"

The veteran farmer nodded, a touch wearily.

"Well, yes – I suppose so," he replied, his very real reluctance sounding in his voice.

"Great," enthused the visitor. "Then I'll be back, say at 3 o'clock, to collect it?"

"What, 3 o'clock? No chance," rasped the veteran farmer. "I doubt I'll be started by then, let alone finished. I've not started my lunch yet – and there's no way I'm going to rush that, not on a hot day like this. The day's at its hottest about now; give it an hour and a half, or so, and it'll probably begin to cool a bit."

"But, but, but that'll mean you won't be finished until late afternoon, possibly early evening," spluttered Toby. "There's no way I'll have sufficient time to bale my hay then; I'll be lucky to do half of it. I know it's a bit rude of me to say this, Harry, and I mean no offence, but couldn't you start earlier; couldn't you have a much briefer lunchtime?"

"I could, no doubt, but I won't," retorted the farmer. "I love to have lunch under this tree on a hot day – both of us do. I hate hot weather, Toby, and this is as hot as it's been for years. This is the one spot I find I can relax and cool down. I'll not be baling any hay until mid afternoon, when it should be a bit cooler and I'll feel more relaxed."

Annoyance and frustration showed, momentarily, on Telford's features, but he quickly managed to force a pained smile. He shrugged his shoulders.

"Well, you're the boss, Harry. I'll leave you to it and perhaps look back later this afternoon if that's all right? Beggars cannot be choosers," he mused to himself as he turned to leave. He stopped though, when Harry spoke again.

"I've just been thinking, Toby," said he – in absolute truth, an excellent idea having just come into his sharp brain. "We can come to a compromise on this. I mean you want to borrow my baler and the only thing stopping you taking it right now, is the fact that I'm going to bale mine first – and I shan't be starting for a while yet; so you'll be waiting for several precious hours with little to do. Well, why don't you hurry things along by baling my hay yourself. It's stood in the yard ready to go; if you go right now, you'll finish not a lot later than I will have started. Then you've only got to come to the yard, hitch it to your tractor, and away you go; A reasonable solution, surely?"

Telford looked none too certain that it was, but after mulling it over for a few seconds, slowly nodded in agreement.

"I'm not sure it's ideal, Harry – but it is a way forward, true. And, as you say, I'll just be kicking my heels, hanging around for it; so, yes, I'll do it – I'll bale your field first. Which one is it?"

"You'll have come past it – it's back down the road about two hundred yards on the right. It's all ready to go and hopefully shouldn't take too long. Thank you Toby."

With this, the younger man was gone, half running down the side of the house to the yard. Just a few seconds later came the roar of a tractor engine, and then the Waltons saw the tractor and baler trundle down the driveway to the road.

"Well, that was a neat move, Harry," said Janet, a touch of admiration in her voice, before handing him a plate laden with slices of bread which she had baked herself – a regular occurrence – a large wedge of cheese, an almost equal amount of butter and a dollop of sweet pickle. Her husband made his thanks, then set about it with enthusiasm – to him there was no better lunch on a hot day.

Finishing his meal, he raised his glass to the air.

"Here's to Toby – may he do a good job with that hay," he grinned, then drank the remainder of the contents. He put the empty glass back on the table top, quickly opened another can, poured it out, and then sipped it appreciatively.

"Do you know, maid, this certainly beats baling hay!"

"I expect it does; there's a price to be paid, though," Janet stated. "When he's finished ours, he'll be hammering away at his own; there's no knowing what damage he'll do to it."

Harry gave a slight nod, smiled somewhat enigmatically – but said not a word. And he was to say nothing for some time, the heat and the lager inducing sleep. It was possible he would have slept for hours had not the raucous roar of a tractor engine destroyed his reverie. He opened his eyes and gazed about him; Janet was just a few yards away, dead-heading roses, and that which had disturbed him was making its way noisily along the short drive from the road to the house.

Tractor and baler came to a halt; its driver alighted hastily, and was soon approaching the picnic table.

"Everything all right?" asked the farmer in affable fashion.

Telford's reply was a curt shake of the head – certainly the thunderous expression on his face suggesting that things were anything but.

"The damn baler's broken down," he rasped. "Almost finished – another ten minutes work at the most, and it's broken. One of the belts has snapped. It's so infuriating – I mean, how am I going to bale mine now? By the time you, or I, of course," he added hastily, "go to Tavistock and get another, most of the day will be gone. That's if they've got one, of course. It's an old machine – it could be that they don't keep them in stock."

"Quite right there, Toby," answered Harry truthfully, "there's no way they'll keep those in stock."

"No, no, they won't. I'll have to try and borrow from somebody else," said Toby. Momentarily he paused – then his face lightened. "Malcolm Baldwin," he cried, speaking the name of the owner of the largest farm in the parish. "I'll go around and see him. He bought a brand new baler just a couple of months ago; that's what I've been told anyway. Yes, that's what I'll do, I'll borrow his; I'm sure he won't mind."

He glanced first at Harry, then at Janet.

"I'd better be off – there's no time to waste," he said, "the day's going on. Bye Harry, bye Janet." With that he was gone.

"Bye Toby, and thank you for baling my hay," said Harry laconically, being acknowledged by a cursory wave of the hand as Toby turned the corner of the house and made for the yard. Within seconds his mighty machine emitted a throaty roar, was propelled down the drive, then on to the road and was driven as fast as it would go in the direction of Baldwin's farm a mile or so away.

Janet stopped the dead-heading, then came down and sat opposite her husband. She looked at him for a few seconds, then asked a question brought about by more than forty years of marriage.

"You've got that know-all look about you, Harry. You knew it was going to break down, didn't you?"

Her husband grinned. "Well, I knew it was more than likely. I hoped, though, it would keep going until he'd finished ours. Still, there's hardly any left. I noticed lunchtime when I was checking around that the belt was fraying badly, and wouldn't last much longer. I was going to change it before I started the baling – there's one on the old machine that'll fit. There'll be none in Tavistock though, not for that old machine – Toby was quite right about that. When he came lunchtime and wanted to borrow it I was about to tell him about the belt and make it a legitimate excuse for him not borrowing it. Then suddenly I saw it as a way to get somebody else to bale the blasted stuff on a baking hot day. It worked quite well," said he with a happy smirk.

"So he's going to borrow Malcolm Baldwin's?" mused Janet.

"He'll be lucky," said a grinning Harry. "I saw Malcolm this morning in the village when I got the paper. He planned to bale this afternoon, he told me. Twenty acres he's got. That'll take him right through to almost dark. There's no way poor Toby will be able to borrow that one."

"Perhaps it will teach him a lesson," opined Janet.

Harry got up, shook his head and said simply: "I doubt it, maid. Folk like him never learn lessons, do they? Still, I feel quite affectionate towards him at present – he enabled me to have a quiet, peaceful, relaxing afternoon."

With that he sauntered out towards the yard and the stricken baler; it would take him ten minutes to fit a fresh belt, and a similar time to finish the baling; quite enough effort and work on such a hot day.

IV

Men, Ancient and Modern

Alfie Draper was not a modern man – and he was moderately proud of the fact, ever ready to speak of it to any who would listen. Not that he was altogether boastful, but he often felt an obligation to his generation to state, without reservation – assuredly without apology – that there was much to be said concerning the ways he, and his male peers adopted when they were young men. This applied to many aspects of life, and most certainly to the raising of children. "It's the mother's job to raise the kids," said he, to many a current young dad. "The father's job is to provide for them and to give them security; put bread on the table, clothes on their backs. Day to day care of children is best done by a woman; after all, you don't see a ram raising a lamb – a bull feeding a calf, do you? No – it's contrary to nature and nurture – and that's never wrong."

Having turned sixty, he was the senior member of the firm now, in terms of age – and by a good deal, as well. There were about a dozen other fellows employed, but except for a brace in their forties, the others were in their twenties and early thirties, several of them with young children.

Alfie got on well with them all, although in reality he did not see that much of them, as he was mainly out on the road travelling the lanes of West Devon and the Tamar Valley calling mainly on farms and smallholdings in his capacity as an Agricultural Engineer – something he was exceedingly good at, a factor well known to the company's main customers. Also, the son of a farmer, he was able to 'talk the language' of men and women who lived from the land. Indeed, as he often pointed out – he by birth, experience and nature, was one of them. Still, even in the agricultural community, he noticed that young farmers got involved in the raising of their children in a way in which their fathers never would have. In fact, he was astounded one morning when, turning out to a farm close to Bere Alston to nurse a sickly tractor, Andy Parsons, the farmer who met him – a young fellow probably in his late twenties – and showed him what the problem was, promptly informed him that he was off into the house to feed the baby, and there would be a cup of coffee awaiting him in the kitchen when he was through. After thanking him for the promise of strong beverage, Alfie asked the customer – trying hard to keep incredulity out of his tone – why it was he who was going to feed the child. "Missus not ill, I hope, boy, is she?"

"No – no, she's fine," he replied. "No, I go in about this time every morning to give him a bottle; up until about a month ago, Jackie was breast feeding – so I couldn't make a great contribution then," said he with a laugh. "Now, though, I can; and I enjoy it – and I'm sure he does as well. Basically it's a bonding exercise, isn't it. I feel it's important for a father to be as involved as much as he can in the upbringing of his kids. Clearly I wasn't involved much before he was born, but I can be now – and I love every minute of it. Folk say to me that you've got to seize every moment you can when it comes to bringing up children, because they grow up so quickly – especially these days. I certainly intend to and, except if there's some kind of emergency on the farm, or with the livestock, I make sure I have quality time with him every day."

With that he was gone, leaving a stunned engineer in his wake. About half and hour later, the tractor restored to full vigour, he went to the kitchen to wash his hands and have his fix of caffeine. Knocking on the door and being invited to enter, he was to receive yet another shock to his system; for an empty feeding bottle was stood upon the kitchen table and beside it lay a fine baby – having his nappy changed by his father, the little one's mother over by the large Rayburn stove.

"Hello, Mr Draper," she said cheerily. "I expect you'd welcome a cup of coffee – and a few biscuits as well. It's a bit chilly out today."

The engineer agreed that it was, and expressed his gratitude for the welcome victuals. "Thank you, Mrs Parsons – this is most welcome. I've got to the age now when the cold gets into my bones. Still, it's lovely and warm in here; Rayburns are marvellous for that, aren't they – throwing out heat. Nothing warms a room – even a large one like this kitchen – as well as they do."

The farmer's wife agreed. "Oh, yes – you're absolutely right. And it's so important to keep the place warm when you've a young baby." She looked towards the far end of the table where her husband was just finishing changing the child. "I imagine it's a long time since you've changed a nappy, Mr Draper," said she, inadvertently implying that he most certainly looked what he was, a man fast approaching retirement – and old age. "Although perhaps you get involved with grandchildren – do you have any?"

He had called at the Parsons' farm several times in the past and had always found her exactly as she was now – kind, pleasant and very direct. "Yes, I do; three, actually. My son Billy and his wife Emma have two – 'A pigeon pair', the boy being 4 and the little maid 2, whilst my daughter, Liz, has one – a little girl, Lucy, about the same age as your little lad there, six or seven months now."

"Oh, how lovely," said she. "Do you see much of them?"

"Yes, quite a bit – especially Liz. My son and daughter-in-law live in Plymouth, and both of them work – Emma part time. So we rarely see them during the week, but weekends we often visit, or get visited. Liz, though, lives only a couple of miles away from us, so we see a good deal of her, especially my wife; Liz isn't working at present, so she comes around a fair bit during week days. I often see them on weekends, especially since . . . well, since, since she's had the baby." He had been about to say since her partner Adam had left her for another woman just three months after the birth of their daughter, but he realised that he would have imparted such information unable to disguise the bitterness he felt at the shameful betrayal of his daughter and grandchild. Such a display of emotion on his part would probably have embarrassed the friendly young couple in whose kitchen he was taking his ease. He rapidly changed the subject, going back to a statement which his hostess had made a few moments earlier. "You're almost right about it being a long time since I changed a nappy, Mrs Parsons," said he. "The truth of it is – I've never changed one in my life; not for my own two kids, nor for the grandkids. I suppose you'd say it's, it's – well, 'a generation thing', I think the cliché is."

"Oh, yes, there's much truth in that," agreed the lady. "Andy's father's never changed one, and I doubt he'll do so now. My own father did, actually – I remember him occasionally changing my young brother. But that wasn't often; he regularly read us stories before we went to sleep, though."

"I used to do that occasionally – usually on a weekend, as during their early years they'd be in bed by the time I got home. My wife, Mandy, would often say that she felt I deliberately delayed my home coming until they'd got their heads down. Not strictly true, mind you, but I must admit that I was never sorry if I arrived home to find them all tucked up and deep in the land of nod."

"Don't you feel you missed a lot, though?" asked the young farmer, earnestly. "I mean – this is a personal question, I admit, but don't you, well don't you feel that it might have affected your long term relationship with them." He stopped briefly, then blurted out, "I'm sorry – I really should not have asked you that – it clearly is none of my business."

The engineer laughed. "No need to apologise, boy – no need at all. It's a very fair question and the answer is simple – I had then, and I have now, a wonderful relationship with my son and daughter; in fact, we've never had a real row, not ever. And we've shared many things together over the years. My son used to go regularly to Home Park with me to see Argyle before he started playing for the village side; he's packed up playing now, so once again we often go together. And Liz and I have always been close; in fact Mandy says that temperamentally, Liz and I are very alike.

Whether that's a compliment, mind you, I really do not know."
He laughed and emptied the hot coffee down his throat – a feat
which brought an admiring comment from his hostess. "Good
heavens, Mr Draper, how can you drink it so hot?"

"My family say I've an asbestos gullet," he replied, grinning
broadly. "I've always been able to drink things very hot. Perhaps
it's a case of 'where there's no sense, there's no feeling.' "

She laughed. "I'm sure that's not the case," she opined,
tactfully. "Anyway, would you like a refill?"

Alfie mused to himself that such a question was like asking
Dracula if he wanted blood. "That would be lovely, Mrs Parsons,
thank you. Nothing better than a couple of cups of hot, strong
coffee on a cold morning." Quickly, she refilled the cup and
handed it to him, for which he thanked her – and for the offer,
accepted, of more biscuits.

"I suppose in your days, Alfie," said Andy – himself, with the
changed baby back in his cot, sipping away at a steaming cup
filled from the large cafetière standing on the Rayburn: "Well, I
suppose there was no such thing as paternity leave, or the like. I
reckon mothers were left to get on with it right from the start –
from birth. Being self-employed, clearly I wasn't able to take
any statutory leave from work, but fortunately both sets of
grandparents live nearby, whilst for the first week I did nothing
more than was desperately necessary on the farm so that I could
spend as much time as possible with mother and child." He said
the last words with immense affection and much pride, gazing
firstly at his attractive wife, then in the direction of his sleeping
son.

"Paternity leave? Paternity leave?" The engineer said the
words as if they represented the foulest fate that could ever afflict
mankind. "Good grief, no – nothing like that, thank the Lord. The
very thought of it terrifies me. A couple of lads at work have
taken it over the past year or so – one of them, his wife had twins.
They both came back to work saying they'd enjoyed it, but I'm
very dubious about that; to be frank, they both came back looking
as if they'd just finished six months' active duty in Afghanistan."

"Oh, Mr Draper, how you exaggerate," chortled Jackie

Parsons. "I expect they were tired, yes, but I bet what they said was true – I bet they enjoyed it immensely, and came back to work totally fulfilled. Oh, I think it's a wonderful thing, paternity leave. It means that fathers can bond with their children and become deeply involved in their lives right from the earliest days. I mean, if they don't have such leave, it means that, except for being present when the baby is born, they are unable to become part of the child's early life."

Alfie Draper emptied his second cup of coffee and, slowly getting to his feet in preparation for a return to his van to drive the half dozen miles to his next call, said, a quite serious expression upon his face, "All that's different as well. Prospective fathers very rarely were present at the birth of their children. Some hung around the hospital or maternity home – read the paper, or had a cup of tea or suchlike, but it would be highly unusual to be with your wife when she was giving birth. In fact, doctors and midwives actively discouraged it; the last thing they wanted was an agitated, expectant father getting in their way whilst they were going about their work. With our son, I dropped my wife off at the maternity home and by the time I'd parked the car and got inside, she was in labour. They gave me a cup of tea, and in less than half an hour he was born. So I went in to see mother and child, stayed with them for about half an hour, then went back to work. With my daughter, I was, believe it or not, even less involved. I dropped Mandy off at the maternity home, saw her safely into the care of the staff there, was told that it could be a few hours before the baby was born, so went back to work again. It was about mid-morning when I left her; about three in the afternoon I phoned to see if there was any news, was told she'd had a girl, assured everything was well, carried on at work until knock off time, went home, changed, had some tea, then went to visit them both in the evening." He shrugged his shoulders – "That's the way it was then; mothers seemed to be quite happy to have babies without fathers being present whilst the fathers generally were happy not to be there, and future relationships between mum, dad and child did not seem to be damaged in any way. I have to say that I felt in no way deprived that I was not there watching and assisting the birth – the opposite in fact; it was the last thing I would have wished to do."

His hosts both had expressions of mild horror on their faces. "Really – is that the way it was, Alfie," rasped an almost incredulous young farmer. "I mean, it sounds almost – almost – well almost, barbarous. I cannot imagine not being there with Sarah when our dear little lad was born; I'd have felt, well – cheated." He said the final word with some passion, the old engineer well aware that it was not a word he used lightly. Alfie smiled gently.

"The world changes, doesn't it – all the time; what is custom and habit now, in ten years time might just be a distant memory, something different having taken its place. To a large extent one goes with the flow – or put another way, you either bend with the wind, or you break. Anyway, I must be off – I've got quite a bit on today, just like yourselves; after all, there's always plenty to do in farming, any day of the week, any week of the year. Thanks for the excellent coffee and biscuits – I'm well set up until lunch now. The old tractor should be all right – just call me if there are any further problems with it." With that he raised his right hand, returned their "Good byes", went out of the kitchen to his van, and set off for his next call.

That one also serviced successfully, he proceeded to make a further four calls – all of which saw the old engineer solve the myriad problems which confronted him – before returning to the depot, parking his van then proceeding home. It had been a good day and he was feeling quite happy with life in general; a man imbued with the innate caution of the born countryman, he really should have distrusted such emotions. His mother, who had been a positive person seemingly usually able to ignore the problems which came her way, would often say, happily, "God's in his heaven – and all's right with the world." He thought of her words as he turned off the road and parked in front of his house on the edge of the village, and mused that, in reality, it was a saying which in her final couple of years, was not at all apt. For little then had been 'all right' with her world, she having to fight a long, ultimately losing battle against lung cancer.

And just an hour after arriving home, all would assuredly not be right in his – and Mandy's – lives either. They had just finished their evening meal and were conversing relaxedly at the table, sipping glasses of excellent wine, when the phone rang. Mandy, who was expecting a call regarding the next gathering of the WI – of which she was a member – walked quite slowly out into the hallway to answer it; in less than thirty seconds she had come back into the dining room, far quicker than she had left it, an expression of major alarm upon her good looking face.

"That was the police, Alfie – they phoned from Derriford Hospital – it's Liz and little Lucy; they've been involved in a car crash; they're both in hospital. The police say that Liz is conscious and gave them our phone number – they want us to come right away." It was a request upon which instant action was taken; for within a minute, the Drapers were in their car and nosing out onto the road. In less than half an hour, they were parking up in Derriford's vast car park.

Reaching the reception area, they were directed towards the accident and emergency ward in which would be found their daughter and grandchild. Hastening – almost running – the couple rapidly arrived at A and E and, on entering, espied a policeman standing in the reception area and assumed that it was he who had summoned them to the hospital. Once approached, he confirmed that is was, indeed, he who had made contact and explained what – to the best of his knowledge – had transpired to cause Liz and Lucy to end up in hospital. "From what I can gather, Mr and Mrs Draper, your daughter – with the baby in the car cradle on the back seat – were driving towards Tavistock from their home, and were on that straight bit of road with the high granite wall to the right, when a dog suddenly ran out from a gateway causing your daughter to both swerve and brake. Apparently she was going quite quickly – at least 50 miles per hour, which in fairness is in no way excessive on a reasonably straight bit of road like that – and having swerved, was unable to apply the brakes sufficiently to prevent her hitting the wall with considerable force – so hard, in fact, that the car is a write-off. Fortunately, there was another motorist who was only a couple of hundred yards behind her, and he immediately phoned for an ambulance."

"How are they – do you know?" The question from Mandy – ever a lady excellent at being able to master her fears and anxieties – was terse, but spoken in an even tone.

"I don't know, Mrs Draper – but there's a lady approaching us who probably will." With that, he pointed to a doctor who had just come out from a side room some twenty yards away. "Doctor," called he. "This lady and gentleman are the parents of the lady – Elizabeth Draper – who, with her baby daughter, were involved in the car crash. Naturally, they want to know how they both are."

"Of course you do," said the medical woman with a smile. "Please come this way." They followed her to her office nearby, where she ushered them to chairs, then closed the door behind her. Sitting at her desk, she rapidly came to the point. "Well, first the good news; your granddaughter is fine – something which proves the value of present day car seats. We have given her a thorough examination and I'm pleased to say there's not a scratch on her. Your daughter, however, has quite serious injuries; though, I hasten to add, nothing that surgery cannot put right, of that we are confident. Fortunately – and surprising considering the force with which the car hit the wall, or so the police informed me – she has sustained no broken bones. She does have internal injuries, however, which will require surgery this evening. Whilst we cannot be completely certain until we have operated, the X-rays suggest that whilst her internal injuries are extensive, they are not complicated; so once we have done our repair job, she will soon be on the mend – although it will be several weeks before she has fully recovered."

"How long will she be in hospital, Doctor?" asked the ever practical Mandy.

"Two to three weeks, I would say – with the latter being the most likely. Even then, we would not send her home unless there was someone to look after her; does – does she have a husband, or a partner?" The doctor asked the question, clearly, only because she had to; it was in the natural course of things, nothing to do with her as such. In this instance, however, it was important

49

she was made aware of Mandy's home circumstances – whether, if she was released from hospital, there would be anybody at home to take care of her.

Aware that it was a subject which brought the worst out of her usually even tempered husband, Mandy gave the answer before he could: "No – there's no husband or partner; she lives alone, just her and the baby."

"I see; there could be a problem there, Mrs Draper," said the doctor, thoughtfully. "As I said just now, when she does leave here, she will need someone at home to care for her – for the first week or two, at least. And she would certainly need help with the baby."

Mandy's reply was instant. "She can come and stay with us – she and Lucy. We've plenty of room, haven't we Alfie?"

Her husband, slightly taken aback by the direction the conversation had taken, was a touch slow in giving the only possibly reply to the question his wife had just asked – "Yes, yes, I suppose we have, really; plenty of room, yes." His mind, though, had been concentrated most severely. A baby in the house – it had been decades since there had been such a young life there, except for occasional visits over the past few years. Still, it would not be too bad. Liz would be there recuperating, so she would be in overall charge, with Mandy just helping out. His involvement need be no greater than it had been when his son and daughter were very young.

He was to be proved wrong, however – and rapidly apprised of the fact. "That all sounds most satisfactory," replied the doctor in positive tones. "However, this is, as I said just now, at least a fortnight away. What is more pressing is what becomes of baby Lucy during that time. Clearly, being fit and well, there is absolutely no need for her to say in hospital. Your daughter would, no doubt, be pleased to have her nearby in one sense, but it is not the best environment for a baby if they are healthy. We could call in social services, of course – they would find a temporary foster home for her. It would be better, though, if a member of your family could care for her for just a few weeks – would that be possible?"

"We've got a son and daughter-in-law," retorted Alfie, somewhat nervous again as to the direction in which this discussion was heading. "They live here, in Plymouth – not more than half a mile from here to be exact. Perhaps – perhaps they would be . . ."

What they may or may not have been willing to do was destined never to be revealed. For Mandy, with a black glare at her husband, interjected with some asperity, "They won't be able to look after her; they've got two children of their own, and also they are both working. It would be impossible for them to look after a baby, except possibly at weekends. No, we will have Lucy at home with us. We've a cradle still – up in the loft, Alfie, isn't it?" Again she glanced sharply at her husband.

He nodded – "Yes, I fancy it is – I've not been up there for some time, but I remember putting it up there years back and I'm sure we've not got rid of it."

"No, we haven't – it's always a useful thing to have around, in case someone with a baby comes to stay. When we get home, you must get it down from the loft, Alfie; then we'll clean it up and get it ready for little Lucy." Mandy had the bit between her teeth and Alfie, essentially a man who sought the quiet life when it came to domestic issues, did not demur.

"Yes – yes, there's no problem there as far as I can see," said he softly – though with a notable lack of enthusiasm.

"Can we take her home this evening, doctor – after we've seen our daughter, of course?" Once Mandy was enthused, she desired action. Also, if truth were told, the thought of looking after her granddaughter for a couple of weeks pleased her greatly – although she was well aware that being a lady of somewhat mature years, she would not want the work and responsibility for too long.

The doctor smiled. "It's splendid that you are able to have the baby with you. However, I feel that it would be advisable for her to stay in overnight so that we are able to monitor her, just to be on the safe side. In the morning, the consultant paediatrician, Mr Jenkins, will be around, so he'll be able to give her a final check. I would say that Lucy will be ready to be collected by

51

noon. Now," she said, getting to her feet, "let me take you to see your daughter before she goes down to theatre. I'm sure she will be so pleased to see you and to know that Lucy will be in your safe hands. I know that she has been more worried about Lucy than she has about herself."

Mandy and Alfie's visit to their daughter was brief; for she lay in her bed looking exceedingly poorly, clearly in need of the surgery which was to take place immediately. With the news, delivered by her mother, that Lucy would be collected the following morning and would stay with them until she was reasonably fit and well once more, her face, though still ashen and contorted with trauma and pain, lost the expression of anxiety that had been there. "Thanks Mum – Dad," she whispered. "That is such a relief – such a relief." With that she had closed her eyes; her parents then left her to rest, and the medical staff to minister to her.

The following morning, Alfie phoned his work and told them he'd not be in that morning because of the accident to his daughter. He was going to cry off for the day, but Mandy had said that once everything was ready for little Lucy – the crib in place in their bedroom, some of her clothes and foodstuffs collected from Liz's bungalow – then she would not need any further assistance from her husband until he came home in the evening. He was, and always had been, as useful as a leaking bucket when it came to childcare and she informed him of such – "I don't need you under my feet, Alfie; you'll be far more trouble than Lucy. So it will be best if you go to work – I can always call you in an emergency."

The morning had been hectic; firstly the phone call to the hospital to enquire regarding the condition of their daughter; there the news had been good – the operation had been successful, even though her internal injuries were a little worse than they had thought. Assuredly she would be kept in for at least a fortnight – probably longer. Also, the Paediatrician had examined Lucy and was content that she was in robust health and could be released from hospital. So, following a brisk lunch, Alfie had – with Mandy's blessing – left the house with alacrity, and proceeded to work; he then spent an afternoon out and about, making calls on farmers, feeling much relieved that care of his young granddaughter was in the hands of his most competent wife, and would appear to have bypassed him.

That fate is ever a 'fickle jade' is well known, but Alfie Draper had never before thought of it as being malevolent. Yet, such was the only conclusion he could draw the following morning when just prior to setting off from his depot, he was called to the phone in the manager's office. "It's your next door neighbour, Alfie," explained the company's young Managing Director, Mike Gooding. "She says it is urgent."

The engineer took the handset, a feeling of alarm shrouding him. "Hello, Chrissie – Alfie here." He was right to feel the way he did, for Chrissie Crawford who, with her husband Harry and their teenage son, Johnny, had lived next door for the past five years or more, imparted serious news.

"Alfie," said she, "I'm sorry to say that Mandy has had an accident; I don't think there's any need to alarm you too much, but I feel you need to come home. Unfortunately, she has fallen down the stairs and injured her right wrist – it could be broken. Just after it happened, she phoned me to ask me to come right over as the baby was crying and she felt the priority was to make sure the little mite was taken care of before she herself received attention. I managed to pacify Lucy – I think she had wind. I was going to phone for an ambulance, but Liz asked me to phone you instead which is what I'm doing."

"Yes – yes – of course, Chrissie; thank you – thank you for the call and for looking after the little maid; I'll come right home – ten minutes at the most." With that he replaced the receiver, quickly explained the situation to Mike Gooding, then rushed off to his car parked nearby, the Managing Director's advice that he was not to worry about work until problems were sorted out, ringing in his ears.

Speed limits were cast to the winds as he thundered through the Devon lanes before swinging off the road and screeching to a halt in front of his house. He jumped from the car at a pace which belied the fact he was on the brink of old age and was soon in the house. Chrissie Crawford was standing in the hallway, a sleeping Lucy in her arms. "Hello, Alfie," she said. "All's quiet on the baby front, I'm pleased to say – Mandy's in the lounge."

"Thanks, Chrissie," he replied, breathlessly, and rushed past her to see his wife. He found her sitting in an armchair, her face white and drawn with pain.

Looking up as he entered, she said softly, "My word, you were quick; you must have broken every speed limit in the district."

He rushed forward to her chair, then went down on one knee, asking desperately, "How is it, maid? How do you feel? Why didn't you get Chrissie to phone for an ambulance?" The questions poured from his lips as his eyes swept over her, she holding her right arm closely to her, almost like an embrace. She answered the last enquiry first:

"I didn't want an ambulance as I was more worried about Lucy than myself. Fortunately Chrissie was home and she came around immediately. She's been wonderful, Alfie. After she pacified Lucy, who had started crying, she wanted to phone 999, but I didn't want them – I wanted you, because I want to go to hospital in my own time, not in an ambulance with sirens wailing and lights flashing."

"What happened?"

"It was all done so simply; I was going upstairs to comfort Lucy when, no more than four stairs from the bottom, I suddenly remembered that I had the nappies downstairs – I assumed that such was the reason for her crying; so I turned on the stairs to go back down, somehow I lost my footing and fell down them. I'd have been all right – it's no great distance, after all, but I put out my right hand to save myself and found my wrist sort of crumpled under my weight. I fancy I've broken it, Alfie; it's already swollen greatly and it's very painful."

"Then I must get you to hospital right away – you really should be there already. You need to have painkillers and have it put in plaster – or whatever they do. Come on maid – you need attention now, this minute."

His wife nodded. "Yes, I know, and I'm ready to go. Fortunately Chrissie has so kindly agreed to look after Lucy until we come back. She's my priority, Alfie – our priority. If Chrissie wasn't here we'd have had to take her with us, but now we can leave her behind and collect her from Chrissie's when we come back – which is much better; she's spent enough time in hospital already."

"She'll be fine with me," said their neighbour, seemingly delighted to be cuddling a young child. "I'll raid your larder for baby food, Mandy, then take her next door. She'll be all right with me, so you've no need to worry, neither of you. Mind you, it's as well that it happened now – Harry, Johnny and I are away on holiday in a couple of days. But hopefully by then you will have got things organised."

Alfie Draper nodded – "Yes, yes, I see what you mean. As it is, we'll get right off to the hospital knowing that Lucy's in the safest of hands." With that, he eased his wife to her feet, guided her into the hallway, putting a warm coat around her shoulders – it wasn't a cold day, but the shock had caused her to shiver most noticeably. He guided her to the car, saw her safely into the passenger seat, then drove off at a steady rate in the general direction of the hospital.

The return was made about four hours later, with the diagnosis they had been given a little better than expected, for Mandy had not broken her wrist – rather, she had suffered a severe sprain. The medics had encased it in heavy bandages rather than a plaster cast and given her painkilling tablets to be taken as and when needed; and it had been emphasised to the very active lady – who temporarily, was caring for an infant grandchild – that her right arm needed total rest for at least ten days. They had almost reached home before the full relevance of this struck her – and when she articulated it to her husband, it hit him with the uncompromising power of a sledgehammer.

"I suppose you realise, Alfie, the situation we find ourselves in," she said, getting instantly to the point. "We've a baby granddaughter to care for, for at least a fortnight – probably longer – and because of my wrist, most of the physical side of caring for her will be beyond me. Which means, I'm afraid, that you will have to do most of it; Billy and Emma might be able to help a bit weekends, when they're not working – they're always very thoughtful – but that doesn't alter the fact that most of the time it'll be down to us, my knowledge and your labour. You said just now in the hospital that Mike Gooding told you to take as much time off as you needed, so clearly there's no problem in that direction."

"Well – well, yes, true," mumbled her husband. "But it's not open-ended; and it's a very busy time at present. It's probably all right for me to be away for two or three days, but it's not fair on them if I'm off for any longer than that." He made sure that he was looking directly ahead at the road – then the entrance to their house, as he guided the car to the parking place at the front; it was no time to look in his wife's direction, for he knew that her eyes would be boring into him like twin lasers. Why, oh why, he asked of himself, had he told her that he could take, relatively, as long off work as he desired. The anticipated tide of words swept over him as he applied the brake, and turned off the ignition.

"Alfie, you should be ashamed of yourself; your daughter's in hospital with serious injuries following an accident, whilst your dear little granddaughter, just a babe in arms, has nobody to care for her – although, to be exact, the Social Services would do so; they would take her and put her with foster parents for a few weeks – total strangers who might be caring, but then again, might not. But it seems as if that wouldn't bother you."

"Oh, but it would – it would," he retorted, hastily. "I wouldn't allow that to happen, Mandy, you know that. I mean, you know me well enough to realise that there's nothing I wouldn't do for the little maid – for all the grandkids, and for Liz and Billy, as well. They, and you, are everything to me. All I was meaning just now was that I clearly have a responsibility to my employers – but, well, clearly, my family must come first, and will come first. I'll phone Mike Gooding in the morning and say that it could be several days – at – at least, before I'm at work again. I promise, maid – I'll do it first thing in the morning."

If there was one thing in his life which he usually tried to avoid, it was the upsetting of his loving, generous but feisty wife. Putting his all too selfish feelings before his sense of what was right – and expected of him – he had upset her in major fashion, and he knew it; thus his raising of the white flag, and hasty retreat.

Fortunately, Mandy's fury evaporated as rapidly as it had risen. "I'll keep you to it – that phone call in the morning. You really will have to stay off work until I've recovered sufficiently to be able to care for her on my own. Until I am, all I can do is to supervise her care, with you as my hands, Alfie – you must see that, surely."

"Of course, yes, of course," retorted he, hastily. "And I will be your hands, maid – no problem."

"Good, right, now if you'll help me out of the car and give me the key to the front door, I'll open up and perhaps you'll go next door to Chrissie's and collect Lucy and, of course, thank Chrissie for all her kindness."

This Alfie did, although he needed no instructions from his wife to do so. "I'm delighted to have been able to help," came the reply from his ever charming neighbour, as he stood inside her front door receiving the bundle that was a sleeping Lucy. "To be honest, Alfie, I've enjoyed having her. I hope one day Johnny will present us with a grandchild or two." She smiled then shook her head. "Do you know, I almost wish we weren't going on holiday in a day or two; I would have enjoyed helping you and Mandy to look after this dear little girl until her mum was back home again."

Alfie resisted the very great temptation to tell her the truth – that he too regretted most desperately that she was going on holiday, saying, merely, "I hope you have a great break, maid, all three of you. And thank you again for all you've done; we'd have been in a rare old pickle if you had not been here."

"My pleasure," said Chrissie, as Alfie, holding his grand-daughter tightly, exited the front doorway. Chrissie followed him: "Tell Mandy, if you will, that I gave Lucy her bottle and changed her, no more than an hour ago – so she should sleep for several hours before she needs tending to again. Good luck, Alfie." She said the final words appreciating, even more than was he, just what lay in store for him on the baby care front in the short term.

It was to be over six hours before the moment of truth arrived – just after 3am, to be exact. He was awakened by none too gentle prodding by his wife – "Alfie, wake up, do – the baby's crying."

Her husband, his brain still partially anaesthetised by the ministrations of morpheus, stirred with immense, and noticeable reluctance; he was on the point of replying, "So, what about it?" but realising that such was not the right attitude, he slowly, stiffly and reluctantly got out of bed and followed Mandy – who had risen with some alacrity, despite the nagging pain from her wrist which defied the painkillers she was taking.

"If you go and pick her up, I'll go down and warm some milk for her." The grandfather went to the corner of their large bedroom, lifted the wailing child from her cot, and slowly, carefully, followed his wife downstairs.

The bottle of milk, warmed rapidly in the microwave, was handed to him as he sat on a hard chair in the kitchen, holding the noisy scrap of humanity in his arms. Mandy passed the bottle to him, asked him to squirt just a modicum into her left hand, pronounced its temperature as being ideal, then watched intently the very rare – but not totally unknown – sight of her husband feeding a baby.

Lucy was assuredly hungry, the contents of the bottle disappearing within a few minutes. "Good, good," purred her grandmother, "she enjoyed that."

Her husband nodded, then got to his feet. "Right, that's done – I'll carry her up the stairs." It was a bold move, and certainly worth a try – but he was not confident it would work; it didn't.

"Not yet, Alfie," said his wife, sharply. "She needs changing. I know you've a poor sense of smell, but even you must be able to smell that." And he could – most definitely he could. He mustered an expression of surprise, however, and muttered – dejectedly, and untruthfully:

"I don't smell anything, maid."

There was no escape, however, and he knew it. In the next few minutes, Mandy would, he realised, be witnessing something which she really had never seen before – her husband changing a nappy. It was not a sight for those of a nervous disposition. A man who could handle the smallest parts of a tractor engine with all the lightness of touch and assuredness of a concert pianist, when attempting to change his granddaughter was, to quote his wife's words, "like a cow handling a musket."

Despite the running commentary of instructions which sallied forth from Mandy, he found the exercise exceedingly difficult. "Good heavens, Alfie, you really are cack-handed. How you would have managed when our children were babies, I really don't know. The disposable nappies these days are so much easier to put on than the linen ones then, with the big safety pin which kept them in position. You should give thanks that those days have gone. Still, not to worry, you'll soon get the hang of it."

These words, though, lacked accuracy. For, whilst he did improve a little, he never did really 'get the hang of it'.

In fact, as he was to say for years afterwards, he was too old to 'get the hang' of such matters – an 'old dog', confounded by 'new tricks'. And there were so many of them, with the following afternoon finding him confronted by another dark mystery. After a seemingly endless stream of tasks, great and small, looking after Lucy and sorting out everyday problems and chores in the house, he lumbered into the lounge and slumped down in his favourite armchair – shattered. Still, all was silence on the Lucy front so, with a bit of luck, he could have a respite – albeit probably brief – from his oppressive labours. He was accurate regarding the brevity of his rest. For in less than five minutes after occupying his chair, Mandy came into the lounge from the kitchen and sat in the chair opposite him. Still suffering some pain from her bandaged and slinged right wrist, she cuddled the injured limb to herself as if that was also a baby.

"Alfie – I'm sorry I've not mentioned it before, but you'll have to do the roast. It'll need to go in very soon now – in fact," said she glancing at the clock standing on the mantlepiece, "the lamb needs to go in now."

Her husband sat up in his chair with a speed and rigidity which suggested a powerful electric current had been passed through it. "Roast – I didn't know anything about a roast," his voice registering a rare combination of shock, weariness and despair.

"We always have a roast one evening of the week, Alfie, as you well know; and you enjoy it, I do know that. And there is a plus from your point of view; for again, as you know, we usually have the remainder of the meat cold the following evening with some boiled or mashed potatoes. So, in effect, if you do the roast now, you'll largely take care of tomorrow's dinner as well."

Mandy had made a great effort to make her voice sound positive and upbeat – but it had no soothing effect on the nerves and humour of her husband. "But I've not the slightest idea how to do a roast," he rasped. "I've never done one in my life; I don't mind helping to peel the spuds and carrots and suchlike, and do the washing up afterwards, but to actually cook it – I've not the faintest idea how to do it."

"Then it's time you did," retorted his wife, a distinct lack of sympathy in her tone. "It'll be just like changing a nappy, Alfie," she continued, in a slightly less abrasive tone of voice. "Once you've done it, it will have few fears for you the next time."

"Well, I've already changed Lucy three or four times, and I still can't really get the hang of it; and it will be the same with a roast, even with you there to tell me what to do. Look, maid, I know it's down to me to cook something for us to eat, but what do you say I do some egg and chips, perhaps with a few beans. Even I can knock that up – and I know we've eggs and oven chips, because we got some when I went shopping with you last Saturday. When you're away, I often do that sort of thing for a meal."

"When I'm away," she retorted, referring to her occasional forays to visit and stay with relatives living in Wales and London, "I always leave you with a fridge full of prepared food. Just now and again you might run out and have to do yourself something with chips, or beans on toast or some such thing, but it's not often as you well know."

"Well – well, no, I suppose it isn't," he conceded, "but what I'm getting at is that I know what I'm doing when preparing a meal such as that. I mean I can do it all in less than half an hour, without any hassle – and without having to bother you to keep coming out to tell me what to do." He added, clearly as an afterthought.

"It's no bother, Alfie," said she in a tone which suggested that the subject was not open for discussion. "And it has to be a roast tonight because the piece of lamb has come out of the freezer. I took it out a couple of days ago and intended to have it yesterday evening; obviously, because of my fall, it didn't happen. So it needs to be cooked now – you know as well as I do that any meat that's been frozen needs to be put in the oven sooner rather than later. It can lead ultimately to food poisoning if you re-freeze it."

Alfie knew his wife was absolutely right – but even if he hadn't, all will within him to resist this penal servitude of baby care, housework and, now, cooking had been crushed. So he gritted his teeth, tried to ignore the relentless stress, invoked the 'Dunkirk Spirit', thought of England – and got on with it.

It is said that 'It is a long lane that has no turning', and the glimmer of hope in the darkness for the suffering engineer was the positive news emanating regarding the progress being made by both his wife and his daughter. For they appeared to be improving faster than the medics had predicted, although still far too slowly for Alfie. However, just nine days after her fall, Mandy was able to deliver to him the best news he had heard in many a long year, as they sat having their breakfast. For a couple of days she had shed her sling for longish periods, though not totally, but on this rainy morning she uttered the words which to him brought unblemished joy – "I think I'll leave off my sling altogether, now Alfie, and see how I get on. Also I'll tend fully to Lucy. If I've no problems with my wrist, then you'll be able to get back to work tomorrow – not a thought which you will find upsetting, of that I'm sure." She smiled but gave him a knowing look as she spoke the last few words.

Her husband grinned, and nodded – "You're right there, maid. I love my grandkids dearly, as I do my children – but looking after them is the most over-rated pastime known to mankind."

The news got even better that day, for Mandy found she felt no reaction in her wrist – save for mild pain – even though she had put it to numerous tests in terms of the many things she had to do. Then late afternoon, when she had contacted the hospital to check on her daughter's condition, she had been given the positive tidings that her progress was such that, providing she had no relapse, she would be able to come to them to recuperate that weekend – and that whilst she would have to take things very quietly, she would be able – and assuredly she would wish – to do most of the caring for her baby daughter.

Thus, the following morning it was a happy Alfie Draper that turned his car into the car park at the company depot. Returning the cheery greetings from colleagues, he walked rapidly through the workshops and was soon sitting in a swivel chair in the presence of Mike Gooding.

"Good to see you, Alfie – it really is; you've been missed," words which were absolutely true, for whilst there were several first class engineers on the company's books, none had the touch, and, of course, experience, of the most senior member of staff.

"Well, I've missed it, I have to admit – and I find it hard to say, adequately, just how glad I am to be back."

The Director laughed. "Well, that's gratifying in one respect – it's good to know that a senior member of our team like yourself is happy in his work, but if you're honest with yourself, I bet you'll miss caring for your granddaughter just a bit. I mean, when I talked to Mandy on the phone a few days ago, to see how things were, she said you were doing an excellent job in looking after Lucy – and also cooking and preparing meals, apparently something else that you'd never done before. It seems to me, Alfie," said Gooding, his demeanour adopting a semi-serious aspect, "that despite what you've been saying to we younger fellows over the years regarding your horror at our being 'modern men' that deep down you're a modern man as well. I bet now you can see where we youngsters are coming from in this – how good, enjoyable, fulfilling it is to be involved in the day to day raising of your kids – and, regarding cooking and suchlike, how absorbing, and in a way relaxing it is to cook, create dishes and good food and so forth. Am I not right?"

The old engineer got to his feet, picked up his list of calls for the day, then glanced down at the young man sitting on the opposite side of the desk and said, "Mike, if I had to choose between turning out at midnight to try to repair a tractor in the middle of Dartmoor in a blizzard, or change a nappy in a nice warm house – I'd choose the tractor every time. As to the kitchen and food, I can assure you that to me there is no joy in cooking and there's little pleasure in eating any meal that I've prepared. No, boy, I'm not a modern man – rather, when it comes to all that business, I'm more like neanderthal man, and you can rest assured I'm not going to change now." With that, he smiled down at a somewhat bemused colleague, raised his right hand in a gesture of farewell and proceeded towards his van and the glorious freedom of the open road.

V

Humbug

To anybody who would listen – and they got fewer as he had said it so many times before – Warren Blake would always claim that the biggest traitor to his beliefs of anybody in all of fiction, was Ebenezer Scrooge.

For the man, apparently, constantly articulated hatred of Christmas – famously describing it as 'Humbug' – only to cave in and embrace the festival following a mere trio of bad dreams. The hardy Devonshire farmer, however, was made of sterner stuff. For he had detested the Yuletide even in his teenage years and, now, aged 55, he anticipated no change. Even as a child he had been no lover of the festival, never especially fussed regarding presents and suchlike – unless he could eat or drink them. And his parents had not been overly keen on Christmas, either, although neither possessed the antipathy towards it that lay within their son. One of the problems, being farming folk, was that Christmas Day was much like any other – even for a child; cows needed to be milked, stock fed and sheltered and, on occasions, new born lambs delivered. And always having a love for the farming way of life, Warren had no problem in carrying out the numerous winter chores which were always there, no matter what the weather.

Then and during the years and decades which followed, he became ever more antagonistic towards the great annual 'winter jamboree', growing increasingly angry and resentful at the amount of money which some people threw at it – often going into debt; the buying of presents which so often were neither needed nor appreciated, the laying siege to supermarkets to bring home mountains of food and drink, so much of which would be wasted (the food, that is); the sending of cards and messages of goodwill to folk one disliked, the massive, frenetic over indulgence, the sickening hypocrisy – all of this, and more, consumed the farmer during the festive season, and never eased until the New Year was past (another falsely optimistic, deceitful, nauseating occasion, in his view).

His attitude might have been different had he brothers or sisters – or if he had married and had children of his own. He had, though, always managed to avoid matrimony and parenthood. There had been girlfriends over the years – several – but none whom he had ever wished to wed. Also none, if truth be told, who had ever seen him as husband material. He had, though, enjoyed life in this way, taking holidays in most parts of the world; he reasoned that he worked hard for his living, and thus deserved them; and a few times every year he would have long weekends in London, taking in a show and a first class meal or two in a hotel of like quality.

He had farmed on his own following his father's death some twenty years before, and had lived on his own in the big old farmhouse since his mother had died – on his 45th birthday. He did have a lady, Dorothy Davie by name, who had kept house for him for six or seven years, coming in for a few days most weeks.

She kept the farmhouse immaculate – helped by the fact that he was unusually tidy for a man – did his washing, and would have at least one major cooking session each week, putting an array of culinary delights into the deep freeze for him to devour at his leisure. "She's the only woman in my life," he would boast over a pint in the local pub. "I pay her well," – which he did – "and I need no other." He was a regular at the local hostelry which, in a village that saw fewer changes than most others in the West Devon area (due possibly to its relative isolation on the peninsula between the Tamar and the Tavy) had quite a high number of such, many of whom, like Warren, had lived there all their lives. And he was a popular one, despite his acerbic hostility towards the Yuletide which usually set in towards the end of November.

In fact, his repudiation of the Christmas festival, was looked upon by many as an important part of the celebrations, when they would stoke him up with a few extra drinks, wind him up a touch, sit back and listen to him hurl abuse at Santa Claus and all who loved him.

The Yuletide, though, was but a long receded memory – or a distant prospect – when Warren Blake was to experience his life-changing moment; was to see his life turned turtle – by a woman.

It was the last day of June and the farmer was watching Wimbledon on television. Just a few years earlier he would have been far too busy with the care of livestock, and the myriad tasks that came a farmer's way on a June day to have been able to indulge himself watching sport on a summer afternoon. These days, though, he lived the life of what he termed a 'gentleman farmer'. Inheriting the 120 acre holding from his parents, he had, even during the difficult years of the nineties and the early millennium, made a tolerable living, being a very able custodian of the land. His present semi-retirement, however was mainly due to his good fortune in being able to sell five acres of his land on the far side of the farm, close to the village, for the development of domestic housing.

A very large cheque had been deposited into his bank account – certainly sufficient to keep him in reasonable comfort for the rest of his days. Loving the land the way he did, however, he had no intention of giving up farming; he took much of the tie and drudgery out of it though, by selling off his dairy herd and instead growing some fifty acres of corn – not due to be harvested until early August – and keeping a number of store bullocks which, most of the time, required merely a daily casting over by an experienced eye. That inspection, on the quite frequent occasions when he was away on holiday, was carried out by Alfie Turner, a septuagenarian who had worked some forty years on the farm until his retirement a few years earlier – but who still worked a few hours most weeks.

As the British Women's Number One played yet another dire

volley in a one-sided match dominated by the Bosnian Number Twelve, he heard – just – an insistent knocking at the open back door. Slowly he arose from his armchair, sauntered out into the kitchen, then into the porch beyond. He glanced at the open doorway – and for a few seconds stood transfixed. For a truly lovely woman stood there, gazing in. Dressed in a white top and blue trousers – both clearly of quality – she exuded grace, beauty and, indeed, breeding. He noted her slender figure, the quality cut of her dark brown hair, and then, as she spoke, a dazzling smile – one which his mother (an unusually cynical lady, was she) would have said owed more to a good dentist than to nature.

"I am so sorry to disturb you," said she, her voice soft. "I can hear that you are watching Wimbledon."

"Oh – oh, don't worry about that," he replied, "I'm glad to have an excuse to leave it, to be honest – one of our British ladies is being hammered."

"It can be depressing it's true – although I do enjoy it. I should really be watching it now, and not bothering you – but I've had a bit of an accident. I was on my way home from the village shop when, not knowing the roads too well, I took the corner far too fast – the one some 300 yards or so along the road – skidded on some mud and ended in a shallowish ditch by the roadside. I was just wondering if you had a Land Rover or perhaps a tractor with which you could pull me out."

He dragged his mind away from its task of trying to discern her age – probably mid-forties – and made a reply. "Yes – I've got both. I reckon a tractor would be best – it can be surprising how difficult it is to pull a vehicle out of a ditch. I'll be right with you." He did not bother to turn off the TV set; rather, he rapidly thrust his feet into his wellington boots and then sped out into the yard, aware – apart from other considerations – that he was probably partly responsible for the accident; the mud upon which her car had skidded having almost certainly been deposited by the large wheels of his tractor that morning, the weather having been a touch damp that week.

Within ten minutes, he had the car back on the road, the tractor pulling it out with ease. A virtually brand new Audi; the lady was extremely relieved that it appeared not to be damaged in any way.

" I really don't know how to thank you, Mr er. . ."

"Blake – Warren Blake; call me Warren."

"Right, I will – and I'm very pleased to meet you, Warren. I'm Helen Compton – I've just moved in to Barley Cottage so by country standards we are near neighbours – it cannot be more than a quarter mile from where we are now."

"No – that's right. I'd heard the cottage was sold – it's been empty for over twelve months, since old Mrs Dawkins died."

"I only moved in two days ago," she said, in her easy manner. "I've moved down from Bristol. I was born in Devon, though – near Exeter – but moved away to the South East with my parents as a child. So I'm returning home in a sense, and it is so lovely here, on this peninsula. Still, I must not take any more of your time. Thank you again Warren – I am so grateful to you."

"No problem – my pleasure. Any help I can give – now, or at any time, just let me know. Living on my own I'm my own boss, so don't be afraid to drop in – or phone me. Tell you what, I'll give you my number." From his trouser pocket he pulled a ballpoint pen and a somewhat grubby piece of paper, and wrote it down.

"Thank you," she said taking the note. For a second she hesitated, then appeared to come to a decision. "Warren, you've been so kind to me – I was wondering if you would join me for a drink one evening; say in the local pub, then neither of us will have to drive."

The farmer was stunned; this beautiful woman was, in effect, asking him out. He recovered himself quickly, though, and voiced his pleasure at such an invitation.

"Great – yes I'll look forward to it."

"Tomorrow evening, perhaps. Say about eight. And I warn you now, that I'll be taking advantage of your local knowledge to acquaint myself with the local people and area." With that she was gone, leaving behind her a middle-aged man who had been smitten in a fashion which had never before come to him in his entire life. He felt it was summed up by the words of an old music hall song which his father used to sing after a good session in the pub – 'When he thinks he's past love, it is then he meets his last love, and he loves her as he's never loved before.' He had to admit though, that in this instance it was his first love also, and he knew even then, that she would be the only love of his life.

As a widow, Helen could never say Warren was the first love of her life – but he was certainly the second. Her husband of twenty-one years, Michael, with whom she had had a son and daughter (both now grown up), had died of cancer just three years earlier and grief still lingered within her at the time of meeting the farmer. Following this, though, the sadness of the past evaporated; she began once again to look forward to life rather than back.

So an unlikely romance developed and flourished with surprising rapidity; indeed, within just a couple of months of their meeting their romance was the talk of the still tight knit community, especially in the pub where the long serving landlord, Jake Fuller, had known Warren for the best part of twenty years. Indeed, the astonishment that such a steadfast bachelor as Warren Blake was clearly in love was surpassed only by the fact that Helen, clearly a beautiful, sophisticated, cultured lady, was obviously in love with him. And it did not appear she was chasing him for his money, even though he was a 'good catch' in that direction, for it was well known she was an accountant – as had been her husband – and that she still practised that well remunerated profession from her home.

With all this love in the air, news that the farmer had proposed to her, and she had accepted him, came as no major surprise, although there were still some in the village who were unsure what she saw in Warren. The answer she gave, to the few who had the presumption to ask her, was that she found him kind, gentle and thoughtful plus he was intelligent and excellent company; also she found him physically attractive – six foot tall, well built, good looking and, as his mother always said, he 'scrubbed up well'.

They planned to marry early in the New Year; Helen would sell her cottage and move into the large farmhouse. The wedding would be held in the Parish Church, the service being conducted by her brother who was rector of a parish in Dorset. Whilst clearly not having the calling of her sibling, she had always been a strong believer, and had often given her time to organisations connected with the church. Seeking to continue in similar vein locally, she had volunteered to help with the Sunday School which was flourishing, as was the church itself, under the leadership of a young, enthusiastic vicar, Simon Straw. And the subject of the Sunday School came up as the couple sat, wine glasses in hand, before a cosy log fire one evening in November.

"I found out last week, Warren, that the Sunday School doesn't have a Christmas Party. Imagine that – no party." Her future husband both imagined it and classed it as an act of wisdom – but he did not say so. He had gathered already, from comments she had made, that Helen was probably as keen on the Yuletide as he was averse to it.

"I'm going to see the vicar tomorrow and suggest we have one – he'll agree I'm sure. I don't mind arranging it. Hard work, of course – but I'm sure you'll help me, Warren. It's such a lovely time of year after all."

The farmer looked aghast – "Me, help," he croaked. "To be honest, Helen, I'm – well I'm not the greatest fan of Christmas. Never have been to be honest."

"Nonsense – of course you like it – who doesn't like Christmas? Jake the landlord said to me a couple of evenings ago when I was waiting for you in the pub that you loved Christmas. I was saying about having a party for the Sunday School, and he said how he was sure you would help as you were the life and soul of things at Christmas."

The farmer felt crushed; his future wife had taken the landlord's mischievous comments at face value – there was no escape. So he was involved erecting trestle tables, putting out chairs and performing the multitudinous tasks involved in organising a children's party.

However he drew some solace from the fact that nobody other than Helen knew he was helping. To maintain anonymity, he needed to be absent on the day itself – a Saturday afternoon some ten days before Christmas – when others would be there, preparing the teas and so forth. The day before this, however, Warren played what he saw as his ace, by convincing Helen that urgent farming matters would prevent him from attending the party – beginning at five – but that he would meet her in the pub afterwards.

Fate, though, was in malevolent mood. For at 4.45 on the afternoon in question, just as he was about to watch the football results, the phone rang – and he was undone.

Within a couple of minutes he was outside and ambling dejectedly towards his Land Rover. He espied Alfie Turner carrying a bale of hay towards a loose box which housed a sickly steer. "I've got to go, Alfie – blasted nuisance. It's the Sunday School party – about to start any minute. The vicar was going to dress up as Father Christmas and give out the presents; the trouble is, though, he's just phoned Helen to say that his car's broken down in Exeter and there's no way he'll be able to get back in time. So she's phoned and asked me to do it; I don't want to, but it would seem there's nobody else. I . . ." His voice tailed off, suddenly aware that he had just imparted news which he did not have to divulge to a man who, within the hour, would be passing it on to the landlord and clientele of the pub; not a man to keep a secret, Alfie.

The older man grinned, then shook his head. "You – you're going to be Father Christmas?" he chuckled then moved off about his business with the wry observation – "There's no limit to what a man will do for the love of a woman."

It was past nine o'clock when Helen and Warren entered the pub – a touch weary. Games had been played, teas consumed and presents received – then the recipients sent home in festive mood. The debris had been cleared up, the hall returned to something approaching order, and the organiser and her future husband had gone for a well-earned drink. Helen sat down near the fire, whilst Warren went to the bar, ordering wine for Helen and Scotch for himself.

Jake Fuller put the drinks down on the bar before the farmer, then waved away the proffered note. "No, Warren – have these on me. You've earned a Scotch if what Alfie told me a little earlier is true. Warm and thirsty work dishing out presents clad in a thick red suit and fluffy beard – and handling a bunch of kids. Everybody here is highly impressed that you – you of all people – were prepared to go against all you've believed in, all your life, just to keep a bunch of kids happy; isn't that right folks?" He looked in the direction of a score or more of customers, the great majority of whom were both local and regulars as he said the words. From the motley squad there were wide grins, noddings and some murmurs of assent.

The farmer smiled, somewhat sheepishly, picked up the glasses, muttered "Thanks Jake," to the landlord, then "Thanks folks," glancing in the general direction of the other patrons. Turning away he moved towards the fireplace – and Helen.

He stopped momentarily as the landlord spoke his name – "Warren," said he, a mischievous grin playing around his lips. "We got something to say to you – just one word – that which Scrooge would have used." He looked away from the farmer, towards the rest of his customers, cried "One, two, three – go!" and joined in the raucous, though impressively synchronised shout of "Humbug!" This was followed by laughter and the raising of glasses in genial salute to the farmer, before the landlord moved away to serve his customers. Carrying the drinks over to the fireside, Warren sat down beside the woman he loved. He raised his glass in a toast to this lovely lady who had come – so late – into his life, then, briefly, he closed his eyes and thought back over the day. It had been mind concentrating, somewhat stressful – even traumatic in its way; the worst part of it though, certainly the aspect of it which really unnerved him, was that simply – but alarmingly – he had enjoyed it.

VI

The Sat-Nav

George Davis was to modern technology what Genghis Khan had been to peaceful co-existence – and fully admitted it. The 'wonders of modern science' were, to him, exactly that – wonders which were beyond his comprehension, and would ever remain so. Not that his home lacked the equipment of the hi-tech age – the opposite in fact; for there was a quite up to date computer and printer, a state-of-the-art digital television set and similar radios; an almost brand new iPod, and two mobile phones. These were present in the house thanks to the insistence of Susie, his wife of almost thirty-five years. She was virtually the opposite of her husband, seeing these wondrous modern appliances as lanterns lighting the path which led to progress and which made everyday life far more comfortable, eradicating so much of the time-consuming drudgery of basic tasks.

Susie had been, for a decade or so, secretary to the local branch of the Women's Institute, and found that during the past couple of years, since the purchase of the computer, with its word processing powers, her secretarial duties took but half the time they had previously, and also that she was encouraged once again to do something which she had performed tediously, in long hand, some years previously, write short stories – a couple of which she had had published in a local magazine during the past six months. The iPod provided her with her favourite choral music when she went shopping, or was doing housework, or out in the garden, whilst her mobile phone was a constant companion, she ever being a lady who enjoyed human contact and ready communication. As for the television, the complex world of using, or recording onto DVDs, held no mystery to her.

No, this fraught, mysterious, indeed alarming technical world of the twenty-first century to George Davis, suited his clever, quite confident wife very well indeed. Her enthusiastic embracing of such wonders influenced her husband not at all, he showing no interest in such things. Indeed, he would trumpet to anyone who would listen – in explanation rather than excuse – that he was a 'Dinosaur with Luddite Tendencies' when it came to the scientific mysteries of the modern world.

The computer he looked upon as a monster standing threateningly in the corner of a former bedroom, which – son Danny and daughter Linda having flown the nest several years previously – had been converted into a study; he ensured that for safety's sake, he went nowhere near it. Whilst he liked music, iPods held no allure, and as to a mobile phone, the last thing he ever wanted was to be constantly contactable. Although semi-retired, he still spent two to three days a week on the road calling on the rural community in general, and farmers in particular, as agent for three different agricultural and horticultural suppliers, selling everything from fertilisers to seeds, hay to light farm machinery.

The companies who employed him were all of a mind that it would help them immensely if he carried a mobile phone, each of them quite willing to supply one. He thanked them for the offer, but pointed out that he possessed one, and had done for some time, having received it as a Christmas present from Danny a few years earlier.

Susie had received hers at the same time and, instantly, recognised that the positives involved in using it greatly exceeded the negatives. It was, however, impossible to convince her husband of the multitude of benefits which could come from using such a piece of equipment. Mind you, she had to admit to herself that it was partly her son's fault that his father shied away from using something which could have been of great value to himself, and to those – both in terms of business and family matters – who wished to contact him. Not that she would ever have said so to Danny – such comments would have seemed most ungrateful to a son who had spent generously on such gifts to his parents. The mistake he had made, however, was to make operating the mobile sound far too complicated. She remarked to her Linda that had Danny just pointed out to his father how to make a call, and the button to press when receiving one, even the reactionary parent would probably have given it a chance, he being close to his children, and assuredly, not wishing to appear ungrateful for what was clearly an expensive gift. Danny, though, had enthusiastically tried to show his ever more bemused father all the tricks the sophisticated item of modern communication was capable of performing. It could take photos, take messages, texts, of course, and all manner of information could be gleaned – including latest scores in football matches. And it was probably this attribute, described by Danny at great length, which finally turned his father irreconcilably against it. "He made the mistake of saying to your Dad, Linda," opined Susie, "that at any time during a game he would be able to find out how Argyle were getting on. Well, you know your father, when it comes to Argyle – when he's not actually there watching them, he never wants to know how they're doing. Being the pessimist he is, he always assumes they are losing, so he prefers to wait until the end of the game when it's all over, before he knows the score. Silly though it sounds, and silly though it certainly is, I do believe that that was the deciding minus for him – the mobile phone was put in a drawer beside the bed and has remained there ever since."

"That really is silly, Mum," replied her daughter, shaking her head sadly. "I know Dad has this dislike of technology – although I think fear would be a more accurate word – but he would find a mobile phone so useful. In fact, I don't know how he copes without one – especially on those days when he's working. I mean, what does he do when he's out on the road if he needs to phone somebody?"

"He uses a public phone box – if he can find one; they certainly get fewer. If he can't find one, then he just waits until he gets home." Susie glanced at her daughter and noticed the slight shaking of her head, and the expression of mild despair upon her face.

"I know what you're thinking, Linda – it makes no sense; but, then, that's your father. He's always been the same regarding technical things and I fancy he's too old to change now."

"Well, if you can't change him Mum, then nobody can," stated her daughter. "I mean, he always seems to listen to you in most things, and rarely goes against what you think or feel. Yet he does in this – it's strange."

"It is indeed – but, as I said just now, that's him; that's the way he is with gadgets and suchlike – and he'll not alter."

Susie's appraisal of her husband's character and reaction in terms of his resistance to technical innovation was put to the test just a couple of months after her conversation with Linda – on George's birthday. As it happened, it fell on a Sunday, so son Danny, with his wife Tess and their two children, had travelled down from their Bristol home, whilst Linda and son-in-law Jack had made the shorter journey to West Devon from their abode in a village close to Exeter. Susie had cooked a sumptuous lunch, whilst their son had brought several bottles of wine to which George did ample justice.

It being a lovely day in early May, lunch had been eaten in the garden – at great length – to be followed by the opening of presents. He always hoped on his Birthday, and at Christmas, for gifts of liquor having a taste for good single malt whisky, brandy and decent port – and rarely was he disappointed, such gifts going some way towards assuaging his yearly intake. This year was no exception, Susie being especially generous in her purchasing of a goodly amount of the expensive liquor. Gazing happily at the bottles arrayed before him, he drained his glass of an excellent Merlot, accepted without demur the refill offered by his daughter, then turned his attention to his son who had produced – from where he wasn't sure – a square box covered in gift wrap.

"This is for you, Dad, from Tess, the kids and me – Happy Birthday."

"Thanks, boy," said he, grasping Danny's right hand affectionately. He then pulled himself slowly to his feet – already feeling the effects of the copious quantities of wine which he had consumed, kissed his daughter-in-law – "Thanks, maid." – waved to their two boys who were hurtling around the garden – "Thanks, Lads." – then sat down heavily on the patio chair and proceeded to open his present. Never a man to linger over unwrapping gifts, the paper was soon ripped off and he sat gazing, somewhat nonplussed, at the cardboard box he held. There was an illustration on the lid of, presumably, the contents – a picture which his somewhat bleary gaze, and slightly hungover mind, was unable to fully comprehend. He looked at his son – "What is it Danny?"

His son was too polite to point out that it stated boldly what it was on the lid. "Open up and have a look, Dad," he said – which is what George did. The lid open, he reached in and pulled out the contents – and reached the conclusion that it was an electronic gadget, a shortish lead with a small plug attached being the main evidence of such. For several seconds he sat gazing at that which he held in his hand, not instantly recognising it. In fact, had he been put on the spot, he would have had to admit that he had not the slightest idea what it was. He had no need to speak, however – his wife, whom, he conceded, knew him better than he knew himself, was perfectly aware that he had not the slightest idea what he held in his hand.

"George," said she, a touch sharply, "look on the cover of the box – it tells you what it is on that. By the look on your face, you've not the slightest idea of what you are holding."

He followed his wife's instructions and looked at the box. "Oh – oh, I see. It's a, a, er – it's Satellite Navigation." The words stumbled from his lips, whilst his expression appeared even more confused and not just because of his intake of wine; to be fair, he had heard of such things, but he was hazy, to say the least, as to what purpose they performed.

His son, seeing his father floundering, instantly came to the rescue. "We thought a sat-nav would be an ideal gift, Dad, 'cause it'll guide you when you're on your travels. Not that you need any guidance when you're travelling locally – throughout Devon, in fact. But when you go further afield, I know that sometimes you find it hard to locate exactly where you're looking for. I mean, you do, I know, often have problems locating where we live in Bristol. You're all right when Mum is with you, because she's a good navigator, but on those occasions she comes up to stay with us for a few days, and travels by train, with you driving up on your own to bring her home – well you invariably get lost and spend a fair old bit of time going around the city looking for where we live. This is now in the past, for all that is needed is for our address to be entered into the sat-nav – I'll do that – and it'll take you there by the quickest route. And anywhere else you go – on holiday, for instance – all you've got to do is enter the address into it, and it'll take you there, giving you instructions – minute instructions, as well – as you go along. We've got one and we find it absolutely vital, don't we Tess?"

His wife agreed, with considerable enthusiasm. "Oh yes," said she, "it really is wonderful – it takes such a load off your mind if you are looking for somewhere."

"That's a wonderful gift, isn't it George," interjected Susie – the tone of her voice suggesting that a reply, instantly, was required, and it would be very wrong of him to give any response other than a most positive one.

"Yes – yes, it is," came the response. "It'll – it'll – well, it'll be very useful in the future; as you say, Danny, I never seem able to find your place, so it will certainly solve that problem and, like you say, we'll also find it useful when we go away on holiday."

George said the words with as much enthusiasm as he could muster – and with infinitely more than he felt. He doubted not that this was a very efficient and most sophisticated item of modern equipment – but he was far from convinced that it was for him. Granted, he did tend to get lost when trying, on his own, to locate the abode of his son and daughter-in-law in Bristol, but he had always managed to find their home in the end; and if he was honest, the worry of trying to operate this wondrous, but arcane, piece of technology would worry him far more than it did to take a wrong turning, or two. Clearly, though, it was expensive – and it was thoughtful and generous of Danny to buy it for him (although very much in character). So he would say all the right things before his gathered family – and then, in the fullness of time, place the sat-nav in the drawer alongside his mobile phone.

His daughter, who was always very perceptive, appeared to read his thoughts. "No putting it in the drawer with the mobile phone, Dad," said she, a mischievous smile playing around her lips.

"No – no – no, maid. No, I won't be doing that," he retorted, as convincingly as he could – but not with total honesty. For he had to concede that he could not view the use of such a complex piece of equipment (and, in his experience, every machine ever made was infinitely more complex and demanding of technical knowledge than their advocates ever conceded) with anything other than apprehension. Granted, it would help that Danny was going to key in his address – but he still feared that to operate it would cause him grief.

Following his birthday lunch, George placed the sat-nav, in its box, on the hall table; it wouldn't hurt there for the time, he mused. He would allow a few weeks to pass, then quietly take it upstairs and place it as company for his mobile phone. This he did, and not receiving any comment from his wife, assumed that she had not noticed his subterfuge. In this, though, he was very wrong; indeed, he had been most foolish even to think she might not have noticed what he had done.

She said nothing to him about it, however, until a few minutes before he was about to transport her to Plymouth one warm Saturday morning in August, to catch the train to Bristol to stay with Danny and Tess for a week. As he picked up her case in the hallway, prior to placing it in the boot of the car, she made her point; "I notice that the sat-nav is in your drawer with the mobile, George," said she, a touch of sharpness in her voice. "I trust you are going to use it when you come up to Bristol next weekend to pick me up. Danny has set it up to give directions to his house – there's no way even you can get lost if you use it; anyway, he'll be very hurt if you don't use it – I shudder to think how much it cost. But, more than that, it was a very, very thoughtful gift.

Promise me you'll use it, George. All you have to do is put it in the car, on the dashboard, plug it in and turn it on. You will do that, won't you?"

"Yes – yes, of course I will," he retorted, hastily. And he would – he had no desire to upset Danny, and even less to antagonise his wife.

And he was good to his word. The following Saturday morning saw him installing the sat-nav in the car – sticking it to the inside of the windscreen, whilst resting it lightly on the dashboard. He then plugged it in to the socket which held the cigarette lighter – an accessory which they had never used. Checking he had locked both front and back doors and closed all the windows in the house, he returned to the car, got in, belted up, started up – then proceeded down the short drive to the road. He glanced at his watch – five minutes past ten; just right, for unless there were major traffic problems, he would be at Danny's place by twelve-thirty at the latest, in good time for the lunch to which he had been invited. Not for the first time in his life, he was to be proved wrong – 'The best laid plans of mice and men,' he mused to himself later that day.

Danny Davis looked at his watch – one o'clock, and no sign of his father. Susie, aware that a roast lunch was ready, expressed her exasperation – anger, in fact. "Where has he got to," she rasped, not expecting an answer to her question. "He promised me he would be here before one. He also promised he would use the sat-nav. I'll be so angry with him if he hasn't."

"Well, Mum, if he said he was going to, then he has," stated her son, simply. "Dad's always a man of his word."

His mother nodded – "Yes, that's true, dear. He always keeps a promise, perhaps there's been an accident on the motorway, or something like that; or perhaps there is very heavy traffic – yes that's probably the explanation."

"I doubt there's any point in phoning him – it's unlikely he'll have his mobile with him." Danny realised that what he had stated was totally superfluous – it was as certain as night following day that his reactionary father would not have with him his mobile phone. Indeed, so obvious was this, that his mother did not even bother to comment. Rather, she looked at her daughter-in-law who had just come out of the kitchen.

"Tess, dear, I'm so sorry that he's late. The trouble is that whilst he will probably be here soon, there's no certainty of it. So I would suggest that we go ahead with lunch now – clearly it's ready; in fact, it smells lovely."

"Are you sure? I mean it won't hurt to wait a little while longer – perhaps a quarter of an hour; it's not going to dry up in that time."

So they did as she suggested, but one-fifteen came and went and still there was no sign of George; thus, lunch was served, devoured and enjoyed, although it would have been appreciated and savoured even more had George joined the three adults, there being a pervading – and increasing – worry over the continued absence of the 'Pater Familias'; an apprehension which manifested itself by causing a dearth of conversation during the meal, unusual in a family to whom communication was ever important.

For Susie, apprehension began to turn into worry. Following lunch, she helped wash the dishes – after congratulating her daughter-in-law on the excellence (as always) of her cooking – then glanced again at her watch. It was just fifteen minutes shy of three o'clock and still neither sight or sign of her husband. Two emotions battled within her – anger at his extreme tardiness and an increasing concern for what might have happened to him. Indeed, the second emotion began to get the upper hand – so much so that the thought flitted through her mind that if the absent George failed to arrive by, say, half-past three, then perhaps the police should be informed.

No sooner had thought of such quite dramatic action entered her head than a sound which they all quite desperately wished to hear rent the tense silence – the front door bell rang. Susie moved quickly towards it, but was beaten to it by her son, the pace with which he sped betraying the very real concerns he had regarding his father's absence, even though he had gone to some lengths to try to camouflage it. He turned the latch, thrust open the door – and was confronted by George.

"Dad," he cried. "Thank heavens you're here; we've been very

– well, well we began to get a bit concerned that you'd not arrived yet." No need, he mused, to make a drama out of it.

"Sorry, boy – so sorry to be so late." George Davis stood upon the doorstep looking more than a little sheepish. His son beckoning him to come in, he entered, shaking hands with him as he did so.

No sooner had Danny closed the door behind them than he was confronted by an extremely irate wife. "George, where have you been? You promised you would be here for lunch and you turn up half way through the afternoon – we've been worried sick; and Tess went to all the trouble to prepare a lovely meal – and you weren't here for it. It's too bad of you George, it really is."

Trying to pour oil, his daughter-in-law quickly came forward, kissed him on the cheek, and said, "Well, you're here now, and all in one piece – that's the main thing. I'll make a cup of tea, and you can tell us what happened."

"Thanks maid," he replied, trying hard to avoid his wife's angry glare. He was certainly unable to avoid her sharp tongue:

"You just don't realise how worried we've been – we thought something had happened to you. In fact, we were on the verge of phoning the police," she snapped – aware there was a slight exaggeration in those dramatic words, although it was certainly true that she would have involved the constabulary if he had been much longer.

"Come through to the garden, Dad. It's too nice to be cooped up indoors – Tess'll bring tea out to us in a minute; and seeing that you've missed lunch, a nice piece of sponge will do you no harm."

"Thanks, boy, that'll be lovely." A man possessed of the sweetest of teeth, George had said many times that next to Susie, Tess was the best creator of sponges and fruit cakes that he had ever known.

His wife and himself followed Danny out into a sunny garden and, after he had greeted his grandsons who were playing football on the back lawn, he sat down on a comfortable patio chair – and sought relaxation. His wife, however, had other ideas; she wanted an explanation for him being over two hours late – and pointed out that they could, and should, have been informed that he was going to be delayed, much earlier.

"If you only carried your mobile phone, George, you could have contacted us and told us you were going to be late. You really must stop this nonsense about them – about all technology, in fact – and come into the modern age."

"Well, I intended to phone you – about a quarter to one, it was," he explained, softly, still highly embarrassed at being so late. "I was going past a phone box, so promptly stopped and went into it to phone you. The trouble was, though, that – that – well, to be honest, I realised that I just couldn't remember Danny's number. So even if I'd had my mobile I still wouldn't have been able to contact you."

"But we would have been able to contact you," came the instant, and irate response. "That's the point, George; you forget that communication is a two-way business."

"Yes – yes, of course; I hadn't thought of that, maid," he replied, truthfully. "Ah, here's Tess." The sight of his daughter-in-law carrying a large tray laden with cups, saucers and a quite magnificent looking coffee sponge, cheered him immensely – it promised much needed sustenance, and a welcome break from Susie's interrogation. That promise, though, was only half fulfilled.

Sustenance in the shape of a cup of tea and a large slice of delectable sponge, soon came his way, and he wasted no time in sampling both. Susie was quiet for half a minute, as she took delivery from Tess of the steaming beverage, spoke to thank her daughter-in-law for it, then to decline some sponge – being more than adequately filled by the lunch – before returning to the attack. Placing the cup and saucer upon the white plastic table stood before her, she fixed her husband with a flinty stare, and asked the question which vexed her most of all: "What happened with the sat-nav, George? You did use it, didn't you – as you promised you would?" She had no doubts as to what the answer would be – he did not break his promises.

Her husband swallowed, rapidly, his mouthful of sponge, and fixed his wife with a look pregnant with a combination of frustration and despair. "Of course I used it, maid. In fact, rarely for me when it comes to technical matters, I put total faith in it. Trouble is, it didn't work – well, not properly anyway."

"Didn't work, Dad?" his son was all attention. "You mean, there's something wrong with it? I don't know how that's happened. I mean, as you'll remember, I got it operational the same day as we gave it to you – and I entered our details into it then. All you had to do was turn it on, Dad – in theory, anyway."

His father nodded, and again began to look a little sheepish. "Yes – yes, that's right, boy; and there's nothing wrong with it really – or there doesn't seem to be, anyway. No, I fancy that I might have made a slight mistake – and, well, I wasn't sure how to put it right, to be honest."

"Oh, George!" exclaimed his wife, just two words, but uttered in a way which gave evidence of her deep-seated frustration that she had endured almost forty years of such incompetence from her husband in virtually all matters of a practical nature. "You really are hopeless."

"Well, I – I – I really don't know what went wrong, maid. It was just, well, bad luck really," he said, somewhat without conviction. "I mean, I fixed it in the car before I left home, and plugged it in and so forth, as you showed me, Danny. But I thought to myself that I didn't really need it working until I got way up the M5 to just a few miles from Bristol. After all, even I know my way to Exeter, then the motorway to Bridgwater and beyond; I just thought it would be a bit distracting having an automatic voice telling me, for a hundred miles or more, where to go when I didn't need any advice. So I left it off until I got to about ten miles from Bristol, my plan being for it to guide me off the M5, then through the dreadfully complicated bit of entering the south side of the city and journeying across it to you here on the north side."

He stopped for a few seconds, accepting Tess's offer of a refill of tea, and another generous wedge of that triumph of a sponge. He thanked his daughter-in-law warmly, took a large bite out of the culinary delight on the plate before him, chewed, swallowed – then returned to his protracted explanation as to why his relatively simple and straightforward journey had turned into such a disaster.

"Well, I was just a few miles from Gordano's Services when I decided to put it on. Obviously most of my attention was on the road, so I just glanced at the sat-nav sitting there and reached across to push the on button. Well, not being able to concentrate properly, clearly I must have pushed the wrong button, 'cause nothing happened. I let it go for a minute or so, thinking that there might be some delay because I was in a blind spot, or some such thing. It was nothing like that, though, so, with the road in front of me relatively clear, I slowed a bit, then, giving the sat-nav my full attention, I reached over and definitely pushed the on button. Within a few seconds the small screen showed a map, so I then put my full attention to the road in front of me, and awaited verbal instructions on how to get here to 27, Cheltenham Avenue." He stopped and smiled wanly, then shook his head.

"You mean the voice wasn't activated, Dad? You got no instructions?"

"Oh, it was activated all right, boy – yes, there was no problem that way." He ceased briefly, then fixed his son with a quizzical look: "Tell me, Danny, is the sat-nav multi-lingual?"

His son shrugged his shoulders non-committally. "I'm not sure, Dad," said he, "but I expect it is. Such things are these days; I mean I think it was made abroad, and it's a fair bet that it sells in a wide range of countries. Why?"

"Well, just as I was approaching Gordano's, the lady spoke to me in that melodic, clear voice of hers – great you might think. The trouble is that she spoke to me in Spanish and, of course, I couldn't understand a word she said. Not long after, I came off the motorway, pulled into a lay-by and tried to get her to speak English again, with no joy, even though I did keep pressing the same button I had pushed before when thinking it was the on button. I did manage to get rid of the Spanish mind you – but for what sounds like Russian, which is even worse. So I cut my losses, switched it off, and tried to find my way here without any electrical assistance – and not very successfully either, which, when taking into account the time I took, becomes most obvious." He stopped talking, shamelessly accepted yet another generous slice of coffee sponge, and awaited the comments of despair and frustration which would, he was certain, follow in generous manner.

In this, he was wrong; for his dearly loved spouse gazed at him for what appeared an age, her face unusually expressionless; then suddenly, she burst into gales of laughter – to be followed by Danny and Tess, all of them overwhelmed by the absurdity and sheer comicality of the situation. "Oh, George," said Susie after the gale of mirth had subsided to a squall, "You really are priceless – and hopeless."

Her husband smiled – a touch wearily and bleakly. It was true, of course – on a Richter scale of ineptitude, he would push the needle to the full ten. His son looked in his direction, and amidst further laughter, made the pertinent observation – "Well, at least you'll be all right going home, Dad. You'll have a human sat-nav sitting beside you. She won't speak Spanish, and she'll certainly know the way."

His father nodded. "Yes, boy, too true – and thank heavens for it as well. For not only will she guide us home, she'll be able to buy me a coffee at one of the services as well. I fancy I've earned one to break up the journey, after the traumas I've suffered today." With that, he quickly looked away so as not to be turned to stone by the withering glare which he knew would be aimed by his wife in his direction, muttered half under his breath, "Blasted technology – nothing but trouble," then promptly filled his mouth with yet more of his daughter-in-law's delightful concoction. He was destined not to enjoy it, however. For, finishing her cup of tea, then replacing it upon the saucer, Susie made reply to her husband.

"Yes – I'll buy you a cup of coffee at the services, George – though why you want it, I really don't know; it tastes like sump oil. But I've no problem in doing that, if that is what you want. What I will not do, however, is guide you out of Bristol. It's a nightmare guiding you anywhere – you've no sense of direction, and you go much too fast. By the time I've located the road we need, almost invariably we're past it. So, no, I will not navigate for you. Rather, you can ask Danny here to show you how to key in our address for the return journey, and then abide by its instructions – and in English, Danny, please."

Her son grinned. "Well, yes, if that's what you want. I'll go through it with you in a minute, Dad, when you've finished your sponge."

His father nodded, too polite to say that the delicacy had turned to ashes in his mouth. Still, there was, he knew, no escape – he knew his spouse well enough to know that if she said she'd not navigate, she assuredly wouldn't. Even if they headed in the direction of Newcastle, she would not intervene. Finishing his snack, he gave himself up to his fate.

Half an hour later, his son – a most patient young man – felt confident that at last he had got through to his obtuse father how to programme the sat-nav. And, miraculously, he had. For his parents enjoyed a carefree, almost relaxing, journey home, the calm, precise, reassuring voice of the lady in the sat-nav guiding them, in just over two hours – including a coffee stop at the services – to their front door. From then on, George Davis used the device regularly – sometimes to venues to which he thought he knew the way, finding that the remarkable machine often guided them via a quicker route. No man was ever a greater convert to this technology than he. His wife, though, whilst both pleased, and somewhat astonished at the enthusiasm he showed for it, erred on the side of caution – after all, she knew better than anybody the extraordinary levels of incompetence which her husband could reach when it came to 'new fangled gadgets' as he often labelled them. So wherever they went, every time George invoked the sat-nav, she had upon her lap, sitting in the passenger seat, a route map opened to encompass their destination.

VII

The Church Organ

Frank Goodman was a farmer, and possessed the independent spirit – plus considerable toughness of both mind and body – usually to be found in this hardy breed. Little worried him, little fazed him and even less frightened him. He was also a fellow who could drink as hard as he worked, the landlord of 'The Ferret and Fox', Alan Small, claiming that he had never known anyone who could hold Scotch as well as the middle-aged farmer, whilst his language could be somewhat forceful as many an erring referee at Home Park, Plymouth, learned to his cost.

There was, though, another very different side to what was quite a complex man. For he was, and had been throughout his sixty years upon this earth, a devout Christian; and whilst clearly capable of articulating a dazzling array of expletives when motivated sufficiently, never did he 'take the Lord's name in vain'. And rarely did he miss church on a Sunday either, having been known to leave weather threatened summer hayfields before the gathering in had been completed, to attend evening worship.

Such dedication had seen him elevated, some twenty years previously, to the position of churchwarden whilst for the past twelve years he had been Chairman of the Parochial Church Council, an office which, during the past three months, had occupied more of his time than he would have wished – although he did not complain for he was aware that he would not be occupying the position if he did not wish to.

The problem was that back in the winter, just months before he was due to retire, the Rector of the Parish, the Reverend George Maxwell – a Devon man born and bred, thus ideally suited to the role of spiritual leader of a predominantly rural area, the Tamar lying to the west and south, and Tavy to the east with the powerful grandeur of Dartmoor to the north – had gone down with pneumonia and, surprisingly in a reasonably fit man, still a couple of years short of his allotted three score and ten years, had died from it.

Thus, somewhat more hastily than they would have wished, the PCC had been faced with the complicated and somewhat fraught process of selecting a new vicar. The result of this, after numerous long, exhaustive meetings and interviews, had not really been to the liking of the chairman – or two other male members of the committee, both similar to him in that they were of mature years and were men who had been born and bred in the parish, and who had spent most of their lives there.

The trio had favoured appointing a fellow just turned fifty, married with two grown up children, who had come late to the ministry after working many years in Devonport Dockyard, and who, for five years, had been a curate in a Plymouth parish. However, when he had not gained majority support, they changed their backing to the support of a woman candidate, a lady in her early fifties who had been a curate in a large rural parish in the north of the county and who was well acquainted with the kind of problems which beset the folk who dwelt in rural West Devon. She, though, also fell by the wayside; the committee in the end, going for youth and good looks.

Not that Frank would ever be able to prove such a charge, but as he said to the brace of elderly colleagues with whom he had been of like mind throughout the entire selection process, "You don't need to be Sherlock Holmes to work it out." For the Reverend Simon Sheldon was twenty-nine years old, six feet in height, very well built and was – something which even the chairman had to concede – very good looking. He had been a curate in an inner London borough, and was now looking to gain his own parish – a rural one if possible.

The four ladies on the committee – all of whom had resided in the parish for less than a decade – backed him the instant they saw him, whilst the two other males on the PCC, relatively young chaps, gave him their support because they felt it was time to go for youth, the parish in their eyes, having stagnated a little in recent years under the long serving George Maxwell, a belief reinforced within them when Simon promised, if appointed rector, to bring 'new ideas' and a 'fresh approach' – a policy statement which cemented the opposition of Frank and the other two veterans. "People with new ideas are often a menace," as one of the trio, Cliff Jackson (at seventy-one, the oldest member of the committee) muttered succinctly – and prophetically. He was strongly supported by Goodman and the third old hand, Harry Watson.

The changes were not long in coming, none of which gained Frank's approval, but none so outrageous that he felt forced to 'man the barricades', as they mostly involved modest changes to the order of service. By far the worst one in his view – and in that of many others – was the young minister's encouragement of worshippers to shake hands with, or, worse still, embrace the person next to them in the pew, then speak the words "Peace be with you", before departing the church. As Cliff Jackson had – in Frank's view – so rightly said, "You don't go to church to fraternise with whoever's stood beside you – I mean, you might hate the sight of them."

Such alterations were but tinkering, however, compared with the bombshell the young vicar was to detonate before the PCC some six months after taking up the post – an explosion which had, following the meeting, driven the chairman into the Ferret and Fox even quicker than normal. He stumbled up to the bar, slumped down onto a stool, and, unusually for him, ignored the cheery greeting from the landlord.

"Whisky, Alan. A double – please," the final word coming as an afterthought. The landlord thrust a glass against an optic – twice – and put it down before the farmer.

"I'll put it on the slate, Frank," said he, the merest glance at the customer's face informing him that the last thing the farmer wanted at present was to be bothered with sorting out payment for what was clearly a desperately needed drink. "What's up?" he enquired. "You look like you're – well – in shock, almost."

"In shock? That's an understatement – I just heard the worst idea that's come the way of this parish probably in my entire lifetime. In fact I can still scarce believe it." The farmer ceased talking just long enough to drain the whisky, then pushed the empty glass back the way of the landlord.

"Another, Frank?"

"Yes – yes – a double again, I need it – in fact, I fancy I need a full bottle. Never heard anything like it – never in all my days. That young vicar's a – a – a vandal," he spluttered. "He's a disgrace to the cloth he wears."

"Why, what's he done?" asked Jack Corbett, the local plumber who lived just across the road from the pub and was, in his wife's eyes, an all too regular customer of Alan Miller. "He's not run off with the organist has he?" Whilst the words were said in jocular fashion, there was an element of possibility about them as their organist, Alison Bentley, about forty, was rather attractive and most pleasant; she was also a very good organist. She was, though, devoted to her affable husband, so her elopement was a most unlikely happening.

"No – no – it's not the organist," retorted the farmer, shaking his head in disbelief. "It's the organ – he wants to get rid of it."

"Get rid of the organ?" The voice was that of Jamie Tancock. "He can't do that, surely?" So shocked was the man at the news, that he left the 'one-armed-bandit' in the far corner which was, to him, ever one of the main attractions of the pub, and returned to the bar. "You can stop him, Frank, surely – you as Chairman of the old Parochial Whatsit." Official titles of organisations were invariably a major challenge to the likeable but somewhat feckless Tancock.

"I can't stop him on my own, but the committee can stop him – the PCC. The trouble is, though, there's a majority supporting him." Frank shook his head in bewilderment. "Right from the very beginning I thought this chap would be trouble – but I never dreamt just how much. Over a hundred years old that organ is –

91

and gives out the most glorious sound you can ever hear; and he wants to get rid of it."

"But what about the hymns and so on – a church has got to have music," Jamie insisted, Jack Corbett nodding his agreement in the background, before lowering his fifth pint of the evening.

"A piano – part of the time anyway. His plan, a great deal of the time, will be to have local pop groups there; happy-clappy nonsense – that's what it'll be. Dancing, I don't wonder, in the house of the Lord – people dressed like hippies. It scarcely bears thinking about. We've got to move with the times, he says – get youth involved and all that. Not that there's anything wrong with encouraging younger people to come to church and take part and suchlike. But you don't destroy tradition – and – and beauty to do it. Anyway, if this is the way it's going to be, then the PCC and me will part company. Mind you, they'll probably be glad to see the back of me – Cliff Jackson and Harry Watson as well, they also being against it."

"But why are the majority of the committee supporting it?" asked the landlord; he personally was not fussed about the issue, but having kept the Ferret and Fox for some fifteen years he was aware that any controversial issues in the village tended to have an adverse effect on business. Folk who would normally drop in for a leisurely drink spending much of their free time planning and fighting campaigns instead.

"Because they see Sheldon's way as being the way forward – the way to fill the church again. Young, trendy, in touch with youth. Mind you, as I said just now, there's nothing wrong with bringing in a few younger folk – we get some in now, but we could certainly do with more. The trouble is that the way he plans to do it means that for everybody he attracts under forty, he'll lose double over fifty."

"It can't be allowed – it's got to be stopped," rasped Jamie Tancock in aggrieved tones. "We cannot have the church without an organ."

"I didn't realise you were a church-going man," retorted Alan, a grin playing around his lips.

"What do you mean – of course I am. I was married in that

church, as was my daughter Julie last year. And when I shuffle off, I've no doubt I'll have the words said over my coffin there as well. I might not go very often, but it's still my church, Alan. I was born and bred in this village, as were many others – it's their church as well." The words were spoken with such force and eloquence that further conversation was stilled – albeit briefly.

The silence was broken by Maurice Craig, a softly spoken, courteous man, both liked and respected, who had for many years been headmaster of the village primary school until his retirement a decade or so before. Although not Devonians, he and his wife – who was the president of the local Women's Institute – decided to stay in the village following their retirement, and Maurice was in the habit of dropping into the pub some two or three times a week, invariably imbibing a couple of rums with blackcurrant, service in the Royal Navy as a young man having heightened his taste for the spirit.

"Mr Tancock is right, in my view," said he from his seat under the window some five yards from the bar. "I cannot claim to be a believer myself – although my wife is, a strong believer – but being a Christian, active or otherwise, is not essential when it comes to appreciation of the importance of a church to a local community – or the beauty of it, either. This church is over 500 years old; it is a beautiful building and I congratulate Mr Goodman and his committee for keeping it in such a good state of repair – no easy or cheap task in this day and age. As to the organ – well I have often attended recitals in the church over the years, classical and church music being very much my taste. And yes, it does have a glorious tone to it – one can sit in that church and feel the music coming from it washing over one. Inspirational; it would be an act of vandalism to get rid of it. I do hope that other members of the PCC come to realise that – to understand also that they are all trustees, not owners, of the church. They administer it on behalf of the people of the parish, and their duty is to them, not to the whims of an ambitious young clergyman who will, in due course, almost certainly move on in pursuit of his career, leaving behind his mindless desecration."

Alan Small was always to say that the retired teacher's

comments – brief though they were – were the most profound and articulate he had ever heard in his public house. It certainly was the spur for action on his part, for the very next day a large pad of lined writing paper lay atop the bar, and his petition to save the church organ began, everybody coming into the pub being encouraged to sign it, with very few refusing. The landlord's example was followed by other businesses in the parish; Millie Bird, who ran the Newsagents and General Store, had her own pile of paper laying on the counter and found the hardest part regarding the petition was stopping some customers who shopped on a daily basis, signing every time they came in. And the local Garage and Filling Station, run by Frank Goodman's first cousin, Dan, also joined in the campaign to get as many signatures as possible, whilst the Post Office lent support by laying a petition to save the organ on their counter alongside the one to save the Post Office itself – from Government cuts.

The campaign to save the organ soon gathered sufficient momentum to generate a demand for a public meeting, which was convened in the Parish Hall one Friday evening and attracted a massive attendance, with almost a hundred people unable to find a seat – thus stood at the back. Without a solitary voice of dissent, a resolution was passed that the PCC should be informed, in the strongest of terms, that the people of the parish objected to the selling of the organ, and that they should reverse their decision to do so. An official letter was written by the organisers of the meeting and handed to Frank Goodman, as chairman, so that he could take it to the next meeting of the PCC the following week. Neither the farmer nor his two fellow committee members, who opposed the 'mindless desecration', had attended the public meeting, or signed any of the petitions, well aware that it was important that the pro-selling majority on the PCC could not claim even the most tenuous of cases that the trio had helped foment opposition to their scheme.

Thus is was, with a clear conscience, that Frank presented to the next meeting of the PCC, for perusal, the letter of fierce objection from the public gathering in the Parish Hall, plus the petitions bearing in excess of 3,000 signatures, all opposing the vicar's plan.

94

Frank, usually being quite a shrewd judge of folk's reaction had been confident that when the "Desecration Six" (as Alan Miller described them) realised just how much opposition there was in the parish to their scheme – virtually total – they would reverse their decision and tell Simon Sheldon that the organ would remain where it had been for generations. He could not have been more wrong, for five of the nine again voted for the organ to be sold, saying that opposition to the scheme had been stirred up deliberately (not stating who had orchestrated such a campaign) and that folk would support it when they found out exactly what the vicar planned for the future – "A church more welcoming to people of all ages and backgrounds than it is at present." The only one of the original half dozen not to support it this time was the youngest member of the committee, an affable young fellow – David Partridge by name – who abstained, saying that he still thought the vicar's plan was a good one, but that he was not sure they should carry it out in the face of such overwhelming opposition. "Perhaps the Bishop should be asked to make a decision," he had said, lamely – and been totally ignored.

The three stalwarts had been taken aback by the decision – and all felt that the battle was on the brink of being lost. In fact, Frank Goodman, in a rare defeatist mood, said that there appeared nothing else that they could do, and intimated that it was probably time for him to resign as both Chairman of the PCC and as a member; his long stint as Church Warden – a role which he enjoyed – was also likely to end, he feeling that there was no real prospect of him ever being able to establish a decent working relationship with any man of the cloth so insensitive to the views and wishes of others. This, he admitted to himself, really was a shame, for in many ways he liked the young rector, and only the issue of the organ – albeit, a major one – stood between him and willing acceptance of a young man who was always courteous to one and all, friendly, hard-working, most approachable and most anxious to return the church to where it had not been for many a long year, one of the main centres of village life.

The retention of the organ, though, was central to Frank's

future service to the Church; if that went, then so would he – his conscience would demand it.

Sadly there were few doubts it would, indeed, go. The PCC – or the unswervable majority, to be more exact – had decided the organ should be sold, and advertisements were due to be inserted in such relevant periodicals as *The Church Times*, very shortly regarding its sale. The battle, as Frank Goodman saw it, had been lost.

He was to hear news, however, which lifted his spirits higher than they had been for some time. It was brought to him on a Monday afternoon, just after lunch, as he stood in the yard putting much needed oil in the strategic places of a dung spreader. A neat, but old, blue Ford Escort sped into the yard and swept to a stop just a few feet from him. The driver's door was thrust open and Cliff Jackson alighted with an alacrity which spoke well for the fitness of a man past seventy.

The farmer smiled. "You've never been a slow mover, Cliff, but I've not seen you move as fast – not even when you played football." (Jackson had been one of the best right wingers the village football club had ever had, a player with great pace and the possession of a skill which, had he possessed the desire, could have possibly got him on the books of a lower division professional club.)

"I've got news, Frank, and I didn't want to waste any time in letting you know," said he, slightly out of breath. "It's about the organ – we can still save it, if we go about it the right way – and if the district council are kind."

"Save it – how," croaked the farmer, suddenly excited and desperate to hear his visitor's news. He knew Cliff well enough to know that he was not a man to exaggerate. If he said there was a way to save the organ, then for sure there was.

"You know my youngest sister, Jenny." Frank nodded. He knew Jenny very well; in fact he had been very keen on her back in his youth, she being around his age, and the best looking girl in the parish. She had, however, had her head turned by a uniform, marrying a naval officer based in Plymouth. His career had taken them both around the world, but since his retirement

96

some ten years before, they had lived near Tiverton, and, being relatively close, he knew that Cliff and she visited each other on a fairly regular basis. "Well, as you probably know, she's on the district council up there, Tiverton way – has been for the past five or six years. Anyway, she and her husband, Mike, came down for dinner yesterday, we not having seen each other for a couple of months. Well, to get to the point, I told her about the new vicar and the selling of the organ and so on, and how the village was up in arms about it and how it looked as if, despite all the opposition, it was a lost cause, and the organ was going to be sold. Then she asked something that none of us have even thought of – nobody in the village either, strangely enough; she asked if the organ was 'listed'. I said I didn't have a clue, and she said right away that I should find out, making the point that if it was, it would be difficult – in fact almost impossible – to sell it or get rid of it in any way."

"I've never thought of it, Cliff," retorted Frank, hope strongly rekindled within him. "But if it is, then it could change everything – we could yet save it. I must find out – I'll phone the council right away."

"It's been done already – in fact, better than phoning, I went into Tavistock this morning to the council offices, and saw the Conservation Officer; very helpful he was, too."

"And is it listed?"

"No, it's not, but hopefully it soon will be. He checked local listings on his computer and was very surprised to find that, somehow, it was not amongst them and, in his view, such an old and beautiful organ should have been, just as the church is, of course. So he said he would put the process in motion right away – this very day – to get it listed, and is confident that it will be, and very shortly."

Cliff Jackson delivered the news with all the pleasure and excitement of a man who had just won the lottery, whilst the farmer's reaction to it was similar, although, being a Devonshire farmer, there was at the back of his mind a feeling that such apparent good news could yet turn to dust.

His touch of pessimism, however, seemed not to be justified.

e

For the organ did achieve listed status, and remarkably quickly at that. In fact the stout armour of official protection was put in place before the PCC had received any bids for the ancient instrument. Joy abounded throughout the parish when the saving of the organ became known, and "amongst heathens every bit as much as amongst Christians," as Alan Small had quipped, in his wry fashion.

Possibly the only Christians who were not joyous were those members of the PCC who had consistently voted for the sale. For some reason, it had become almost a matter of principle amongst them, and a high level of resentment festered with the group – "Why should the council be allowed to interfere in what is essential a private matter," their most vociferous, and unrepentant member, Hilary Fuller, had said in the village Post Office one morning.

The sharp retort from the post mistress that affairs concerning a parish church were very much the business of the entire community, led to a fierce argument which led to the PCC member stating, in furious fashion, that she would never again enter the Post Office Stores as long as it is run "by a stupid, offensive woman like you."

Her final passing volley to the shopkeeper was fired like tracer bullets. "And I'll not resign either – nor will any of us who supported selling that decrepit organ, we've already decided that. We'll stay and we'll live to see the day – not that far away – when others will see sense, and realise we were right all along about the organ; they'll realise that it is an anachronism, a relic of a by-gone age; then they'll agree with us, and it'll be sold." She stormed out and slammed the door behind her.

The Reverend Simon Sheldon, the man who had created all the fuss regarding the organ was, strangely, in no way fazed by the listing of the mighty instrument – although clearly it was a most effective brake on his ambition to be rid of it and be able to create a very different type of music. Being very much an adherent of the 'You win some – you lose some' school of thought, he moved on, rapidly and without a backward glance. For he had many other positive ideas for the future of the church and the parish which had no connection with the retention, or otherwise, of the organ, so proceeded to pursue those. None of them involved radical changes, so over the following months he was able to carry out many of them with little interference or criticism from the PCC. In fact, his general policy of making the services and procedures of the church a little more in keeping with the twenty-first century was accepted by even the more reactionary members of the committee (and the community) for the best of reasons – they seemed to work, the average congregation on a Sunday showing a rise in numbers of almost fifty per cent compared with those of old Reverend Maxwell in his latter years.

He further endeared himself locally – in fact, it was possibly the 'coup-de-grace' – by joining the local football club and proving to be one of its best players, a tough tackling and excellent attacking full-back; and he attained the status of being a local icon when one November Saturday afternoon, he got himself sent-off for committing a 'professional foul'. Dropping in to the pub that evening for a pint – as he did on occasions – he was treated like a hero, and if he had lowered just a quarter of the liquor he was offered, then he would undoubtedly have left the pub in such a state that the Bishop would assuredly have been told of it – which would have done nothing for the career of the young, ambitious man that he was.

The fellow who had first made the stand against the disposal of the organ, was glad to see things get back to normal, with church affairs occupying but a smallish portion of his busy life, rather than dominating it as had been the case for nearly three months. Frank Goodman, though, was to say always that he felt he was in some way to blame for a further calamity at the church which was to revive the dispute over the organ; for he made, in his eyes, the simple but crucial mistake of allowing himself to feel content with life, even a touch optimistic regarding the future – alien and inappropriate emotions for a farmer. "I tempted fate," said he, "and look what happened."

The catastrophe which re-opened many of the wounds that had largely healed during the twelve months and more since the battle of the organ, occurred one crisp Sunday evening in early autumn in the midst of one of the principal services of the year – Harvest Festival. The large congregation – the church being almost full – were in the middle of celebrating, and singing, that "All is Safely Gathered In, 'Ere The Winter Storms Begin," when suddenly the organ died, emitting what sounded like a deep thunderous groan. With admirable presence of mind, Dick Coleman the choir master, immediately turned away from the choir, faced the congregation and conducted them through the rest of the hymn, most folk keeping to the tune and the timing quite well in consequence.

Following a hasty word with Alison Bentley who still sat at the organ, an expression of bemusement upon her face, Simon Sheldon informed the congregation that unfortunately the organ had 'packed up' and so they would have to carry on the service without it. However, he stated that there should be no great problem as the only remaining hymn was *Bread of Heaven* and everybody knew the tune to that one. Still, to help them keep in time, Mr Coleman would again conduct. Thus did the service proceed – relatively smoothly – to its conclusion.

Immediately following it, the vicar, Frank Goodman, Alison Bentley and the choir master got together in the vestry to discuss what should be done. Why the organ, which, to the farmer's long and comprehensive knowledge, had never failed before, had suddenly 'broken down' now, he had not the slightest idea; nor did anybody else. The organist, though, knew a man who possibly would – her husband Stephen, also an organist, who, not wanting the commitment of regular playing, would cover for holidays, illness and such, in churches and chapels in the West Devon area. He was also, stated his wife, quite knowledgeable regarding the workings of such mighty instruments, and, if there was not much wrong, he might be able to repair it – he had done such in a chapel near Tavistock just a few months before.

Thus did Stephen Bentley, the very next evening, come round and have a look – and a tinker. His views were not encouraging when he came around afterwards to report to Frank Goodman, who had arranged to meet him in the pub.

Sipping a large glass of red wine, of which he was both a lover and a connoisseur, he gave the PCC chairman his dismal report. "I can't say exactly what it is, but I do fancy it's rather major. I've checked most of the simple, easily rectified things it could be, but everything there seems all right. Now, I'm no expert as I've said to you before, but I have a feeling it has failed deep in the organ – something major. Only that, I feel, would explain why it broke down so suddenly and so completely. It'll need stripping down by an expert to start with, who then will guage what is wrong and what is needed to put it right. If new parts are required – and I fancy they will be – it'll not be easy to source them; this, after all, is a very old organ. Nor, I'm afraid, will it be cheap."

He was assuredly correct in both predictions. For Frank, acting upon a suggestion from Stephen – who knew the correct people to contact regarding anything to do with most musical instruments, and especially organs and pianos – gave him the name and phone number of a specialist company in Exeter, about the only firm west of London, in Stephen's view, with the knowledge and expertise to be able to tackle such a complex challenge as that posed by the ancient instrument.

The fellow who came to apprise from what the organ suffered was slight in build, totally bald, bespectacled and about sixty years old. A man called Conway, he was, according to Stephen, an acknowledged expert in the field of repair, restoration and maintenance of elderly organs and was also a director of the company. It was as well that he was small, as he spent most of the day worming his way into holes which would have fazed a cat, to get into the 'bowels of the beast' as he put it.

Frank, ever conscientious regarding his position of Church Warden and Chairman of the PCC – and well aware that the organ was still there largely due to his original stand against its sale – spent the day shuttling to and fro between his farm and the church (some half a mile), keeping the expert fuelled with heavily sugared tea brewed in the vestry, and becoming ever more depressed thanks to Conway's habit of seemingly perpetually shaking his head in disciplined despair and saying, "There are serious problems, Mr Goodman – inevitable I'm afraid, in an organ as old as this."

In fairness, the time he took to assess exactly what the problems were tended to back up his doom laden comments. For he had started his inspection at 9.30 and, except for a few tea breaks, and less than half an hour for him to eat his packed lunch, he did not finish until just before 4 o'clock. He went into the vestry, washed his hands, took off the overalls he was wearing, put on his jacket and joined the churchwarden who was leaning against the piano which occupied what little space there was between the organ and the front pew and was the only, and rather inadequate, source of music in the church at present. Despite its shortcomings, however, Frank had been very grateful to Stephen Bentley for his loan of it to the church to tide them over until the organ had been repaired – or other arrangements had been made – he possessing another piano at home which was newer and which he preferred when it came to giving lessons, which was one of his sources of income. The piano had been transported to the church on Frank's hay trailer, its lifting on and off near rupturing the churchwarden, Bentley and Cliff Jackson in the process.

The expert had a grave expression on his face, but seeing as he had had such all day, the farmer didn't know whether this was a harbinger of bad news, or was his normal look. Before the question on his lips could be asked, Conway had answered it. "The positive news, Mr Goodman, is that we can repair the organ. It will not, however, be cheap – in excess of £10,000 for certain. I will, of course, work out an exact quote for all parts and labour, which will be with you within a few days. This is a quite magnificent organ – many a cathedral would covet one of such quality and power as this; it is though, as we all know, very old. Thus most of the new parts which are needed will not be available. Granted, one or two of the smaller ones can reasonably easily be accommodated by adapting ones which we fit into modern organs. The main one at the heart of the organ, deep within it and thus hard to get at, will have to be specially made at our works in Exeter – a highly skilled, time consuming and expensive business. As will be the fitting of these parts, and the general overhaul and servicing of the instrument, crucial if you are to get the best out of it."

Thus was Frank Goodman, Chairman of the PCC, left awaiting an estimate which he knew he would find deeply depressing; and he felt even lower when the realisation came to him that he would have to take that massive potential bill to the PCC to seek their views as to how such a huge amount of money could be raised, or, to be realistic, if it could be raised at all, in the foreseeable future. For certain, he and his two companions in the 'Gang of Three' who had originally opposed the selling of the organ would be roasted by the 'Monstrous Regiment of Women', led by Hilary Fuller.

The organ expert was true to his word, the quotation for the repair of the organ reaching the farmer exactly three days after his visit. It made alarming reading. Frank immediately phoned Cliff Jackson, then Harry Watson, and agreed to meet them in the Ferret and Fox that evening, when he would divulge and discuss the amount which needed to be raised to sort out the organ. Certainly it was a time to have his allies about him – to have their support and ideas.

Thus that evening found the trio sitting quietly in the pub, sipping their beer and puzzling as to how the church could ever come up with the money. "Over twelve grand," sighed Watson. "I reckon it might just as well be twelve million for all the chance we've got of raising that amount. It could take years – many."

"Yes," agreed the chairman. "Hopefully Stephen Bentley's loan of the piano is a long term one; we'll certainly need it for the foreseeable future."

"Twelve thousand, eh." The words were said by Alan Small, who had been hovering nearby wiping a couple of tables. "That's what they want to put the organ right – or, at least, I assume that's what you're on about." The landlord, like virtually everybody else in the village, was well aware that an expert had spent a day earlier that week assessing the reasons for the organ's failure and how much it would cost to put it right. As it had been public pressure that had done so much to stop the sale of the instrument, it was only natural that their interest remained keen; and it was equally right they knew the sum required to put it right. Thus none of the trio were in any way offended by Small's somewhat obtrusive question – he, and the rest of the village, had a right to know.

"Yes," admitted Frank, "or £12,010 to be exact. It's funny, isn't it, that no matter how big a quote or a bill, they always put in a few odd quid to make it sound as if it's all been worked out to the nearest single pound."

Small nodded. "Yes – true enough," he agreed with a grin. His expression suddenly became grave. "It'll take some finding, won't it – that kind of money?"

There was rapid agreement from all three that it would, indeed, take some finding. Conversation ceased for a brief period, all of them deep in thought. They were raised from it by a softly spoken, "Excuse me, gentlemen;" Maurice Craig, having imbibed his usual nightly brace of rums, was standing before them. The retired headteacher looked a touch embarrassed. "It's just that I could not help but overhear your conversation with Mr Small concerning the sum of money required to bring that magnificent organ back into play. I think I've had an idea that could be of some help to you – but it's something I would wish to discuss with my wife first. Neither of us ever make any decisions, especially where money is concerned, without both of us discussing it first. I wonder if it would be possible for us all to get together here tomorrow evening – say, about 7.30. I usually get here at that time and I am usually away by about, well 8.15 or so. I'm a touch long in the tooth to be out very late."

His approach caught them off-guard for a few seconds, but Frank Goodman soon overcame his surprise and said, readily, "Yes – that'll be fine as far as I'm concerned. I don't know about you gents." He looked across at his companions as he spoke. From them there came hasty nodding.

"Yes – yes, no problem," said Cliff Jackson, and like assent was given by Harry who could not speak as he had a mouthful of pork scratchings.

So the appointment was made for the following evening, with none of the three having the slightest idea as to what Maurice had in mind, although they did have a certain feeling – perhaps a certain hope – that it could be something to their advantage. And they were to be proved correct.

The three PCC members assembled at about 7.15, got some drinks in, and paid for a rum for the retired headteacher who arrived to drink it just before 7.30. The quartet sat in the far corner of the bar and, taking a sip of their drinks, the church trio gazed expectantly at Maurice Craig who, likewise, took a small measure of his liquor. He placed the glass back on to the table top, then looked at his expectant audience.

"Thank you, gentlemen, for coming along tonight," (words he spoke out of courtesy more than anything else, well aware that attendance at the pub was no hardship to them). "It is appreciated – and thank you for the drink. As I mentioned yesterday evening, I could not but overhear your conversation regarding repairing the organ – £12,010, I believe was mentioned."

Frank nodded his agreement, then said, "I reckon we can raise the tenner – it's the twelve grand that's the problem." He followed the words with a wry smile.

The former teacher smiled, then said, "Yes – I can imagine that is something of a challenge. Well, it could be that I am in a position to offer a solution. I said nothing yesterday evening, even though an idea had formed itself in my mind; I needed firstly to talk it over with my wife – something I have now done. Fortunately, she was in total agreement with what I was thinking – which I thought she would be; she is a regular worshipper in the church as you will know and as I've told you, I am a great lover of church organ music. The restoration of that wonderful instrument is of considerable importance to us both. So, without more ado, I'll give to you our idea of a financial way forward regarding putting the repair work in hand. Twelve thousand pounds is what you need – that, certainly, is the sum I heard you mention last evening." Frank Goodman nodded his agreement, as the ex-headteacher continued. "Our offer, gentlemen – my wife and myself – is that we are willing to pay for the repairs to the organ."

"All of it – what, twelve grand?" Cliff Jackson's tone betrayed his incredulity. "Why, that's – that's fantastic."

"Well, we are very fond of that organ, as I said just now. And whilst we are far from being wealthy, we are comfortably off. We both had long careers in the teaching profession, and retired on decent pensions. And as we were not blessed with children, we have had no draw on our resources in that direction." He said those words with a gentle smile playing around his lips, and a brief shake of his head – clearly the saving of money was no compensation for their lack of family. "Our idea is this, gentlemen; when the work is done and the organ is in full working order again, I will give you a cheque for the twelve thousand. Now half of it will be a gift; the other half, however, will be, in effect, a loan – £6,000 – interest free to be paid back when convenient to yourselves. I'm sorry we cannot make it all a gift; but with us both now into old age, we do have to be certain that we have sufficient funds to cover all eventualities. However, we are not going to put any time limit on it, for we are confident that such an honourable body as the Parochial Church Council will ensure that the money will be paid sooner rather than later."

"Yes – yes – yes, of course it will," spluttered Frank, astonished at the sheer munificence of the offer. "We will ensure the money is repaid to you as soon as possible – perhaps a certain amount each month. We could set up a standing order."

His two colleagues nodded their agreement, instantly; indeed, so relieved were the pair they would have agreed to virtually anything.

Promptly, Frank got up from the able and went to the bar, where he ordered another round of drinks – including a double rum for the benefactor. As he said when he had returned to their table with the liquor – and glasses were raised for a toast towards the successful, and speedy, renovation and repair of the organ, "You deserve a dozen crates of rum for what you have done for us all, Mr Craig."

Drinks were consumed and, as they prepared to leave the pub, Frank informed Maurice Craig that his so generous offer would be put to the PCC later that week when they had a meeting. "I would be astounded if your marvellous offer is not accepted instantly – with both relief and immense gratitude."

106

The first of the Frank Goodman's predictions proved accurate – the offer was accepted instantly by the PCC. In fact, it was accepted with virtually no discussion – something which surprised the chairman, as he had anticipated at least a discordant note from Hilary Fuller, although she did comment that "beggars cannot be choosers"; there seemed, however, to be little relief and a shameful lack of gratitude.

Following the vote – unanimous that Maurice Craig's offer be accepted – Frank Goodman insisted that a letter be sent to the Craigs expressing the deep gratitude of the committee for their remarkably altruistic offer. Also, a letter was to be sent to the organ repair company that their estimate for the work had been accepted, and that the work should be put in hand by the company within the seven days promised by them if their quote was agreed. The prediction that the work would take a maximum of three weeks to complete, meant that a revitalised organ would, in theory, be once again giving out its magnificent tones within a month. To set things in motion, virtually instantly, Frank stated that he would phone the company the following morning, tell them of the committee's decision, and say that this would be confirmed by letter within a day or two. "It'll mean that they'll be able to put things in motion right away, which could cut down the period of repairs by a day or two, at least," opined the chairman. Frank glanced around the members of the committee, saw there was no dissent to his suggestion, so moved rapidly to 'any urgent business'.

"I have nothing to raise here," said he, "and nobody approached me before the meeting to say there was something they wished to bring up, so I assume there is nothing." Before he could declare the meeting closed, however, the strident tones of Hilary Fuller assailed his ears:

"Yes, there is something, Chair," she retorted. "Something of considerable importance." She noted, with satisfaction, the momentary expression of intense annoyance which flitted across his face, partly activated by the fact he was not able to bring the meeting to a close, but caused even more by the fact that she had addressed him as 'Chair', a word which, she well knew, he detested. If a man was in the chair, then 'Chairman' was the word which should be used, was his view; if a woman, then, logically, 'Chairwoman'; to address someone as 'Chair' was to dehumanise them – a chair, after all, was a conglomeration of wood upon which one sat.

"Very well, Mrs Fuller," said he, icily. "Although I would point out that it is customary, and good manners, for a member of the committee to mention before the meeting if there is an item they wish to bring up under any urgent business."

"In the normal run of things, I would have done so, Chair, but the proposal I am about to make is such that I do not feel it would have been helpful, in any way, to have mentioned it earlier."

"I would remind you that it is completely contrary to the spirit of any meeting to make a proposition of any item unless the committee has had prior notification of it – or unless the matter is of great importance or urgency." Frank Goodman spoke in a tone of severity which was unlike him, but which nonetheless he was good at summoning on those rare occasions when it was needed – and he was certain that it was most assuredly necessary when dealing with the acidic, and devious Mrs Fuller.

The lady was in no way abashed. "It is both very important and urgent, Chair," she rasped, "and it needs to be brought to the committee immediately."

"Very well," replied Frank Goodman, making no attempt to disguise the hostility he felt to both Hilary Fuller and her 'urgent business', whatever it was. "Say what you have to say, Mrs Fuller."

"Thank you, Chair," replied she, putting subtle emphasis on the 'Chair', and again noting with satisfaction the expression of anger on his face. "I feel it my duty to bring this matter forward on behalf of what, I believe, is a majority of this committee. The fact is that we are in a financial mess, and the reason for it is the necessity of having to spend £12,000 to renovate the organ. Granted this will, initially, be paid by Mr and Mrs Craig – and theirs is certainly an exceedingly generous gesture. Only half of it is a gift, however, with £6,000 having to be repaid in the near future – a very substantial amount for a smallish parish such as ours, at the best of times, and, with us also having to find money for repairs to the roof and to address dry rot in the vestry, this assuredly is not the best of times. The reality is, if we are honest with ourselves, it is difficult to know where the finance needed for all these things will come from. I know that the Craigs have said that there is no urgency regarding repayment of their loan, but it has to be repaid sometime – and I doubt it will be any easier next year that it is this. Now, the reason we are in this mess, Chair, is simple enough – it is because the organ is listed and therefore cannot be removed and, clearly, needs to be kept in working order. If it were not listed it would have been removed from the church months ago and the massive problems we face now would not have arisen; we would not now be afflicted with major financial worries and, on a wider front, this church with our active, progressive vicar, would have moved on into a new era. And the reason it is listed, Chair, is down to yourself and a few other members of this committee. With their assistance, you took action to get the organ listed without any consultation with this committee; basic courtesy alone should have persuaded you to bring such an important matter to a meeting of this committee – a special one if necessary; even worse than this, I feel that you over-stepped your authority, along with your colleagues, in pursuing this matter with the Planning Department of the District Council – this is a gathering of equals, Chair, not a dictatorship. With all this in mind, I feel – and I have thought long and hard about this – that I have no alternative other than to propose a vote of No Confidence in you as Chair of the PCC."

Her voice had scarcely tailed off before Jane Carter, staunch ally to the proposer, had thrust her arm in the air. "I second the motion, Chair," cried she in her rather shrill way.

So stunned was the chairman over this development that several seconds elapsed before he responded to the motion before the committee. "This is a motion which I did not foresee, that I have to admit, and I suspect it has been well debated by several members of this committee long before this meeting began." These were words spoken by Frank Goodman with a large measure of bitterness – if not anger. "With that in mind," he continued, "I see no point in debating it further – all members of the committee will, I am sure, have fairly set ideas as to whether or not they have confidence in myself as chairman of the PCC. So, I put it to the vote – all those in favour of the No Confidence vote regarding me, please show."

Five arms shot skywards – with almost indecent speed.

"And those against."

Loyally, but clearly dejectedly, Cliff Jackson and Harry Watson raised their arms; like Frank, they were somewhat 'shell-shocked' at the turn of events. "It was an assassination," was the way Harry described it afterwards and the vanquished chairman could only agree.

"The motion is carried," said Frank Goodman, a touch of despair in his voice. This was truly a bitter moment for him. His long and deep involvement as both member and Chairman of the Parochial Church Committee being of immense importance to him.

He rose slowly from his seat, glanced about him, opined, "I fancy my time will be better spent in the Ferrett and Fox," wished all a curt "Good evening," then walked slowly from the scene.

No sooner had he left the room, than the piercing tones of Jane Carter rent the air. "I assume Mr Goodman, by leaving the meeting, having been defeated in a No Confidence vote, indicates his awareness that he is no longer the chair of this committee. Such an important office as this clearly cannot be left vacant, especially with all the problems which confront us; I propose that Mrs Fuller becomes Chair of the PCC – do I have a seconder?"

David Donnelly, a fellow in his forties, raised his right hand to acknowledge his seconding of the motion; he did it with a marked lack of enthusiasm, but felt that probably it would have been better if the organ had gone when its demise had originally been mooted. Only having been in the area for about four years, and a member of the committee for two, he was, however, a little embarrassed over the unseating of the chairman. Still, he mused to himself, Frank Goodman had to be replaced, and whilst he was not a great fan of Hilary Fuller, she was undoubtedly efficient and would probably make an effective chairwoman.

"All those in favour of the motion," said Mrs Carter, and four arms were thrust into the air. Hilary Fuller, confident there was no way the vote could be lost, opting for decorum by not voting for herself. "All those against." Frank Goodman's steadfast allies raised an arm apiece, fully aware that their cause was well lost, but determined to remain loyal to a man who had led the PCC with dedication, vision and integrity for so many years.

"Mrs Fuller is duly elected as Chair of the PCC." Jane Carter made the statement with an air bordering on triumphalism – which was what she felt, for she was convinced that her good friend Hilary would make a far better Chair than Frank Goodman and, something which she would never admit, even to herself, she had not forgiven him for the incident a few years previously when a bullock had somehow escaped from one of his fields (situated only about 200 yards from where she lived) got into her garden – her pride and joy – and caused mayhem. Frank had apologised for it but not, in her view, with any sincerity – although he had paid her £100 in compensation. To her, though, no amount of money could adequately compensate for the desecration of a garden it had taken years to create; so now, in her eyes, she took a modicum of revenge. The newly elected chairwoman moved briskly towards the front of the large room to occupy the chair of office, whilst Messrs Jackson and Watson moved even more quickly towards the exit – then through it.

Briefly they stood outside trying to come to terms with the audacious *coup-d'étet* launched, and accomplished by Hilary Fuller – one which meant that she and those of like mind were now well in control of the PCC and, thus, able to dictate the future direction in which the local ministry moved, a fact neatly annunciated by Harry Watson in his brisk, understated way: "It's not been the best of nights, Cliff, not for us, not for poor old Frank, and worst of all, not for the future of this church."

His sombre companion nodded his agreement. "Sadly, you're right – and at present I cannot see any way of altering things. That woman has been cleverer than a bag of monkeys. There's got to be something we can do, Harry – but at the moment I've not the slightest idea what it is. Still, first things first," said he, a touch more brightly; "I'm in need of 'Scottish Wine' – a nice single malt will do me a power of good, I fancy."

Watson nodded his agreement. "I'm with you there, boy – but I've a feeling it will take more than one to ease the pain of all the nonsense that's taken place this evening."

With that, they turned and walked at a steady pace in the direction of the pub. Within ten minutes they were sitting there at a table with Frank Goodman, drinking whisky and all gazing morosely in front of them. The displaced chairman sat there, almost trance-like, saying very little except, about once every minute or so, "I still can't believe it – I just didn't see it coming." His companions said nothing, both deeply immersed in their own gloom.

Harry Watson was the first to break the silence – save for Frank's regular, and monotonous lament. "It's just occurred to me – we should tell Maurice Craig about what's happened. He'll not be happy about the change of chairman; keeping in mind his great love for the organ. I mean, from his point of view, the man who has fought so hard to save it – you Frank – has been replaced by the woman whose only ambition is to destroy it. And destroy it she probably will – she's a very devious woman."

Cliff Jackson fixed him with a keen gaze. "I can't see how she can do that, Harry, now that it's listed," he said.

Watson shrugged his shoulders. "Well, my brother-in-law used to be on the planning committee of a council across the Tamar and I remember him saying years back, that if somebody is determined to get around listing laws, there are ways it can be done – and Hilary Fuller would seem to me to be the sort of person who will, if for no other reason than sheer cussedness, make it her business to get the listing order lifted, or, at least, weakened."

Jackson nodded his agreement, "I see where you're coming from," said he, before reaching for his whisky, emptying his glass, then moving to the bar to get refills. Whilst there, he enquired of the landlord whether or not Maurice Craig had been in that evening. Harry Watson's reference to the fact that the church's benefactor would be unhappy regarding Hilary Fuller's usurping of the chairmanship, playing around his mind somewhat. Alan Small shook his head – "No, he's not been in; they're away on holiday, he and his missus – won't be back for a fortnight or more."

Returning to their table, Cliff distributed the drinks, then sat down, deep in thought. Possibly a minute or more passed without a word being said, until Frank Goodman, having tipped back his Scotch, returned his glass rather noisily to the table top, leant back in his seat, and said something fresh; "When I get home, I'm going to write out my resignation from the PCC. It's clearly time to make a break. There's plenty of other things I can waste my time on," the last sentence was spoken in a tone pregnant with bitterness.

Harry Watson nodded his agreement – "Yes, Frank, I feel exactly the same way; my resignation will also be in the post tomorrow. I've had enough of all the conspiracies and internal politics that seem to be going on in the background when it comes to that committee. It's time to break free, I fancy."

Cliff Jackson emptied his glass, then looked at his two companions. Slowly, he shook his head. "No, don't do that – not yet at any rate. Five minutes ago I would have agreed with you both, and my resignation would also have been in the post tomorrow, but something you said, Harry, a bit earlier has played around my mind a bit, and I fancy there could still be a way in which we can yet turn the tables regarding the 'Foul Fuller' and her ghastly crew. I need some time to pursue it though – to see if there is a way we can get rid of her before she does any lasting damage to the church, and this parish. It could be there is nothing we can do, but I do have an idea which is, I believe, possibly worth pursuing. Nothing ventured, nothing gained as they say. Now, the next meeting of the PCC is four weeks tonight. Can I suggest that none of us resign until then – that's if we resign at all? If things don't work out to our advantage, then we can all go to the meeting, resign in person, then storm out – a bit of a dramatic exit will do no harm, for it will at least show Fuller and her fans that we are not prepared to go quietly. If, though, things work out as they might, then it could well be her and that blasted

Carter woman – at least – who have to go."

The man spoke quietly, as was his way, but with utter conviction. Both of the fellows who listened to him had known him a very long time – in Frank's case he could not remember a time when he had not known him. The possessor of a shrewd, intelligent brain, still as sharp as a razor, with an ability to do the *Times* crossword almost as fast as Inspector Morse, they were aware that wisdom dictated they gave the older man the month he desired, and then take things from there. So both Frank Goodman and Harry Watson went home to their wives with some small conviction flickering within them that there was still some future for them on the Parochial Church Council.

The renovators were true to their word, beginning work on restoring the mighty organ to magnificent order the following Monday. No longer being chairman, and deciding to keep a low profile until the next meeting, Frank was not party to progress reports – or otherwise – regarding the vital work, but on his still regular visits to the Ferret and Fox, gossip and hearsay made no mention of works in the church, which had to be good news as assuredly he, and all the regulars, would have been informed by the landlord (a man who usually was aware of all happenings in the parish) if things were going awry. He saw Harry Watson a few times at the pub, but Cliff Jackson only once – some three weeks after his ousting from the chairmanship – when the deep-thinking man informed him, somewhat enigmatically, that the Craigs were back from their holidays, and that he would ensure they were both at the PCC meeting the following Thursday week.

The Sunday prior to the meeting, found the former chairman near the back of a packed church, singing – with no small measure of delight – *Bread of Heaven*, to the glorious strains of the mighty organ, the restoration and repair works having been successfully completed just forty-eight hours earlier. A delighted Alison Bentley, using her comprehensive skills to bring the best out of the huge music box, said that the tone and performance was even better than before. So Frank Goodman went home that night a happy man, and no matter what the following Thursday's meeting might bring, nothing could alter the fact that this

114

wonderful musical instrument should be there to inspire worshippers for generations to come.

Having a busy week on the farm, Frank thought little of the upcoming PCC meeting, although he had to admit to himself that he was a touch curious as to what Cliff Jackson was up to. Whilst he didn't think that even that astute man could move Hilary Fuller out of the Chair, he had sufficient regard for, and confidence in, the fellow's abilities to feel that something of a positive – and, for him, possibly advantageous nature – might manifest itself that evening.

Anyway, he mused to himself as he approached the Church Hall, he would soon find out. Stood outside the meeting place was Harry Watson, who had phoned earlier in the day suggesting they meet up before the gathering, and go in together. What Cliff was doing they knew not, but Harry, like the farmer, had a feeling that something very interesting could happen that evening. The two entered the smallish hall, and took their seats – extremely uncomfortable, being uncompromising high backed wooden chairs, built to last – and settled themselves directly in front of Hilary Fuller, who was sat gazing at the body of the hall from the far more comfortable, padded chair that was the chairman's seat.

Harry leant in the direction of the former chairman and whispered, "Now you know what it's been like for us committee members over the years, sitting on these blasted chairs – whoever designed them should be shot."

"Yes – I'm with you there, Harry. It seems to me that if I cannot be chairman, then it's best I leave altogether – I couldn't face years of sitting on these chairs." He grinned, wryly, in the direction of his companion, although he was by no means certain that he was joking; nor was Harry.

"Evening Frank – Harry." Both men turned their heads at the greeting and saw Cliff Jackson taking his seat beside them. He was not alone, being accompanied by Maurice Craig.

"Good evening, gentlemen," said the retired headteacher, in his ever-courteous fashion.

"Evening, Mr Craig," they chorused.

"Mr Craig has come along this evening because he wishes to

make a statement to the committee regarding – well regarding recent developments," explained Cliff Jackson, an air of suppressed excitement about him. "It is a statement which, I am sure, will concentrate the minds of all of us present here tonight – but one or two especially," he continued, again a touch enigmatically.

Hilary Fuller looked up from the notes she had been making, took in the faces of those attending, seemingly for the first time, noticed – a fleeting expression of alarm momentarily upon her face – the presence of Maurice Craig amongst them, glanced at her watch, then spoke for the first time.

"Good evening, Ladies and Gentlemen," said she, her voice even more strident than normal, brought about, surmised Frank Goodman, by the unexpected presence of the benefactor – clearly a visit which the new chairwoman had not expected. "It's past seven o'clock, so we must make a start. I see that Mr Craig has joined us. You are, of course, most welcome in one sense, Mr Craig. Certainly this committee is greatly in your debt – both literally and metaphorically – for your kind gesture regarding paying for the refurbishment of the organ. However, I am sure that you will be most understanding if I ask you to leave. Unlike the parish or district councils, we are not a public body as such and the discussions we have, along with the decisions we make, have to be carried out in private."

"I am well aware of that, Madam Chairwoman," replied Craig in his gentle way, "and I have no intention of remaining here for more than a few minutes. I am here simply to deliver to you, as Chairwoman of the PCC, a letter which I have written concerning the refurbishment of the organ – a project which, I believe, has been brought to a most successful conclusion. However, it has been brought to my attention that since I made the offer to the PCC, on behalf of my wife and myself, concerning paying for the refurbishment, certain important and potentially disturbing changes have taken place regarding the make up of the PCC. The principal one, of course, involves yourself being elected to the Chair in place of Mr Goodman. Now, in essence, such internal changes are the business of yourselves and nobody else and I do not have the right, or seek the right, to interfere in any way.

116

However, when my wife and I made the offer of the £12,000 – half a gift, the other £6,000 to be repaid over a period of time – it was made when, with Mr Goodman in the chair, the PCC seemed very keen to preserve that magnificent organ. However, now that you are in the chair, Ma'am, things, I fear, could be different. It is common knowledge throughout the parish that you, and some of your colleagues on the committee, were wishing to sell off the organ, only its listing preventing you from pushing through its sale. However, I am informed that whilst its listing prevents the organ from being destroyed, it could still possibly be sold, and it occurs to me that now it has been extensively refurbished, it is a very saleable item. If this were to happen, it would mean that my wife and myself would have drawn quite heavily on our savings just to fund the PCC to be able to bring the organ up to a standard and condition where it would command a high price on the market. Nothing could, or would be further from our intentions; we both wish to see that beautiful musical instrument as part of this church and this parish for generations to come. Now, Madam Chairwoman, I say to you that in no way do I question your integrity, you are clearly a lady of strong opinions and convictions which is something I respect. However, I fear that your beliefs and vision for the future of both this church and its organ are radically different to those of my wife and myself. To put the matter in the very bluntest of terms – we do not feel that the future of our organ as a long term, integral part of our church is safe in the hands of this committee as long as you are in the chair and thus in a position to influence matters as you can at present. Thus, with deep regret, on behalf of my wife and myself, I have to state that unless Mr Goodman is restored as Chairman of the PCC with immediate effect, then our offer of paying the £12,000 cost of the organ renovation is withdrawn. All this is written, in formal terms, in the letter which I hold in my hand, and which I will give you now." Briskly, amidst an eerie silence, he moved towards the chairwoman's table, dropped the letter on the surface in front of her, wished one and all a "very good evening", and departed.

It seemed like minutes before anybody broke the tense silence that Maurice Craig left in his wake, though in reality it was only thirty seconds or so.

"What exactly does this mean?" asked David Partridge – ever the member of the committee who vacillated between the two factions, yet inclined usually to support Hilary Fuller. "I mean – well, what happens now? How are we going to pay for the organ repairs if Mr Craig refuses to give us the money he promised?" He stopped talking briefly, but then added, a most troubled expression upon his face – "I mean, can he refuse to pay after promising that he would do so?"

"No – In my view, he cannot," snapped Hilary Fuller. "He gave a solemn promise to pay it – so he's morally bound to do so."

"Whether or not he is morally bound, is a matter of opinion," stated Cliff Jackson in his measured, unemotional way. "What counts, though, is whether or not he is legally bound – and in that direction, I fear that he is not. For it is as he said – he and his wife agreed to give us the money when Frank here, who is a staunch supporter of the organ remaining an integral part of our church, was chairman. Now, however, our chairman is Mrs Fuller who wanted – and probably still wishes – to sell off that magnificent instrument. Indeed, as I see it – and, I suspect, as Mr and Mrs Craig see it – now that the organ has been restored to its full glory, there could yet be a way in which it may be sold. They have reacted to this by insisting that if the situation which existed when they made their so generous offer is not restored, namely, if Mr Goodman is not reinstated as chairman, then that offer is withdrawn. Which means that when the bill for the £12,010 comes in – and it'll be here within a few days, you can depend on that – we as members of the committee that instructed the company to go ahead and do the repairs will have to pay it out of our own pockets; it'll be the best part of two thousand pounds each."

"Stuff and nonsense," snorted the chairwoman. "There's no reason why we should have to pay it."

"There is every reason, Madam Chairman," replied Jackson, his voice registering no emotion at all – which made it most

118

effective. "Quite simply, if we do not pay it, who does? The church accounts at present are, as we are all well aware, in a particularly parlous state; there's not enough there to pay even the interest on £12,000. No, we put the work in hand – so we, ultimately, are responsible for settling the debt."

There was silence for several seconds before David Partridge, in a somewhat faltering voice, spoke his fears. "I don't want to have to pay out of my own pocket," said he. "In fact, I can't afford to. I've got kids and a mortgage, and my wife recently lost her part time job. There's no way I could find the money."

"Well, as I see it, if we don't do as Mr Craig wishes and re-appoint Mr Goodman as chairman, then we will have no option," opined Harry Watson in his customary phlegmatic way. "It is as simple as that."

"Well, I don't care what the ramifications are, there is no way that I could ever support the removal from the chair of Hilary – er, Mrs Fuller, I should say. Mr Craig's demands are nothing other than blackmail – he should be ashamed of himself, especially as he is a well-respected member of the local community."

Frank Goodman smiled to himself; Jane Carter's rasping defiance regarding Maurice Craig's demands was to be expected. She was not a woman that the farmer liked, but he had to acknowledge that she was a lady always loyal to her friend Hilary Fuller, and who invariably said it as she saw it.

Cliff Jackson's measured tones rose above the murmurings which followed Mrs Carter's outburst. "There is no way that one could call it blackmail. Mr Craig is merely saying – correctly and with total accuracy – that the situation regarding our committee which existed when he and his wife made their remarkably generous offer, has changed considerably, and changed in a way not to their liking. Therefore, he feels justified – and, in my view, is justified – in withdrawing their offer unless the original composition of the committee is reinstated." He stopped briefly, looked around him, then delivered his *coup de grâce*. "With this in mind, Madam Chairman – and I emphasise here and now that this proposal is, in no way, one which you or anyone else should see as a personal attack on yourself – I feel that I have no alternative other than to propose that Mr Goodman once again becomes Chairman of the PCC." Harry Watson was about to raise his arm as seconder, but was beaten by a worried looking David Partridge.

"Yes, well, I am desperately sorry things have worked out this way, Madam Chairman," said he, taking great care to avoid Hilary Fuller's belligerent stare, "but I have no option other than to support Mr Jackson's proposal – so I formally second it."

The chairwoman sat as if turned to stone. The realisation came to her slowly, but came to her nonetheless; she was having done to her what she had done to Frank Goodman – she was being ambushed. There was silence for what seemed an eternity, but was little more than half a minute. Then Hilary Fuller, taking something of a grip on her anger, snapped, "We have a proposal put forward – all those in favour."

All members of the Committee – with the exception of Jane Carter – raised an arm, many of them looking decidedly sheepish.

"Those against."

Hilary Fuller's loyal lieutenant thrust her right arm into the air with a quite superb show of defiant belligerence.

"The motion is carried. Mr Goodman is duly elected as Chairman of the PCC." The words came from the outgoing chairwoman's lips with a venom almost alarming in its intensity. Rapidly she rose from her chair, knocking it over in the process. She gathered up the papers before her, looked around angrily at those whom she considered had betrayed her, rasped, "My resignation from this committee will be in the post first thing in the morning," then stalked from the room.

Instantly Jane Carter jumped up from her chair also, and glared around her. "You should all be ashamed of what you have done – it is disgraceful. You don't want a proper committee here – a democratic body. You want to run it as it has been for far too long – until Hilary became chair. You want to run it as a private gentleman's club, but it's most obvious there are no gentlemen here – only treacherous unprincipled jackals. Well, if that is what you want, then do it. But you'll do it without me – my resignation, also, will be in the post tomorrow." With that she gazed about her, a malevolent expression upon her face, then stormed from the room.

Still stunned by the evening's developments, Frank Goodman rose slowly from his seat, ambled to the front of the hall and settled himself in the 'Chair'. "Thank you Ladies and Gentlemen, for your renewed confidence in me as Chairman of the PCC – it is appreciated."

Cliff Jackson raised an arm. "May I propose, Mr Chairman, that a letter be sent immediately to Mr and Mrs Craig informing them that we have acceded to their wishes and made you chairman once again. This will put in place the money to pay the bill for the organ restoration which will, as was said earlier, be with us any day now, for sure."

There was unanimous agreement to that letter being sent; indeed, there was unanimity on every issue which came before the committee that evening, which surprised the chairman somewhat, but was in line with what Cliff Jackson expected.

"They have the fear of God put into them," explained he, as the trio of himself, Frank and Harry sat at their customary table in the bar of the Ferret and Fox following the meeting, drinking whisky. "It was Hilary Fuller who stirred up two or three of them to be awkward; you'll get no problem from them – for a while – at least."

"What I don't understand is what Maurice Craig was doing at the meeting in the first place," stated Harry Watson. "Mind, as he was there with you, Cliff, I reckon you were responsible for that. In fact, knowing you, and your knack for getting things done, I fancy you engineered the entire thing – Maurice Craig's ultimatum, and the dreaded Fuller's destruction."

Cliff Jackson grinned, then took a sip of his whisky. "Well, no – not really; but I did, perhaps, give things a helping hand. It was you, Harry, that got me thinking – the comment you made here in the pub last month, when we came in following the meeting with the lost vote of confidence. You said that the Craigs should be told as they wouldn't be happy that you, Frank, had been replaced with Hilary Fuller. Mind you, at first, I only thought of informing them as a matter of courtesy, them pledging twelve grand to solve the organ problems. The more I thought of it though, the more I realised there was an opportunity for what one could term, a bit of mischief. After all, as you said Harry, they more than most would be upset at your removal from the chair – and they would be doubly upset that Hilary Fuller had usurped your place, it being she who was so enthusiastic to support the vicar in his desire to get rid of the organ. I mean, she being chairwoman of the committee tasked with safeguarding the future of the organ was a bit like putting a fox in charge of a hen house. This is what I put to them in a somewhat more subtle way. I could see they were unhappy at what had happened, but, I felt, not so unhappy that they would threaten to withdraw funding, which was what I was after as I felt confident that most of the PCC, when confronted with the possibility of each having to dip into their own pockets for four figure sums, would rapidly reverse their decision. So it was then I played my trump card and gave them a touch of what I think is called in modern jargon, misinformation."

Frank laughed. "You're a devious devil, and no mistake, Cliff. What did you tell them?"

"Well, I didn't tell them anything definite. Rather, I gave the opinion that whilst the listing of the organ had meant that it couldn't be destroyed, it was quite possible that now it had been restored, it could still be sold – as Hilary Fuller and a few of the others wanted to do in the first place, and which, now that she was in the chair, she might well push through at a later date – though probably not that much later."

"I didn't know that, Cliff – that's a bit worrying to say the least." The concern Frank felt over such news was clearly etched upon his face. "I mean, what's to stop another 'Hilary Fuller' coming onto the committee with the same desire, to get rid of the organ?"

The older man laughed. "Don't take me too seriously, Frank. To be honest, I've not the slightest idea. All I did was to float this as a possibility to Maurice and his wife. What is known as 'egging the pudding'. In reality, I imagine that the organ being listed means that it has to remain in the church – which is also listed, of course. So I'm guilty of, shall we say, exaggeration; the main thing is that the Craigs believed me, and came to the conclusion that it was vital to get you back in the chair. Once they had come to that conclusion, I suggested that the nearest thing to a foolproof plan that I could think of which would make the committee reinstate you as chairman, was to frighten them into thinking they might have to cover the twelve grand bill out of their own pockets. So Maurice Craig wrote that letter, and came along in person to tell everyone of his and his wife's decision not to fund the repairs if you were not returned to the chair. Mind you, it was something of a risk, as if the majority had decided to stand by Hilary Fuller rather than casting her adrift, then everybody on the committee – including us three – would have had to pay up. I wouldn't have fancied that."

Harry Watson laughed loudly, then slapped his companion on the back. "Brilliant, Cliff – absolutely brilliant. Frank's back in the chair, the Craigs will pay for the organ and – truly a bonus – Hilary Fuller and Jane Carter are going to resign. A triumph – brilliant."

Frank Goodman grinned, then nodded his agreement. "You're right there, Harry. Thank you Cliff – I'm forever in your debt. I've always enjoyed being chairman of that committee and I would have missed it a great deal; Now, though, it's not going to happen – not for a while, that is. Nobody knows what the future will bring," added he, with the countryman's innate caution.

"You're wrong there, Frank," said Jackson. "I know: You are about to go to the bar and order three double Scotches – that is what the future is about to bring, or, at least, the immediate one; am I not right?"

The farmer laughed. "Yes, you're right," said he getting up from his chair and moving towards the bar. Once there, and confronted by the landlord, he changed his mind regarding his order. "I'll have a bottle of Scotch, Alan, please. It doesn't matter about glasses because we've already got them; and what, no doubt, we are about to get, certainly early tomorrow morning, is a hangover, but who cares – it has been a very good evening so far, and a bottle of Scottish single malt will round if off very, very nicely indeed."

123

VIII

The Diet

Don Langley liked food and drink of most kinds, but none appealed to him more than the traditional fare of his native Devon. To him there was no better savoury dish than a pasty which, he always said, originated in Devon. At least, that's what his mother told him, she maintaining that a Cornish pasty contained fish, while one from north of the Tamar, was made 'proper', awash with beef, potato, swede and onion. And there had been few mortals on earth who made a better 'oggie' than she, although overall, her cooking skills were a touch erratic.

Having said this, his wife Tess made a succulent pasty and was, to be fair, far superior to his mother as a general cook. For Tess could produce an excellent roast and – crucial to a man with the 'sweetest teeth' in the land – her cheese cakes, trifles, spotted dick and sticky toffee puddings were to die for, whilst her cream teas could make him 'wax lyrical' (flavoursome homemade light scones and fruity preserves, allied to the only purchased part of the meal, clotted cream). His love of sugary things also made him an inveterate sweet chewer and chocolate eater. He also liked his liquor – especially whisky and red wine, while the odd pint of good local cider slipped down nicely.

These crucial joys of life, however, were destined to be under threat. For, having been feeling a touch 'under the weather' for a couple of months he had finally been persuaded by his worried and persistent wife to make an appointment to see the Doctor –

and had just been summoned by a receptionist to go forth to the medic's lair.

Unfortunately for the patient, old Doctor Black, who had the girth of a sumo wrestler – and, in consequence, was quite sympathetic to dietary excess – had retired after thirty-five years in the practice, his place being taken by a brisk, keen young fellow named Parsons. Within a minute of entering the consulting room, Don was lying horizontal upon a hard couch, being examined, pummelled and generally assaulted by the medical man, who appeared to have about him the type of disciplined violence that would have made him an ideal recruit for the SAS.

The diagnosis was swift, confident and somewhat damning. "You have high blood pressure, Mr. Langley, and the main reason for that is simply that you are at least two stones overweight. It needs to be shed – it can be dangerous for a man of your age to carry too much weight. I see by your notes you are fifty-two – well into middle age now. I'll give you a diet sheet before you go. Do you do much exercise?"

"Well – well, I play the odd round of golf," he replied, "and I'm a season ticket holder at Home Park," he added – without conviction.

The Doctor snorted, "Watching professional footballers run around hardly counts as exercise. And whilst a round of golf does constitute some exercise, it is not in any way exacting – which, frankly, is what you need. No, I feel a regime of running is what is required."

"Did – did you say running?"

The patient's face was ashen; if he'd been a touch under the weather before, he was now feeling on the brink of intensive care.

The reply was brisk – not a man to 'beat about the bush', Doctor Parsons. "Yes, Mr Langley – running. Don't go mad. To start with – possibly a daily run of, say four miles, working up to perhaps seven or eight. Do that in conjunction with your diet and within a couple of months – perhaps less – you'll find you are the correct weight for your height, and age, and you will feel really fit and well; and if you maintain a sensible diet and continue to take brisk exercise, then there is no reason why you should not live well into old age; your health, basically, is very sound. Still I feel it advisable for me to see you in, say, a month, so that I can monitor your progress, so perhaps you would make an appointment on the way out. Good day, Mr Langley, and good luck!" The doctor opened the door for him and as he passed through, handed him a diet sheet. "There you are," said he with, in the patient's eyes, totally inappropriate positivity, "I'm sure you will soon get used to it – there's plenty of good, healthy food you can eat; no need ever to feel hungry. See you in a month".

The door closing behind him, Don trundled out to the reception desk, made his appointment as instructed, left the waiting room, got into his car and drove home.

He realised afterwards that before arriving there, he should have disposed of the diet sheet, and merely told Tess that he just had to watch his weight a little; and as for the running, there was no need for that to have been mentioned at all. The trouble was, however, that he was in such a state of shock that it never occurred to him to do anything other than tell Tess the full story of the traumatic session he had just experienced with the doctor, forgetting that his beloved wife was always a lady of action – and in this instance, scant sympathy.

"Well, Don, I'm not surprised at what he said. You are overweight, as I've told you many times (the truth) and you do not take enough exercise," (again the truth). "Still," she continued, that purposeful tone in her voice which always made him a touch nervous, "We'll start that diet the first thing in the morning – and you can go for a run as well; it's Saturday so you won't have to get up too early. It'll be different on weekday mornings, of course; you'll have to be up about six o'clock, or so, to give yourself time to do the run and then get ready for work. You've got an old tracksuit somewhere, haven't you? I'll search it out," she enthused, without waiting for his confirmation about the tracksuit. (He'd have been unable to confirm it anyway as he had not seen the garment in over twenty years, since his footballing days.)

When Tess Langley did something, she did it well – and with enthusiasm. The challenge was to return her husband to fitness

126

and health – and she was up to it. The following morning Don was awakened by the deafening shrill of the alarm clock. Befuddled with sleep, he stole a glance at the time–piece – "Seven o'clock, Tess – that's all it is," he cried. "We never get out of bed before half-eight on a Saturday – sometimes even later than that. The weekend is when we have a lie in. And we never put the alarm on weekends – unless there's something special on."

"Well, there is," retorted Tess, already out of bed with her dressing gown on. "You're starting your running routine this morning. It's important to do these things fairly early in the morning, when the air is nice and fresh – and it's really lovely out there this morning; May at its best. While you're using the bathroom and putting on your tracksuit, I'll get breakfast."

She disappeared out the door as he arose shakily from his bed; the prospect of a jog around the local undulating lanes did nothing to raise his spirits. He avoided total despair, however, by thinking of his breakfast. They always had a good traditional 'full English' on Saturdays and Sundays – a 'health conscious fry-up' as his son Mark would say. Being more rushed on weekday mornings, they would merely have cereals and toast – though Don did not stint even in this direction, having a gargantuan bowl of cornflakes, sweetened by copious amounts of sugar and irrigated by half a bottle of full cream milk, to be followed by two, sometimes three slices of toast with a layer of best British butter on top.

Suitably clad for the trials to come, Don went downstairs, then into the kitchen – and froze, his gaze transfixed by the horrors exhibited on the table top. For upon it, laid before where he always sat, was a bowl containing a slice of melon and, beside it, another bowl with a meagre portion of cornflakes struggling to make itself seen. He glanced at Tess, then back in the direction of the table, and again in the direction of his wife. "What's all this, Tess?" he croaked, his voice seized with despair. "I mean – well, it's Saturday and we always have a fry-up on Saturdays and Sundays."

"We used to Don, yes, but not any more. It says nothing about cooked breakfasts in your diet sheet. Rather, it recommends a slice of melon and a moderate portion of cereal – which is what you've got; and only semi-skimmed milk should be used." The tone of her voice made it plain that this was not a suggestion, rather a statement of present and future intent.

Her next pronouncement shamed him. "Don't worry," said she, "you're not going to be alone. I'm going to join you – for a while, at least. I'm not much overweight, but losing a few pounds will do me good." Even Don's present persecution complex could not blind him to his wife's nobility. For Tess's figure was sylph-like, as it always had been, she having not put on a single pound during the twenty-six years of their marriage. If she was denying herself when she did not have to, he felt an obligation to go along with her without demur – in the short term, at least. Thus did he sit down and devour his meagre breakfast, and drink the solitary sugar and milkless cup of tea that was put before him – a foul tasting concoction when compared to the strong, white highly sweetened brews (many in number) which he habitually consumed at breakfast time.

Having finished, he got up from the table, and meandered out through the kitchen door to commence his run, Tess's directions concerning his route ringing in his ears: "The football club is about two miles away, so if you run there and back, you'll do roughly four miles. Good luck, Don."

Grunting, "I'll need it," in reply, he walked out to the road, turned left, and broke into a laboured trot.

He was always to say that it was his weakened condition – due to the lack of a decent breakfast – that caused the accident, even though there was no evidence to support this. Whatever, he had gone little more than half a mile when, going past her solitary cottage, he had glanced towards old Mrs Curtis in her garden, and promptly tripped on the edge of a pothole in the road. He had hit the asphalt with some force – and broken his leg in two places. The elderly lady – almost ninety years old – had reacted with both speed and presence of mind. Seeing he was badly injured, she had gone indoors, phoned for an ambulance, then re-appeared carrying a blanket to keep him warm and a cushion upon which he could rest his head.

It all seemed an age ago as he lay in his hospital bed, his left leg – upon which he had had an emergency operation – slightly elevated and heavily plastered. Three days he had been there, and had been warned that it could still be a further week before he would be allowed home. Still, he comforted himself with the thought that it would be a long time before he would be able to run again.

As to his diet, he had not thought about it for the first two days, for he had felt rather poorly and food had no allure at all. Today, though, he was a good deal better, and was feeling a little peckish even though he had devoured a decent lunch. And as he sat there propped up in bed, listening to Tess as she relayed all the local news, his mind kept wandering towards the anticipation of dinner. Even more, his thoughts turned towards chocolate – what he would give to be confronted with a giant bar of Cadbury's Milk (or even a small bar for that matter).

Then, suddenly, he saw it – peeping out of Tess's shopping bag. He could have felt no happier if he had just won the lottery – for, clearly, those troublesome 'sweet teeth' of his were about to be appeased. He knew a box of chocolates when he saw one, and even though he could only see a small corner of it, he knew without doubt that Tess had a carton of such joy in her bag – and probably a big one as well. Clearly his unfortunate condition had driven all thoughts of his diet from her mind. There was a God in Heaven, after all, he mused. To his shame, he found he was willing his dear wife to go; He loved Tess dearly, but at that moment all he could think of were an array of luxuriant chocolates melting in his mouth.

Eventually, after glancing at her watch, his lovely wife got to her feet. "I didn't realise it was so late," said she. "I must be off – I'm going to drop in on Mrs Curtis on the way home." She lifted up her bag and reached inside.

"Mrs Curtis?"

"Yes – to thank her for her kindness to you when you had the accident."

"Too right," he agreed, "she really was a saviour."

As he spoke the words she pulled the chocolates from the bag with a flourish, like a conjuror drawing a rabbit from a hat. "I thought that the least I could do would be to get her a little gift – so I've bought these chocolates. I do hope she enjoys them." Her husband lay stunned.

"I've not forgotten you, though, Don," continued Tess. "So I've got you these." A bag of green grapes was produced, and laid carefully on the top of his locker. "We mustn't forget your diet – especially now you are unable to do any exercise. And they're nice – I tried one in the shop."

She deposited a kiss upon his ashen face, then turned and swept from the ward leaving behind a husband within whom the will to live was under serious attack.

IX

The Turkey

Joe Conway picked up his glass, sipped the whisky therein, returned the glass to the tabletop and gazed morosely – and somewhat unseeingly – at the far wall of the bar of 'The Cat and Feathers'; he was oblivious to the dozen or more folk who populated the smallish room, made even more cosy by the roaring log fire which occupied the ancient fireplace. What a fool he had been – what an idiot; Sally would just about kill him if she knew – and it looked very much as if she would know, sooner rather than later. He had promised to bring one home at the beginning of the week, but had managed to dredge up a few lame excuses for failing to do so. He had another sip of his Scotch, then leant back in his chair. Here it was, just a day and a bit from Christmas – an occasion which, usually, he loved – and he was feeling lower than a snake's belly. It was all so unfair. All he had done was to try to make a stand against robbery – against being ripped off. He didn't mind paying a fair price for a turkey, but he refused to pay the excessive prices being demanded.

Sally, it had to be said, was partly to blame, for she refused to have a cheap frozen bird from a supermarket, insisting on a fresh, free-range, organic one – requirements which meant the price per pound was almost quadrupled. To be fair to her, she had amended her demands, partially, when she heard the cost associated with the term 'organic' that festive period, but insisted on the fresh and free-range aspects – "Frozen turkeys are not the same," said she,

131

"and if they're frozen and not free-range they're horrible – like eating flavourless cardboard."

He had pointed out to her some time before that their guests for Christmas dinner, their son Danny, his wife Kirstie and their grandsons Harry and Charlie, would never notice the quality of the turkey, "As long as there's plenty of it, they'll be happy," he opined, with honest conviction. "I mean, Danny could win a Nobel Prize for eating; he's never fussed what it's like as long as there's plenty of it."

"Nonsense Joe. Danny is very discerning when it comes to food – and Kirstie even more so. When we went to them for Christmas dinner last year, their turkey was absolutely delicious – it almost melted in the mouth. I didn't ask her where she got the bird, but it was clearly free-range. She will expect no other here – and she will get no other." When Sally made a statement with such vehemence – rarely, if truth be told – she meant it; a free-range turkey was demanded, and nothing else would be accepted.

With those instructions in mind, Joe had proceeded over a period of some three to four weeks, to try to complete a task which should have been simple for a man such as himself – a local man who knew great numbers of folk amongst the community throughout West Devon; also, he was an agricultural representative, who spent his working days calling on farmers and landowners from the Tamar to the northern fringe of Dartmoor.

Just a year before he would have been able to pick up a succulent bird of the sixteen to eighteen pounds in weight that he was seeking with no trouble at all – and at a fair price. Those twelve months, though, had seen much change – something which a man like himself who made his living from the farming industry should have anticipated. He was fully aware that new health and safety regulations had come in, but he did not realise they were so draconian that the majority of farmers who had treated the sale of turkeys and poultry at Christmas as a lucrative sideline, ceased to do so. Quite simply to fund the equipment needed to conform with the new regulations was so expensive, it was only financially viable for those who did it on a large scale –

very few in the local area. Hence the turkey supply situation locally – nationally too, or so it was reported – was a simple case of demand for free-range birds greatly exceeding supply; truly a sellers' market. In consequence prices were inordinately high – well above what Joe Conway was prepared to pay. Not that he was desperately short of the funds needed to make such a purchase – no, he refused, as he had said several times in the pub recently, to be 'taken to the cleaners'. Yet he had known for weeks, if he was honest with himself, that if he wanted a free-range turkey, he would have to pay far higher than he had ever paid before. The alternative was to buy a frozen one from the supermarket – still surprisingly low in price – which would suit him (they tasted much the same as free-range to him) but would not be accepted by Sally. She would consider such a turkey to be an insult to Christmas. Indeed, she hated all frozen meat and poultry, saying (wrongly in Joe's view) that only somewhat inferior flesh ended up being frozen.

The trouble with him was that at times such as this, he tended to indulge himself with a Mr Micawber type of mindset, convinced that something would 'turn up'. Not surprisingly, nothing had. A couple of weeks previously, he had done a round of local butchers' shops and been quoted prices even higher than those on the farms – which was something a man of his experience should have anticipated. By the time Christmas week had dawned, the realisation had crept over him that the only way he was going to obtain that which he so desperately desired was to brace himself for pain – and pay the exorbitant sum demanded.

He was destined, however, to keep the money in the pocket. For there was not a solitary free-range turkey of any size or weight to be bought in either the town or on the farms. Those which had not already been sold, were ordered. "A big shortage of fresh birds this year," were the unhelpful words which came from all directions; and there was no chance of gaining a goose or a couple of capons or suchlike instead – there was far more demand than supply for any fresh bird which could be eaten. Anyway, even if there had been, he would not have wanted them especially; there was nothing at Christmas to match turkey meat;

he loved it and his Danny would just about eat one on his own if given the chance.

What a mess, he mused to himself – and he was totally to blame for it. His turgid mental processes were interrupted by the sound of the bar door closing. He looked up to see the burly figure of Steve Sharp ambling towards the bar carrying a largish cardboard box. Old friends, he and Steve had played football together long ago, they now lived less than half a mile apart, and often shared a few drinks in the Cat and Feathers.

Steve went to the bar, placed the box on top, had a brief conversation with Alice, the barmaid, behind it then, turning his head, espied Joe sitting in the corner. "Drink Joe? Looks as if you've a Scotch here – fancy another?"

"Well, yes – perhaps I will, Steve, thank you. I've got to be careful 'cause I'm driving, but a small one'll do no harm."

Within a couple of minutes, Steve had brought two whiskies to the table, plus the large cardboard box. Sitting down, he raised his glass in the direction of his friend – "Cheers Joe. Have a good Christmas."

"Thanks, boy," replied he with little enthusiasm. "You too."

His companion laughed – one tinged with irony – then shook his head. "It's been a right caper so far – Christmas that is."

"In what way?"

"On the turkey front," replied Steve, taking a sip of his whisky. He grinned – "talk about the best laid plans of mice and men. Up to a couple of days ago, we didn't have a turkey; I've been meaning to get one for the past couple of weeks, but you know how it is – I didn't get round to it. Then a couple of days ago, a fellow I work with came in and asked if anybody wanted a turkey. He had won one in a raffle, but seeing as he and his family were going away for Christmas, he didn't need it. A lovely bird too – just over eighteen pounds, and all he was asking for it was twenty quid. Well, as you can imagine, I nearly snatched his hand off. I gave him the money there and then, and collected the bird from his house after work yesterday. This morning, though, my Jackie had a thought – and it was a good job she did. You see we changed our cooker about three months ago, and she suddenly had doubts that a bird that size would fit in the new oven – it is a touch smaller than the old one. Well, it won't – it's much too large. So I've had to buy a smaller one in the supermarket – just in time, because they didn't have many left. That's why I've come in here this evening – I thought that Doug and Liz might well buy it from me – after all, they're doing Christmas dinners here every day, and that includes Christmas Day. Alice, though, says that they're both out for the evening, but even if they weren't, she fancies they are well off for turkey meat. So, I'm looking for someone who wants to buy a turkey."

It took several seconds for Joe Conway to fully appreciate the staggering piece of good fortune which had come his way. He then jumped to his feet with the cry, "I'm looking for a turkey, Steve, desperately."

He opened up the cardboard box and gazed down at the magnificent beast; then he prodded the soft, white flesh with a forefinger, through the cellophane bag which enveloped it.

"It looks like a lovely bird, Steve. How much do you want for it?"

"You can have it for the same amount I paid for it – twenty quid."

"That's a ridiculously low price for a fresh free-range turkey, boy – you'd have to pay three times that amount in a butcher's."

Steve frowned, then shook his head. "No – it's not fresh or free-range, Joe – it's a frozen one. It's just that it thawed out overnight. I took the plastic wrapping and labels and suchlike off it at the time and when we found out it wouldn't fit in the oven, I put it in a large cellophane bag we turned out – that's why it looks like it just came off a farm."

Joe was about to express doubts regarding purchasing it as it was not free-range, but the words of regret were stilled before they reached his lips; for the last nine words spoken by his friend thundered around his mind – 'it looks like it just came off a farm'. That it did; for the birds he had bought in previous years from farms had all been packaged this way; even his Sally would not notice any difference. Granted she might notice a slight difference in flavour – but, then again, she might not. A lot of this free-range nonsense was in the head, in his view; if it looked free-range, then it was free-range. His mind was made up – Dame Fortune had turned a beaming smile upon him, and he was not about to shun her favours.

"I'll take it, Steve, thank you – it looks a lovely bird, it really does." He pulled a twenty pound note from his back pocket and handed it to his companion. "This is a great weight off my mind." He quickly bade his farewells, went to the bar and paid for a double whisky for his saviour, and was home within ten minutes, bearing his priceless cargo.

The following day – Christmas Eve – was one which Joe always enjoyed immensely. Technically, he was working, but custom had long been to do little that day except visit the pub, and having discarded his stress regarding Christmas dinner with the purchase of the turkey the night before, he accompanied half a dozen colleagues to the Cat and Feathers about mid-morning, and left about mid-afternoon, Yuletide bonhomie – along with many seasonal drinks – putting him in the best of spirits. Having had sufficient sense to have left the car in the garage that morning, he walked happily – though just a touch unsteadily – the half mile home.

He went in the back way, took off his shoes, greeted his wife – who was standing near the turkey on the far side of the kitchen, with some exuberance, going over to her and giving her a kiss; then he flipped the kettle on. His cheery greeting went unanswered; rather Sally, gazing at him, in poker-faced fashion, nodded in the direction of the Christmas bird, and asked in a tone decidedly lacking in warmth, "Which farm did you get this turkey from, Joe?"

He was in no state to answer such a searching question. "Well – well – out – out Bere Alston way," he stuttered.

"Really," retorted his wife, tersely. "Tell me – was it cold there?"

Despite his somewhat befuddled brain, he was aware that things were not as they should be. "Well – no, no. It was mild for the time of year, just like here. I mean, it's only six miles away."

"Mild, eh? Then how do you account for what I found inside

the bird just now, when getting it ready to be stuffed?" She reached into a bowl just to the left of the turkey, pulled a small cellophane wrapped pack from it and threw it down onto the worktop in front of him.

It took him only a few seconds to realise that mild though the weather was forecasted to be, for him it promised to be a very chilly Christmas. For there confronting him like the spectre at the feast, was a packet of giblets, clearly still partially frozen; written across it was the legend, 'Bernard Matthews – Bootiful!'

X

Monitor

James Marker glanced at his watch; 8pm and already they were approaching the penultimate agenda item. It had – somewhat unusually – been a good brisk meeting, the reasons for which, in his experienced view, being twofold – five councillors (a third) were absent and amongst them were a couple of the more vociferous members; and secondly, there was a Champions' League match on television and he had not the slightest doubt that many councillors had ambitions to watch, at least, the second half – he amongst them.

Closing the debate and taking a vote regarding the size of the grant to be made towards the repainting of the Tamarside Scout Hut, the chairman then glanced to his right, enquiring of the Parish Clerk, "Any other business?"

Daniel Collins shuffled his papers, as was his habit, cleared his throat – again, his habit – and commenced to reply to the question. A retired solicitor who had been born and bred in the village, down close to the Tamar, and had practised just half a dozen miles away at Tavistock, he carried out the part-time clerk role more as a hobby than for the modest remuneration which came his way. Speaking in his rather slow but deliberate fashion, and gazing intently at the chairman, he said, "I've a letter here from a Mrs Symons, a local resident, complaining about drainage in the playing fields and the broken showers in the dressing rooms. Apparently her son plays for the football club and recently he's been coming home after matches plastered in mud – he's the goalkeeper I believe."

"Yes, that's right, Mr Chairman, he is," interjected Charlie Mullins, a semi-retired farmer who was the council's oldest and longest serving member. "I watch the team now and again and he's not a bad keeper to be fair to him. Mind you, he needs to be useful with what he's got in front of him."

"Yes-yes, I'm sure that's right," stuttered the Parish Clerk, somewhat disconcerted at being interrupted in mid flow. "Anyway, she is demanding action regarding repairing the showers and putting in hand work to solve the wretched drainage problem. As we are all too well aware, Mr Chairman, the showers are beyond repair and have to be replaced – a very expensive business. And the costs of draining the pitches would be immense, well beyond our financial capabilities at present, I feel. However, it is on our list of capital projects to be carried out in the near future."

"Near future?" rasped Councillor Mullins. "Mr Chairman I've been on this council for well over thirty years and the drainage of the playing fields was on the list of future capital projects when I first came on. I doubt I'll ever live to see it done."

"Why can't the Football Club replace the showers?" enquired Councillor Jennie Morton, a teaching assistant at the local school.

"Because they don't own them, Councillor Morton," the chairman replied. "All the pitches and the dressing rooms are owned by this council – the Football Club merely pays an annual rental which is, I must say, quite high. And it's not just the Football Club that uses those grounds – or the dressing rooms. They are there for community use. No, it is we that must pick up the tab. Still, it's early April now and, with a bit of luck, the weather will soon be warmer and drier – so the showers will not be needed as much. Not that this is a long term solution, obviously," he added hastily.

"No – no, you're quite right, Mr Chairman," opined Martin Jackson, Chairman of the Finance Committee. "These showers will clearly have to be replaced in the fullness of time – and after that the pitches will have to be drained. But there are – are – well, complicated issues involved. We really need to look at the situation closely – identify problems, look at various, well, various options and – and consider the implications. I would propose, Mr Chairman, that for the time being we monitor the situation regarding these matters at the playing fields and re-visit them at a later date."

"Thank you, Councillor Jackson; do I have a seconder?" said the chairman, seizing the opportunity with alacrity – with a bit of luck he would be home gazing at his TV screen within a quarter of an hour. Charlie Mullins thrust his right arm into the air with unusual speed – he was as keen as was the chairman to get home.

"Right, we have a proposal that for a while we monitor the situation regarding these matters at the playing fields. I'll put it to the vote." He was about to ask who was in favour of the motion, when he noticed that Councillor Sally Benson had put up a hand to catch his attention. She was the council's newest recruit, having won a by-election less than three months earlier. The local postmistress, she had lived in the village for a dozen years or so, and was widely respected. Indeed, it had been her efficiency, hard work and business acumen that had turned the local Post Office from being a 'lame duck' into a prospering business, both on the Post Office side, and the general store aspect. In fact, the success in the former part of the business had ensured that the Post Office remained open when so many others in the area had been closed. Being the sort of person who only spoke when she had a sound question to ask, or a long considered opinion to give, she had already gained the approval and trust of her fellow councillors.

"Yes, Councillor Benson?"

"Thank you, Mr Chairman," said she, courteously. "It's just that I wonder what is meant here by the word, 'monitor'."

"Well – well – well, Councillor," spluttered the chairman, "it means what it says, really. You know, there are – are somewhat complex issues here, and it is crucial that we – we – we, well, we monitor the situation before we commit public money to a specific action."

"Well, yes, I can fully understand such a policy when

something is not straightforward, but that is not the situation here, is it? You say these are complex issues, Mr Chairman, but they are not, are they? The opposite, in fact – nothing could be simpler. The showers at the playing fields are broken beyond repair; thus they need to be replaced as soon as possible and, as we own the dressing rooms, and rent them to the football club and other organisations, then we should install new showers as a matter of urgency. Not to do so is to fail to fulfil our duty and responsibility as landlords. And once this has been done, then we should look at what I concede is a far bigger and more expensive issue – draining the pitches. This as I see it, is the situation Mr Chairman; there is nothing in it which needs monitoring."

Sally Benson had delivered her views in most articulate fashion and devoid of emotion. She had left the council in general, and the chairman especially, floundering. "Well – thank you, Councillor Benson. You – you put forward interesting points which I am sure have some merit, but I still feel it is important we do not rush into any rash action which we could live to regret. We are talking here, as I said earlier, of the spending of public money; so it is only right and proper we – we – we monitor matters to avoid costly mistakes."

Councillor Benson was not finished. "As I said a moment ago, I can see that there are times when issues need to be monitored to see how they develop but there are other times when action can, and should be taken immediately; this is such a situation. My attention was drawn at the meeting last month, to the use of the word 'monitor'. It concerned deepish potholes in the car park next to this hall; clearly they need to be filled in as a matter of urgency, yet it was agreed that they would be 'monitored'. Now, when I got home that evening, I looked up the meaning of 'monitor' in a dictionary. It stated that it means 'to observe or record the condition of a person of thing'. Clearly there was no need to further record the condition of the car park – it was there for all to see. I have to say that a policy of monitoring in these circumstances – as with the shower and drainage problems we have discussed this evening – was and is merely a policy of inaction; we monitor rather than do anything. I don't think this is at all fair on the people who elect us. It is time the problems we've pinpointed this evening were put right, not 'monitored'."

"I cannot agree, Councillor Benson, that in monitoring something we are merely avoiding doing something," admonished the chairman – quite gently. He had a feeling that this was not a lady to upset if at all possible. "Rather it is the adoption of a policy of – of – of cautious wisdom." He paused briefly, rather proud of the phrase he had just used. "As a public body we do not have the freedom of action which would be that of a private business. If we are in any way profligate then we incur the wrath of the District Auditor. Is that not so, Mr Collins?"

The Parish Clerk, ever the seeker of a quiet life – thus a great adherent to a policy of inactivity – nodded vigorously. "You are absolutely right, Mr Chairman. The District Auditor has immense powers – indeed, if he feels a council has squandered money, there are ways, I believe, in which he can force the individual councillors involved to repay such money out of their own pockets." Collins made the statement in authoritative tones, even though he felt that he was possibly exaggerating the powers of the District Auditor.

There was a pause whilst Councillors took on board the warning the Parish Clerk had just given. It was too good a chance to miss in Charlie Mullins's eyes. The meeting threatened to meander on and he could see himself missing the football altogether. So he played a card which he'd used many times over the decades and one which had usually worked in terms of bringing a meeting to an end – and in muddying waters, also.

"Mr Chairman," said he, "I have to say there is much in what Councillor Benson says. So instead of monitoring the situation at the playing fields, I feel it would be better if we set up a working party to go into matters and report back to the council at a later date. I so move."

The chairman, seeing the proposal for what it was – a speedy way of bringing the meeting to an end – instantly asked for a seconder. Councillor Jennie Morton obliged, and the vote in favour was unanimous, Sally Benson seeing it as a personal triumph; the slothful dragon that was monitoring had been slain – for the time being, at least.

The Chairman, Vice-Chairman, Chairman of Finance and Chairman of Properties and Staffing were rapidly appointed to form the working party, then James Marker declared the meeting closed. Within seconds he and Councillor Mullins were exiting the building in considerable haste. "We should be able to see most of the second half, Charlie, thanks to you. That was a master-stroke proposing the working group. We'd have been there for another half-hour if you hadn't. She'll be a good councillor, will Sally, but I fancy that once she gets her teeth into something, she'll not easily let go."

"Absolutely; there was no way she was going to accept the monitoring policy – and, to be fair, there was a lot in what she was saying. We know what has to be done in the playing fields – but there's no way we can afford to do it unless we put up the Council Tax; and we certainly can't do that – there's elections next May."

The chairman nodded his agreement. "Too right; mind you, when the working party reports back we'll have to recommend putting the work in hand – there'll be no way around it."

"No, there won't; but it'll be a while before you meet, I'll wager," retorted Mullins. "If I know Dan Collins he'll not call a meeting of the working party for months. There's nobody who likes a quiet life more than him; if he had to do a lot then he would have given up the clerkship long ago. And, remember, he's a retired solicitor so he's spent a lifetime in a profession dedicated to prevarication. Rest assured, James, there is no way your working party will bring any proposals to the council this side of the election."

The chairman laughed. "Yes, I fancy you're right, Charlie. I must say, though, that I feel a touch guilty."

"Guilty?" rasped his companion, "there's nothing to feel guilty about, boy. It is simply the slow, but fair, forward movement of the democratic process."

James Marker smiled. "Reckon you're right, boy. Still, I'm away home," said he, moving briskly towards his vehicle on the far side of the car park. "See you at the finance meeting next week."

Here, though, the chairman was wrong for he was destined not to attend that meeting. Indeed, he was not to see the second half of the televised match that evening either. For within twenty minutes of his farewells to Charlie Mullins he was lying in the back of an ambulance speeding towards Derriford Hospital, Plymouth having suffered the trauma of a broken left leg.

Before reaching his motor he had fallen heavily in the car park having tripped on the rim of a deep pothole – one, he mused, painfully, which evidently had not been properly 'monitored'.

XI

Carbon Footprint

"Right, members – we come to any other business." James Marker glanced to his right at the Clerk to the Council, Daniel Collins. "Have we any, Mr Collins?" It was a superfluous question for he was all too well aware that there was an item of business to be brought to the attention of the council – one which, he feared, would greatly disturb the quiet life he always sought and, even worse, prolong the meeting.

The somewhat arthritic Parish Clerk got slowly to his feet. He shivered slightly – brought about largely by the low temperature in the Village Hall where the heating had been installed before the Second World War, but also in anticipation of the combination of outrage and scorn which, he knew, would engulf both the chairman and himself. He cleared his throat, gazed somewhat unseeingly at the eleven councillors sat before him, then said, in faltering tones, "Thank – thank you, Mr Chairman. I've – I've had a letter from the District Council; well, really it's one from Devon County Council, but they sent it to the District for them to send copies to all the Parish Councils in the area. Mind you, to be exact, it's not really from the County either – it's from the Government, and I'm led to believe that they have sent similar instructions to all the counties, cities, unitaries and so on in the country."

"Could the Clerk please get on with it," rasped Councillor Charlie Mullins. "I've got better things to do than to sit here

145

listening to Mr Collins going all around the houses – I've got yaws lambing at home." Although semi-retired, he still kept a flock of Devon Longwool Ewes on his fifty acres, something which kept him and his wife occupied, and brought in 'a few bob' as he put it. Always a man who valued folk being brief – getting to the point – he and the over verbose clerk, who rarely got to the point with even the remotest sense of urgency, had been at each other's throats for years.

Daniel Collins' expression suggested feelings of surprise, offence, even hurt – "I thought I was getting to the point, Mr Chairman," said he. "It is, I'm sure you will agree, important that councillors be made aware of the source of the letter I hold in my hand, and how it has come to us today; and the reasons for it, of course."

"Quite so," replied the chairman, urbanely, "but it would help if you inform members as to the contents of the letter you hold."

"I'm about to, Mr Chairman." He looked even more offended. However, clearing his throat, he proceeded to explain the content of the missive. "Basically, this is an instruction from the Government to all councils throughout the country regarding climate change – global warming, and so forth."

"Oh, no," groaned Councillor Frank Hillman, the local undertaker. "No matter where you go, Mr Chairman, there's this constant barrage of nonsense about global warming; the last three summers have been wetter than normal, and quite cool, whilst last winter, and the one which hopefully we are almost through, have been the coldest for a quarter century or more. It's driving me round the bend, all this talk, all this tripe suggesting we're all doomed."

Charlie Mullins snorted loudly. "You should be all in favour of a bit of doom, Frank," said he with a wide grin. "It would be ideal for your business; you'd be able to retire within twelve months."

"Thank you, Councillor Mullins," interjected the chairman, only too aware that the farmer, although he regularly stated his desire to get home as soon as possible, could, unintentionally, extend a meeting almost as effectively as the Town Clerk. "If you would explain the contents of the letter, Mr Collins, please."

"Yes, yes, of course – thank you Mr Chairman. Basically, the instruction from Whitehall is that every council throughout the British Isles – no matter, what size or at what level – must work out ways to reduce their carbon footprint. As yet we are not being told as to how much we have to save, percentage wise, but that will follow, no doubt, at a later date. What we have to do first, however, is to consider ways that we reduce our, our, well our carbon footprint," he stammered, "and, initially, submit them to the District Council for their consideration."

"What the hell does all that mean?" asked the bemused Charlie Mullins.

"Well, it's crystal clear what is means, Mr Chairman," said Councillor Sally Benson. "It means that in all our operations as a council, we have to use less energy. No instruction could be clearer; the problem will be how to put it into effect."

"Yes, quite, Councillor Benson," agreed the chairman, grateful that somebody had articulated the situation so quickly and so clearly. It was, though, what he expected of Sally Benson; she had been a member of the council for less than twelve months, but she had soon showed herself to be an astute lady of considerable intelligence, with a clear sight of the way ahead.

"As Councillor Benson says, the instruction is straightforward enough, but as to how we do it, I really don't know. Are there suggestions from members?" The chairman cast his eye around – and fixed it upon Charlie Mullins, who was intimating that he wished to speak. "Yes, Councillor?"

"The answer is simple, Mr Chairman – we don't do it. I've never heard so much tripe in my life; as Councillor Hillman said just now, it's a load of nonsense. After all, the climate's always changing – right throughout history it's changed; and no matter what we do, it'll continue to change as well. And there's a school of thought amongst some scientists that actually the climate is going to get colder rather than warmer. Mind you, no Government is going to admit to that, 'cause it's an easy way to put up taxes; they say that something or other is bad for the environment, then they put a hefty levy on it. No, our best policy is to say we'll look into it, then put it on the 'back burner'. Give it twelve months or so, and everybody will have forgotten about it, including the Government. In fact by that time, we could have a different Government anyway."

"Mr Chairman, I really must protest over what Councillor Mullins is saying," cried Councillor Jennie Morton, doing little to mask the exasperation she felt. Normally quite a quiet member, she was nonetheless a clear and deep thinking lady with strong beliefs and views. "I keep hearing this talk about climate change – global warming, call it what you will – being nonsense, and all made up by scientists and exploited by Governments and so forth, but anybody believing this is foolish, frankly. The warning is there for us all to see, for us all to heed, and if we do not then the consequences for future generations – perhaps even this one – could be catastrophic. The Government, quite rightly, are insisting that all Local Authorities do something to reduce the amount of energy they use; and clearly we have to respond to this – we have to take action; I'm sure even a Parish Council such as ourselves can find ways to reduce our carbon footprint, and help the environment – and reduce costs as well," she added, aware that the saving of money would appeal more to some members than the saving of the planet.

"What do you suggest, Councillor Morton?" asked the chairman. "I agree that it is something we cannot, indeed, should not ignore, but I am a little uncertain as to what we can do; after all, we're not Plymouth – we're just a Parish Council which has limited powers, property and responsibility."

"Yes, that's quite right, Mr Chairman," replied Jennie Morton. "There are ways we can make a contribution, though, I'm sure of that. For instance, there are the playing fields we own and administer, with the football pitches and the cricket square and such like – and the children's play area. It could be that we do not cut the grass as often – just as a suggestion; we would save petrol if we mowed it less often, thus cause less pollution – and, of course, save some money as well."

"As Chairman of Finance, I have to say that Councillor Morton's idea appeals, Mr Chairman," said Martin Jackson. "The problem is though, that there will be hell on, especially if we have a wettish – thus fast growing – spring and summer. Folk already complain that we don't cut it as much as we should, as it is. If we reduce the number of cuttings even further then we will be in trouble; and none of us can afford for that to happen – there's elections next spring."

"Perhaps I could put me yaws in there, Mr Chairman," said Councillor Mullins, grinning broadly. "They would keep it down – it would save me a few bob as well."

To his surprise, Jennie Morton took him seriously. "Yes, that's a good idea, Mr Chairman. I know that sheep bite close to the ground, so they would ensure that the grass was very short."

"You can't have a flock of sheep running wild in the playing fields," snorted Martin Jackson. "Just think what would happen if there was a wet day – and we have plenty of those even in the summer; why, there would be hoof prints everywhere, including on the cricket square; they would go ballistic if we allowed that to happen – after all, it took years to get that square as level and smooth as it is, most of the work being done by their own players in their spare time. And there's the dung as well – we can't have the playing fields covered in sheep sh... droppings. There would be hell to pay, and no mistake."

"Well, better that than to be covered in dog muck as it is at present," retorted Councillor Morton with asperity.

The mention of dog fouling brought the normally quiet, laid-back Norman Hillman to life. "Yes – that's right, Mr Chairman," he rasped, irresponsibility of dog owners being one of his foremost local grievances. "What Councillor Morton says is absolutely correct – it's shameful the mess they make in the playing fields. My son plays football regularly as you probably know, and he often comes home complaining about it – and it gets worse; I mean, I used to play years ago, but it was never any problem then. And half the pavements in the village are covered in it; shocking, I'm always getting complaints from folk, naturally enough. What's the Dog Warden doing about it – I mean we still contribute to the District Council for his services, don't we? I never see the fellow; if we're getting no help from him, I suggest we stop paying the District Council and sort the problem out ourselves."

The Parish Clerk looked up from scribbling notes, glanced in the direction of the chairman and gave the information – "I'm afraid there isn't a Dog Warden at present, Mr Chairman – the fellow who was doing it was dismissed three months ago because he was done for drink/driving and thus lost his licence; obviously as he covers a large part of West Devon, a driving licence is crucial."

"How have they not appointed somebody else if the post has been empty for three months?" enquired James Marker.

"Well, apparently, the first advert they put in was illegal because they failed to mention they were equal opportunities employers who welcomed applications from both genders, all ethnic minorities, the disabled and all sexual orientations. So all those who applied to the first ad, had to apply over again to the second. They are about to appoint somebody any day now – or, at least, that's what they told me when I asked them last week." The Parish Clerk made his report in his usual fashion, but, mercifully, far more to the point than usual.

"Thank you, Mr Collins for that – at least we now know why no action regarding the epidemic of dog fouling has been taken," said the chairman in his somewhat understated way.

"But no action ever seems to be taken when there is a warden," stormed Councillor Hillman. "It's a total waste of time belonging to this warden scheme – I move we tell the District Council we want no further involvement with it and use that money to sort the problem out ourselves."

"Well, I don't think, Councillor, that this is the right time to discuss such a matter as dog fouling – what we are supposed to be talking of is how we can reduce our carbon footprint," pointed out the chairman, gently. "I feel that probably the best way forward would be to have the issue of dog fouling, and whether or not we continue to subscribe to the Dog Warden Scheme, put on the agenda for our next round of committee meetings, next month. Will you see to that, Mr Collins?"

The Clerk nodded – "Certainly, Mr Chairman. As you so rightly say, this carbon footprint business, and what we propose to do about it, has to be the priority at the moment."

"Quite right, Mr Chairman," said Jennie Morton with alacrity – global warming and the urgent need to save the future world from it, was ever close to her heart. "This is something we really need to tackle – all of us. As a council there are, I am certain, numerous ways in which we can save energy – the playing fields as I mentioned just now and, of course, the Village Hall in which we are now sitting. I'm sure we could save on heating – turn it down, even turn if off, more often than we do at present. Few things waste energy and contribute to global warming more than central heating and such like."

"Turn it down?" rasped Charlie Mullins, his voice almost choked by incredulity. "Turn it down? Mr Chairman, even with it on full volume, it's still freezing in this hall; in fact most of the time it seems to be colder in here than it is outside. Replacing is what the central heating needs, not turning down, but chances of us being able to afford it in the foreseeable future are just about nil, I should think. We've hardly enough money to pay the bills as it is."

"It is in the estimates to be done next year, Mr Chairman," stated the Town Clerk.

"It's been in the estimates to be done next year for decades, Mr Chairman," snorted Councillor Mullins, in derisory tones, "and I don't doubt that it'll still be there in ten years' time. As we all know, all lists of estimates and priorities, are merely statements of what we would like to do, not what we expect to do. Anyway, we need to make this hall warmer, not even colder than it is now; I'm frankly astonished that we get as many bookings for it as we do – and as we all know, it's the bookings that are really our principal means of raising income. Without them we'd be in an even worse state than we are now."

"Solar panels, Mr Chairman, that's the way forward," stated Sally Benson. "We would have effective heating and lighting for the hall, save a huge amount of money in terms of running costs, and reduce our carbon footprint quite dramatically. It's something we all – and I most certainly include myself – should have thought of long before now."

The chairman nodded sagely. "Yes, it is a good idea,

Councillor Benson – first class, and, as you say, it would save us a considerable amount of money. The problem, though, is the initial capital expenditure. Buying and installing solar panels is, I've heard, a very expensive business. It would take, perhaps, decades before the savings we make would cover the initial costs. I fear that realistically there is no way we can hope to finance such a scheme, worthy though it is."

"We could get grants, Mr Chairman," persisted Miss Benson, never a woman to be deflected easily from the path she had chosen. "For certain there will be Government grants for such things – it would be ludicrous if there are not."

The Town Clerk shook his head. "I doubt very much there will be, Mr Chairman – at least, not for Parish Councils such as ourselves. So often Government grants are aimed at the private sector rather than the public. Home owners might well be able to access grants for installing such things as these panels – they can certainly get them for cavity wall insulation and the like; we've had it done ourselves at home, that's how I know, but with councils it does tend to be different. Governments of all political persuasions tending to feel that if an authority decides to spend money, then the local Council Tax payers should be the ones to foot the bill, even in fields such as this where expenditure would be of benefit to the community in environmental as well as financial terms."

Daniel Collins had made the statement in the confident, authoritative tones at which he could be very good, even though he was by no means sure that he was correct in what he said. There was nobody more aware of this than James Marker. It would not be the first time, he mused to himself, that the Parish Clerk had given information to the Council in such confident tones, only for the councillors to find out, at a later date, that he was totally wrong.

"Thank you for those observations, Mr Collins – they are helpful," said he. "However, as we know, situations and policies change, so I feel it would be helpful if you could check up with, perhaps, the District Council that there are no grants from central Government for such things as solar panels. I agree to some extent with Miss Benson – it does seem strange if there aren't. After all, if we are being exhorted by the powers that be to save the planet, then they really should be giving us some help to do so."

"Quite right, Mr Chairman," agreed Councillor Mullins. "They should be helping, but they won't – you can be certain of that. It's the oldest dodge going when it comes to Governments – they tell us what we have to do, but give us no money to do it with. If we do decide to do these things, then we have to hike up the Council Tax and we get abuse from people in the parish but if we don't then we're in trouble with the Government. Well, I'd rather be in trouble with Whitehall than with local folks – after all, I don't live in Whitehall. No, as I said earlier, I feel that at the present time we should take no action. I move that the letter from the District Council be noted."

From Councillor Jennie Morton there came a cry somewhere between anger and frustration. "Mr Chairman, how many more times does Councillor Mullins have to be told that doing nothing is not an option. The Government clearly are instructing us to take action – to decide how we as a Parish Council can reduce our carbon footprint in all the places in the parish which we own, or come under our jurisdiction, then to formulate policies in accordance with improving the environment, then to put such polices into action. Nothing could be simpler or more straight-forward, Mr Chairman. What the Government want from us – the District and County Councils also, no doubt – is action, not waffle. My goodness, there has been enough hot air expressed in this chamber this evening to put up average temperatures globally a couple of degrees, at least. As was said by Churchill to various Government departments during the Second World War – 'Action this Day.' – Let us seize the moment, Mr Chairman." Jennie Morton ceased as abruptly as she had begun, her face flushed with emotion and a sizeable measure of anger.

"Powerful woman when she gets going," muttered Norman Hillman to his nearest colleague, Charlie Mullins.

"She is that, Norman," agreed the veteran councillor. "I'd rather have her with me than against, boy. Trouble with her is,

153

though, whilst she's a nice enough person, and clearly no fool, she's the sort of woman who wants to do things – and expects all the rest of us to want to do them as well."

The chairman glanced at his watch; he had anticipated that the meeting would be over by eight o'clock, but it was already past half past eight, with no end to it in sight – and there was a brand new 'Midsomer Murders' on at nine. It was time he made a serious attempt to take control of the meeting. "Members," said he in a tone as masterful as he could make it (which made little impact upon the councillors if truth were told), "it really is time we reached some conclusion on this matter – we'll be here until midnight if we continue like this. Will somebody make a proposal on how we proceed, for move forward we must. If nobody does, then I will have to move something from the chair."

Marker glanced around and saw the right arm of Councillor Douglas Dyson rise, slowly, into the air. He had come to live in the parish some ten years before; he was a Devonian born and bred – near Okehampton – but had followed a career in London as a Civil Servant, and clearly a successful one as he had been awarded an OBE a few years previously. Returning to West Devon upon retirement, he had been a member of the Parish Council for just over five years. A courteous, relatively quiet man, he had quickly made his mark as a councillor of common sense with a sure feel as to the role and purpose of a local representative of the people. He was a man to whom most would listen, and with whom few would argue, he usually articulating wisdom and a sense of fair play in relatively economic fashion. James Marker was relieved to see that the retired Civil Servant wished to speak – progress would now be made, of that he was sure.

"Councillor Dyson?"

"Thank you, Mr Chairman," said he, getting slowly to his feet. "I have listened to the debate with great interest, and find that I have sympathies with all sides. However, as has been said by Councillor Morton, we do not have, nor should be expected to have, the option of doing nothing. So, respectfully, may I make the following proposal, Mr Chairman – one which I will explain as I go on.

"I feel that we should bypass the local District Council, and the County, and go directly to Whitehall. As a former Civil Servant, I think such a direct move is infinitely more preferable than going through a third party. If we approach the District Council, whether it be to ascertain the possibility of accessing grants for solar panels and such like, or to get details on exactly what is required of us regarding reducing our carbon footprint – in which areas, by what means, by what amounts and so forth, we will make little progress. There are, after all, so many questions to ask when confronted by a bland command such as is contained in the letter which the Parish Clerk read out just now – if we do that, then the Council's Environment Department will issue their own guidelines, and do so probably without consultation with Whitehall. Understandable, to be fair, as it would mean less work for what is, no doubt, a busy department of a busy council. The instructions they will give will probably be very sensible and fair – but they might not be correct. For the Government might have ideas different from those of environmental officers locally – some of which, sad to say, may not be overly sensible. So we as a council would then be in a position where we had actioned plans and so on – at what for a small authority such as ourselves would be considerable expense – only to find out that we had not done what Whitehall had expected of us, and thus, would have to start again. I speak here from experience, Mr Chairman, having known such situations during my thirty-five years as a Civil Servant in London.

"May I suggest, respectfully, that as I said earlier, we write to the Ministry of the Environment in Whitehall, asking for clarification on the matters which concern us – and may I suggest that we write individual letters concerning our major queries. So often if there are a list of questions in a letter, then only the first will be answered, as different departments will deal with them, and almost invariably the letter will be lost between offices, or lie yellowing in somebody's in-tray.

"So I would say that the way forward is to write to the Ministry first to establish whether or not grants are available for solar panels; then another letter seeking guidelines and advice regarding the scope of a local council such as ourselves to be able to reduce our carbon footprint. And possibly a letter to find out by what percentage we are expected to reduce it – and during what time scale. The letters do not need to be sent in that sequence, Mr Chairman, of course – that is merely my suggestion. Whatever, I feel this is the way forward, and I so move. Thank you, Mr Chairman." Ever courteous, he bowed his head in the general direction of James Marker, then sat down.

A few seconds elapsed before the chairman spoke, so engrossed had he been in what the learned Civil Servant had just said. "Thank you, Councillor Dyson," said he at last. "You have given us sound advice, I feel – and you have also made a proposal which can move us forward. Do I have a seconder?" He glanced at his watch – he could still make it home in time – then at the councillors sat before him. For a few seconds there was no response from the motley collection of councillors sitting there, all of them seemingly deep in thought; and the chairman could understand why – for those who wished to take no action were uncertain whether or not Douglas Dyson's proposal would lead to matters moving forward far faster than they wished, whilst those keen to do their bit to save the world were a touch apprehensive, not sure that the proposals, sound and progressive though they appeared to be, would make things happen within a reasonably short period of time. Eventually, the high esteem in which Douglas Dyson was held triumphed and both sides gave his proposals the benefit of their doubt. Thus did Norman Hillman second them, and saw them carried unanimously.

With that, the chairman declared the meeting closed, and was soon outside hastening towards his car, parked in the recently re-surfaced village hall car park. As luck would have it, Douglas Dyson was parked next to him and reached his vehicle just seconds before James Marker. As the chairman squeezed his key fob to unlock, he hailed the ex-Civil Servant, no more than five yards away from him.

"Thanks for your proposal tonight; without it I fear we'd never have got home. Also, it's a masterly proposal in that you united the entire council, those wanting action being satisfied and those hoping it will go away and never come back, likewise. Again, masterly, I have to say, Douglas."

"That's kind of you, James," he replied with a gentle smile. "Clearly, as you pointed out, a proposal was needed, desperately, so I merely stepped into the breach, as one might say. I had a feeling that most of the councillors, like myself, wished these wretched exhortations to reduce carbon footprints would go away and never reappear. There is, obviously, no way we could make that happen – we have to appear to take action. Now, if we had asked the District, or County Councils, for guidance we would have received it all too quickly – and, as I pointed out, it might not be as accurate as Whitehall would wish. Therefore, we would have put into operation all sorts of nonsense which would cost money, upset people and then find at the end of the day that we had to do much of it again; by that time I would imagine we would have to have bodyguards to walk through the village, so angry would people be." He grinned widely. "So my proposals will ensure that we will not act until we have the correct instructions – and that could be some time."

"How long a time?" enquired the chairman, increasingly aware that he was in the company of a master of prevarication.

"Well, let me put it this way: It takes Whitehall departments, sometimes, months to reply to urgent missives from other ministries located in the same street. So a remote Devonshire Parish Council, which nobody up there will ever have heard of, sending three different letters seeking guidelines, at different times, will be lucky to get replies in the foreseeable future."

"Months, eh?"

"Months? No, my dear fellow, not months – years. Not many of us will live to see these so important questions answered – vital information we must have as a council before we can take any action. Good night, James."

"Night, Douglas – and thank you. A brilliant effort, if I may say." With that he opened his car door, jumped in and was soon off into the night. He looked again at his watch – if luck was with him, he would yet be home in time for the first murder.

XII

Risk Assessment

James Marker – a patient man by any standards – glanced at his watch, then shook his head; he felt almost in despair and found it exceedingly hard to disguise the fact. It was an agenda which he thought would be sailed through in less than half an hour – and he was usually quite sound at assessing such matters. Not this time, however, for councillors that evening had been exceedingly teasy, pedantic and, indeed, bloody minded with virtually every item which came before them, no matter how trivial, being discussed at some length. They had even taken half an hour to decide whether the dry cleaning of the Town Crier's outfit, twenty-two pounds, should be paid out of the Properties Account or from Petty Cash; his casting vote, as chairman, decided the latter.

Still, there was light flickering at the end of the tunnel – "We arrive – at last – at the final item," said he, his voice pregnant with a combination of sarcasm (most rare), weariness and relief. "Any other business? I've not been informed of any. . ." – the words directed to the Town Clerk who sat to his right. He expected that worthy man, Daniel Collins, to assure him that there was nothing else to be considered that evening – but, yet again, he was to be grievously disappointed. The Town Clerk looked a touch sheepish, deliberately avoiding the chairman's eye.

"I'm – I'm – I'm afraid there is an item, Mr Chairman," he stuttered. "I'm sorry I did not mention it before the meeting but I was – was, well, a bit tied up," he ended, lamely. Clearing his throat, he continued, "It only came in late this afternoon and is quite a simple matter which should take up little of our time."

Marker groaned inwardly – he had no trust in any prediction of brevity, especially from the Town Clerk.

"All it is, Mr Chairman, is a letter from the vicar; quite straightforward."

Again the chairman indulged himself momentarily in an internal spasm of mild despair – so often the Town Clerk's assurance that something was 'straightforward' signalled a protracted debate which would devour time in abundance. "What it is, Mr Chairman, is that in July, on a Sunday, the Bishop is coming from Exeter to baptise and confirm some twenty people of all ages, and, if dry, he wishes to carry it out in the river; so he is writing, the vicar that is, to ask our permission."

The chairman's face betrayed some confusion. "Well, yes, that seems a reasonable request, but to be honest, I would not have thought he needed our permission. I know the river runs through our park, but it is surely under the control of the River Authority."

The Town Clerk nodded his agreement – "Yes, quite right – it is. And the vicar will have to get their agreement as well; but the footpath along beside the river – where they will gather, of course, well that is owned by us; so clearly they need our permission to stand on it."

"I've never heard such nonsense in all my life, Mr Chairman," rasped Councillor Mullins, never the most patient of men, especially when there was something on television he wished to watch. "That footpath is just that – a tarmacked route for people to walk beside the river through the park; it's a public right of way. Hundreds of people walk along there every day – they don't have to ask our permission to do it, so why does the vicar need to?"

"Because it's an official event, Mr Chairman," said the Town Clerk, in the weary tone of voice he used, habitually, when explaining to, what appeared to him, obtuse councillors matters he saw as being very simple. "And also, people will be standing still on the footpath – probably taking part in a service as well. As I've implied, with the vicar seeking our permission, then we have to class the request as being official – thus it involves all sorts of laws and rules which would not come into it if they had gone ahead and not sought our agreement. As it is now, we will have to have a risk assessment done."

The momentary stunned silence was shattered by a roar from Charlie Mullins – "A risk assessment – did the – did the Town Clerk say a risk assessment, Mr Chairman?" His voice spluttered with a potent mix of outrage and shock – not unusual in the man – whilst his face looked almost apoplectic. "I've never heard such nonsense in my life. Why do we need such a thing, what possible danger can there be?"

"Well, even if there is no danger, Mr Chairman, we still have to do one – it's the law. But, to be fair, there could be risk there. After all, with all the dry weather we've had lately, the river is very low. If someone jumped in they could suffer a serious injury."

"Nobody's going to be jumping in," rasped Mullins, "it's a baptism, not Olympic diving."

"Why should we have to do one, Mr Chairman, when clearly the river is the vital part here," asked Councillor Jennie Morton. "Surely it is they who should do the risk assessment if such a rather pointless exercise has to be done – not us."

"In matters concerning the river itself, they will have to, Mr Chairman," retorted the Town Clerk. "Most certainly they will – yes, it will require such assessments from them as well as us. The River Authority will also be instructed by the Environment Agency to test the water to make sure there is no danger to health should anyone drink any of it, so they will also have to carry out an analysis of its purity. Also, it's possible they will require an assessment of any impact the event might have on nearby flora and fauna. For example, there could be some rare species of plant life, or birds, or even fish, to be found; it might be deemed harmful to such creatures to permit such a gathering in what is generally a quiet, somewhat secluded spot."

"How can it be quiet and secluded, Mr Chairman – it's only about a hundred yards from the children's play area," snorted Charlie Mullins, his expression still somewhat thunderous.

"Well – well, yes, that's a fair point," conceded the Town Clerk. "All I'm saying is that the Agency might deem it such a place; they are very much a law to themselves. And another matter which strikes me, Mr Chairman, is that we might need to apply for an Entertainment Licence. If so, we must do so right away, as it can take some time to obtain one."

"Are you serious?" exclaimed James Marker, so stunned by the Town Clerk's exhaustive, and exhausting, summary of all the labyrinthine legal procedures which could be involved, that he inadvertently strayed from his customary urbane and patient demeanour when chairing meetings. "I mean, I can't see the Bishop doing a song and dance act."

"Perfectly, Mr Chairman," came an instant reply, the Town Clerk clearly deriving some satisfaction from the situation; he did, at times, enjoy blinding the committee with legal technicalities, well aware that whilst he was not always right concerning such matters, the laymen and women of the Council would be unaware of such inaccuracies on his part. "It's likely there will be a singing of hymns and Psalms which could, indeed, require such a licence."

"Who's going to pay for all this, Mr Chairman?" asked Councillor Martin Jackson, as Chairman of the Finance Committee, a man zealous in his opposition to the council spending public money on anything that was avoidable.

"Well, we must, Mr Chairman, in everything pertaining to happenings on our own property – obviously." The Town Clerk added the last word to register his impatience at having to reply to questions to which, to him, the answer was, indeed, obvious. "I wouldn't think, however," he continued, "that the cost would be too great – although, of course, we will have to hire the services of an expert as there's nobody on our small staff qualified to do it. One good thing, however, is that on reflection, I fancy that we might not need an Entertainment Licence as there's a chance that religious services could well be exempt, even if hymns are sung. It's something I will check, naturally."

"If we've got to foot the bill, then to me it's a non-starter, Mr Chairman," retorted Councillor Jackson. "Now, if the church would be willing to do so, then I'd have no objection to us allowing them to proceed. No public money should be spent on this. I'd put the ball back in their court."

"I don't think that's fair, Mr Chairman," said Jennie Morton, a lady to whom fairness was the overriding consideration in all things. "The church is not a well off organisation – not at local level, at least – and should not have to pay just to use the path by the river to hold a small service. Anyway, most of those who will be involved will be local people who already contribute to the maintenance of the park through their Council Tax. If we give them permission to use it – and there's no reason why we should not – then we must pay for this wretched risk assessment nonsense."

"If we go along the route suggested by Councillor Morton, Mr Chairman, there's no reason why it should cost very much," opined the Town Clerk. "There's a surveyor in the town who we've used before who is qualified to do risk assessments. I know him quite well and I can say, as there are no members of the public or press present, that he'll not be too pedantic regarding identifying risks. He's the sort of chap guided and governed by common sense. I mean we are all aware that the path by the river is totally safe – all we need is someone qualified to confirm the fact. I feel confident he would, and for a moderate fee."

James Marker nodded his agreement. "Yes, yes – that is probably the way forward." He was getting to the stage when he would have agreed to virtually anything just to bring this interminable meeting to a close. He was about to ask for a vote on the Town Clerk's suggestion when he noticed Councillor Douglas Dyson had raised his arm – yet another delay, although he had to concede that it could have been much worse as the former civil servant was noted for his brevity.

"Yes, Councillor Dyson?"

"Thank you, Mr Chairman," said he in his habitually courteous way. "I don't wish to prolong what has been a lengthy meeting, but I might be able to suggest a solution to this problem which would see this council obtain the required risk assessment at no cost at all to us – and by 'us', I mean the Council Tax payer."

"Well, that would be marvellous, Councillor," replied the chairman. "Tell us more, please."

"The fact is, my wife, Melanie, recently retired from a largish building company where she was in charge of all health and safety matters, and she has all the qualifications required to do risk assessments, plus much practical experience of doing them. I cannot speak for her, of course, but I am quite confident she would be happy to do this for the council – and, possibly even more so, as she is a regular church goer, for the baptisms in the park. Furthermore, I am sure she would not expect any payment for it. So if the council are in agreement with this, I shall leave the chamber for a few minutes and contact her to see if she is willing to do it."

The agreement of the council was forthcoming at the speed of an express train – and, unusually, was unanimous. So Douglas Dyson left the chamber, contacted his spouse, returned within the promised few minutes – and informed the gathering that she was happy to carry out the assessment, and would not expect any payment; she would liaise with the Town Clerk. The business of the meeting done, and a satisfactory conclusion reached, the chairman declared it closed – and members departed reasonably satisfied with the evening's work.

James Marker was to say for many a long day afterwards, that he – and the council – should have suspected that something which sounds too good to be true, is usually just that – too good to be true. Not that it cost the council anything in terms of fees. Melanie Dyson was true to her husband's word and charged not a penny for her services in compiling the report; also she completed it in under a fortnight. These were the positives – sadly miniscule when compared with the negatives; of these, James Marker was made aware within an hour of them arriving on the Town Clerk's desk.

It was a phone call which the Chairman of the Council would remember for a very long time, from Daniel Collins, which he took on a bright, sunny June morning – but one which, after a few minutes conversation with a frantic Town Clerk, suddenly felt chillier than a dismal day in January. For Melanie Dyson's risk assessment was such that it would surely increase the risk of cardiac arrest amongst members of the council.

The problem was that she was a lady of considerable zeal – a factor of which the council had not been aware – and had not limited herself to just the inspection of the river walkway where the baptisms were to take place, but had covered the entire park. Her report, according to the Town Clerk, was not for the squeamish. James Marker, though – a positive thinking man – still hoped for the best: "Are you saying, Dan, that there's no way the church can do the baptisms in the river?"

"No James – what I'm saying is that nobody will be able to do anything anywhere in the park for the next few months: Thanks to her risk assessment, we've had to close it down."

XIII

The Fifth Generation

Duncan Curtis finished his tea in silence, thanked his wife, Alice, muttered, "It's a fair evening, maid, so I'll go out and dead-head a few daffs," and then ambled from the kitchen. Putting on his wellington boots, which lay in the porch, he strolled into the garden, glad to feel the warm spring sunshine upon him.

His patient spouse watched the dejected figure disappear from view, then shook her head with a mixture of annoyance, dismay and, perhaps, just a touch of sympathy. It was that team again, she mused to herself; here he was, amongst the best tempered, most easy going people she knew, yet every time that wretched football club lost, he acted as if there was a death in the family.

Mind you, even she had to admit that such defeats had happened with all too much regularity during the past nine months, with the culmination of such failure taking place that very afternoon – they had lost yet again and in consequence, had been relegated. The sole mercy was that this defeat – in the final fixture of the campaign – had taken place away from home (far away, in fact, up in Yorkshire), so at least he had been spared the pain of actually seeing them go down.

Of course, as everyone knew only too well, it had nearly happened last year, they only staying up by a solitary point. And, it had to be said, they only avoided the drop then because of the serial ineptitude of the trio below them, and even the year previous to that, had seen them have a mediocre season, spending the nine months at the fringes of the relegation dog fight, ending up just six places from the bottom.

He bent over and nipped off the heads of blooms well past their best, then glanced about him. Overall the garden was looking in good order, with plenty of colour plus the promise of more. He looked beyond the garden hedge at the glorious Devon countryside around him; assuredly there was no better place to live and, equally, there was nowhere else he would rather live. Yet, despite this, he did have to ask why this area could not provide a better, more successful football club for him to support. Why, for instance, couldn't he follow Arsenal, a great outfit who had never been relegated throughout their long history.

It was his father's fault; for that good and kindly man perpetrated (what, in fairness, his father had done to him as a youngster well before the war) the folly of taking him, then but eight years old, to Home Park some sixty years previously – and he had seen them win.

There was, after that, no escape; he was a supporter, and, unlike serving a prison sentence, there was no time off for good behaviour – a life sentence here meant just that. Mind you, there had been the odd good year, times when promotion had been chased – and, on occasions (infrequent), it had even been caught. Good times, though, rarely visited for long, although their previous promotion had led to six campaigns in the Championship. He well remembered that Saturday afternoon, standing there on the Home Park pitch (against all the rules) amongst a huge crowd following the triumph, along with his son Simon, his regular companion at matches (a fourth generation brainwashed in terms of support). What joy, that day – what a feeling.

His philosophy in life, though, was always to distrust success, happiness and good times, for almost invariably a time would come when the coin would flip over, and failure, even misery, would ensue. It was probably his farming background which had steeped him in such negativity whilst his experiences in a world that he had inhabited for nigh on three score and ten years had done nothing to promote in him a more positive outlook. Such a pessimistic frame of mind caused him to feel that it would be many years before supporters would again have cause to invade the pitch in celebration.

As for himself, it was unlikely in the extreme he would experience such elation ever again – for his days as a season ticket holder were over. Ironically the invitation to renew it for the upcoming campaign had arrived that very morning, just a few hours before their relegation had been confirmed. Aware that an enthusiastic uptake amongst supporters was unlikely, various discounts had been offered for renewal – indeed, a generous 20% off was available for anybody who renewed within seven days. He had, over the decades, managed to shrug off the inclination to pack it all in following previous relegation experiences – indeed, he had, firstly with his father, then on his own and, in recent times, with his son, held a season ticket for over fifty years. Now, though, it was time to call it a day, time to spend Saturday afternoons in a less stressful way, and winter evenings by the fire rather than sitting in a draughty stand with the wind blowing off Dartmoor. It was not to say that he would never go again, but he would pick his games taking note of the side's form – and results – the weather, the quality of the opposition and how he felt.

Alice had sought to dissuade him from such action – or to be more accurate, inaction – regarding the season ticket when he spoke to her of his decision not to renew, following his reading of the missive from the club. Her arguments ran along the lines of, "You'll miss it, Duncan, after all these years," – he being certain he would not – and, "What about Simon? He's been going with you for years – if you drop out you'll be letting him down." He had to concede that this was a far more powerful argument, and that he might well be letting down his son by not renewing. There was often a time in life, though, when changes needed to be made, and this was one of them.

He would continue to take an interest in affairs at Home Park, there was no doubting that – even if he had not wished to, his love for the club would demand he did so. After all, throughout his life there had probably never been a day so bad that a good result could not put right, or one so good that a defeat for the Greens could not ruin. The time had come, though, to do something different – although he had not the slightest idea what that would be. He was sure, however, that he no longer wished to sit in the, often chilly, stands watching his beloved team lose. Whilst Simon would be disappointed he was no longer going, his son, with whom he had always had an excellent relationship, would understand, of that he was certain – well, almost.

Perhaps he would do a bit more in the garden, be a touch more ambitious in what they grew, be a bit more creative; it could certainly be rewarding, gardening – and therapeutic. His reverie was disturbed by what sounded like a car door closing to the front of the house. He groaned – visitors; that was the last thing he wanted; rather, he wished to be left in peace to commune with nature on this lovely spring evening. Slowly he walked towards the side of the house to go around to see who had arrived, but stopped when their visitors rounded the corner and came into view – his son and grandson.

"Simon – Craig, it's good to see you," cried he, enthusiastically. He loved the pair dearly so it was always good to see them. Fortunately with them living just half a dozen miles distant in Tavistock, Alice and he saw a great deal of the pair. He moved forward rapidly, shook his son by the hand – as was his habit – then embraced his grandson. When doing so he was aware, suddenly, of just how overdressed was the lad. For on a balmy evening, whilst Simon wore a short sleeved casual shirt, his son was wrapped up in a raincoat which was buttoned up to the neck. He was about to comment on it but his attention was diverted by his son's enquiry as to what he was doing in the garden.

"Dead heading a few daffs, boy. It's been a good year for them, but now with the warmish sunshine they've just about had it – even late ones." He turned away from the pair and began to move along the path, then into the garden, only to be halted by an exhortation from his grandson:

"Grandad, look at me," came the cry at the top of his voice. The older man did as he was bid, turning 180 degrees to gaze back at young Craig. The sight which met his eyes brought a wide smile to his lips, for standing before him was a grandson, stripped of his raincoat, sporting a pristine dark green shirt, trimmed with white, the 'Mayflower' logo sailing to one side of his small chest.

"What have you got to say to Grandad," coaxed his father.

"Green Ar-mee," came the shrill, piercing cry.

Duncan roared with laughter, then embraced his grandson once again saying, "Well done, Craig – you look great, absolutely great."

"It's an early birthday present really, Dad. He's not six until next month, of course, but he desperately wanted a team shirt, so Carrie and me thought we'd let him have it a bit early – it's only three weeks away, after all."

"He looks good in it – fits him like a glove," said the older man, pride in his voice. He turned and pointed towards the back door – "You go in and show Gran your new shirt, my lover; I expect she'll have a smoothie for you as well. And ask her to put the kettle on." The final seven words were spoken to a rapidly disappearing small, green clad back, speed induced partially by the exhortation of his grandfather to show his shirt to his gran, but more, he suspected, by his mention of a smoothie.

"All well with you, boy?" asked father to son, as they moved slowly along the path leading to the kitchen.

"Yes, fine Dad – despite today's result. Still, we knew it was going to happen, didn't we? Actually, it's about that and next season which brought us round," said Simon – a statement only partially accurate as he omitted to say that he had received a phone call from his mother just before lunch, imploring him to come over and 'talk some sense into your father' regarding renewing his ticket for the following campaign:

"I don't want him moping around and getting under my feet every Saturday afternoon during the winter," being her closing remarks.

Mind you, he had no intention of trying to 'talk sense' into his dad in a direct way – for when it came to following that football club, he understood Duncan Curtis even better than did his mother. In his view, a different approach was required. "I've had it in the post regarding next year's season tickets; if we renew within seven days, there's 20% off – that's a fair saving, Dad. Anyway, I'll be going past the ground on Monday morning, so I

h

thought I'd drop in and get mine, one for Craig, and if you'll let me have a cheque, I'll get yours as well."

"One for Craig?" The tone of surprise in Duncan's voice was most noticeable. "He's a bit young, Simon, isn't he?"

"Well, he's young enough, I suppose – but he'll be six by then; and he desperately wants to go. And the beauty of it is the club have this offer whereby if any adult buys a season, they can get one for a child, under ten, free of charge – a full season with nothing to pay. Fantastic, isn't it?"

The grandfather had to concede that is was, indeed, too good to miss. However, he realised the time had come for him to state his future intentions concerning his own ticket. "I've decided not to renew it, boy," said he – a touch shamefacedly. "If I'm honest, I've been thinking that way for some time; even if they had stayed up I doubt I would have renewed it."

His son had been aware of his father's increasing disillusion, and suspected that, with the relegation being the final straw, a decision not to renew would be taken, even before his mother had told him about it. He was prepared for it – and went on the attack.

"Not go, Dad – not get another ticket? But you must – we've been going together for years; you and me. And next season, there'll be Craig as well. He'll be so upset if you don't go – he's talked about nothing else but going there with me and Grandad." This was a statement which was totally untrue, because the little lad was to learn, for the first time on his birthday, the exciting news of his ticket.

"Upset Craig? Surely not, boy." There was uncertainty in his tone – and now more than just a touch of guilt.

"Of course he'll be upset, Dad. I've told him that when the time comes for him to go to matches, he'll be the fifth generation. Firstly there was Grandad's Grandad, then Grandad's own father, then Grandad himself, then me, then him; and three of those generations will be there together. Despite his age, he understands what it all means – and he thinks it's marvellous that he'll be there with you and me. You've got to go, Dad – for Craig's sake if for no other."

170

Simon felt a touch guilty himself at telling such an emotive – and untrue – tale regarding a non-existent conversation with his young son, but 'when needs must, the Devil drives'.

His father stood still for several seconds before speaking – and when he did so, he talked largely to himself. "Three generations together – yes, I suppose there will be; and there's no reason why they shouldn't have a decent season either. They ended the season with a better side than they began it, even though they went down."

He looked at his son, his mind made up – as Simon suspected it would be. He had known that a frontal attack would have been in vain – Duncan Curtis could be a stubborn man. However, he was also a man who believed in the importance of roots, of family, of dynasty. He nodded – "All right, boy, come on in and have a cup of tea and then I'll nip upstairs and get my cheque book."

"Right, Dad, lead on – a couple of cups will go down nicely, plus a slice or two of Mum's Dundee Cake; there's usually one on the go." One thing for sure, he mused – he'd earned it.

XIV

The Bank

Don Briggs strode along the side of his large bungalow, followed by the limping Hughie Dixon. They turned the corner and were confronted by the spacious back garden, part of it dedicated to shrubs and flowers, but about a third put to practical use in the growing of vegetables. The slightly disabled visitor – his limp down to the fact that his left leg was a little shorter than the right, due to several major operations following a serious motorcycle accident some twenty-five years previously – followed his host along the path dividing the floral from the edible, and stopped a couple of yards from a steep bank at the rear. Don Briggs indicated the problem with a somewhat theatrical sweep of his right arm. "That bank's worrying us, Hughie," he explained. "Several times during the twenty or so years we've lived here we've thought of having a retaining wall built to ensure it doesn't collapse on us, but whilst there have been occasions when it hasn't appeared to be as stable as it might have been, there's never been a time when we felt it could really collapse – until now. This winter's done it."

The builder nodded, "Yes, I know what you mean, boy. Coldest winter for thirty years – probably longer than that. The frost was terrible – it's caused problems all over the place. The power of it to destabilise hedges, banks and suchlike is amazing."

"Quite so," agreed the homeowner. "And it's been made worse by the weeks of heavy rain we had last month. Anyway, me and

Louise looked at it a couple of days ago and we were of like mind that it really was time we had a retaining wall built as that bank at present looks as if it could collapse at any time – and if that happened, it would be like an avalanche."

"Yes, I fancy you're right," came the words of agreement. "There's not going to be a frost for a day or two, it being May, but there could well be plenty more rain – the price we pay for living between the Tamar and Dartmoor, of course – and looking at it, I'm not sure it can take a lot more. No, it's a job that needs doing, right enough – and the sooner the better."

"So can you give us a price, Hughie?" requested Briggs. It was the fifth time he had asked such a question of a builder in the past month – and he still awaited a response from any of them.

Hughie Dixon did not know this, of course, but he would certainly have realised that he was not the first local builder that Don would have consulted – he was never the first one anybody consulted. For his reputation went before him; in his favour was the fact he, generally, was cheaper than most of the others – that was the one advantage of being a 'one man band'. Against him, however, was his innate unreliability (he had been known to start a job, then go on a fortnight's holiday), his poor timekeeping – especially after a heavy night in the village pub – and the, generally, unimpressive standard of his work which, at best, was probably just adequate, at worst, dire. Yet he had been in the building trade all of his working life – and like Don Briggs, he had lived in the village since birth. After leaving school, he worked with his father, also a jobbing builder of no great reputation. Indeed, the son was in many ways, in terms of his profession, remarkably similar to his parent. Had he been able to learn a trade in a proper fashion, then he might have been different, but he quickly fell into his father's way of being a 'jack of all trade' who was, assuredly, 'master of none'. Yet he had made a tolerable living over the years, and now, in his fifties, his two sons having grown up and gone out into the world (neither of them, though, into the building trade), he and his wife, Amber, had a comfortable lifestyle, always having at least a fortnight every year beneath a warm, foreign sun. The secret was, as he

173

always told his family, never to turn down the small jobs – those that so many builders did not want.

"I live on the crumbs from off their plates," as he would say with both regularity and honesty. He did have a weakness greater than any other, however – a chronic inability to give a price for a job without going through profuse indecision and mental torture, something of which Don Briggs – a lifetime friend (though probably not a close one) knew only too well. So when he asked the lopsided builder for a price to put up the retaining wall, he suspected that something of a pantomime would ensue.

He was to be proved correct. The protracted procedure began with Hughie scratching his head; this was followed by a pursing of the lips, then a shake of the head. "It's a fair old job, Don, really; I mean it's going to take a fair amount of material – so it'll take a fair while as well. A brave bit of time, in fact."

"I'd have thought it was a quite straightforward job, boy," opined the homeowner. "Granted, it'll take several blocks and so forth, but it's just a straight wall that's needed – nothing ornate, certainly nothing complicated. And I wouldn't say it needs to be that high – five feet, perhaps, certainly no higher. In fact, it could be that it doesn't need to be as high as that. Chances are that the bank will remain intact for the foreseeable future – it's just that we need a barrier there in case it does decide to collapse."

"Oh yes, yes, it's wise to do it, Don – another winter like we've just had could bring the whole lot down. In fact, another spell of heavy rain could as well."

"So, how much is it going to cost?"

The builder shook his head, then again pursed his lips. "Fair bit, boy, fair bit – it's not going to be cheap. I mean, it's a brave job really – more complicated than it looks," he prevaricated.

"Well, how much is a fair bit, Hughie?" there was slight annoyance in the tone.

The man again shook his head. "To tell you the truth, boy, it could be more than you're expecting – a fair bit more. Price of blocks now is shocking – and several will be needed, I'm sure. and it'll not be quick – no, it'll take longer than you may think."

"How long?" Now, there was considerable exasperation in the tone.

Once again came a shake of the head: "Well – well – well, it could take a brave while; several days perhaps. A lot of it will depend on the weather, of course. I mean, if it rains I won't be able to do anything – you can't build proper if it's raining – especially if it's heavy rain; it can't be done."

"But the fact that it might rain, and you won't be able to work shouldn't affect the price in any way," rasped the customer, somewhat annoyed. "I mean I'm not going to pay you for sitting at home waiting for the rain to stop, am I – it doesn't work like that, Hughie, does it? If you're not able to work it's hard on you, but it's nothing to do with me. All I'll pay for is the time you're actually here working on the wall – is that not so?"

"Yes – yes – yes, of course it is, boy," spluttered the builder. "I don't really mean it in the way you took it. Obviously I'll only charge for the actual time I'm working on it; trouble is, it's not easy to say just how long that will be."

"Come on, Hughie – you've been in the building trade all your working life. All I want built is a simple, straightforward wall – no fancy work, or embellishments or anything like that. Surely you can give me an idea – perhaps just a rough one at present – of how much it will cost; surely you can do that, boy."

Don had managed this time to disguise his previous tone of great exasperation with one of gentle pleading – which appeared to work, with the builder at first shrugging his shoulders, before nodding his head. "Well, I suppose I can give you a rough estimate, Don – it mightn't be very accurate, but I'll do my best."

The homeowner was fully aware that Hughie's quote would be devoid of accuracy – just about everything the man did was failing in precision, but he reasoned that even this obtuse man would be able to tell him the cost with tolerable accuracy, and also be able to erect the simple structure discussed to an acceptable (if only just) standard.

Hughie reached into a coat pocket and produced a stubby pencil, then rummaged in another one. Several seconds elapsed before he produced, like a rabbit from a hat, a VAT receipt for

petrol. He gazed at it, then turned it over; he looked around him,
espied a slim, flat stone, promptly picked it up, rested the paper
upon it, and then, concentrating his mind on the length and height
of the proposed wall – glancing around him as he did so –
scribbled slowly upon the grubby, but blank reverse of the paper
which he would soon have to produce for his accountant when
that long suffering man did the builder's annual accounts.

The best part of a quarter of an hour elapsed before he folded
the paper and placed it back in the pocket from which it had been
produced along with his pencil. He paced along the route of the
proposed wall for a final time, then stopping momentarily to, Don
assumed, imagine what the concrete block barrier would look
like.

It was at this point that the potential customer suddenly
understood why Hughie's constructions so often deviated from
the vertical: It was simply that the man himself was never really
vertical, his shorter left leg causing the fellow to lean slightly to
one side when assessing the precision of that which he had built;
he rarely confused things by using a spirit level.

"Right, Don – I'll be on my way; with a bit of luck I'll be home
before it gets too wet. They give rain and gales for the best part
of the next twenty-four hours – and I fancy I feel a spot or two on
my face already; and the wind's definitely rising."

"Yes, you're right, boy," agreed Don. "We're in for a rough old
night, I'm afraid. Tell you what, I'll phone you this evening for
your quote for the job – you'll know by then, for certain." The
words were spoken with a confidence he did not feel – a doubt
quite justified when he saw the momentary flash of panic contort
the builder's face.

"Tonight – tonight," gasped Hughie. "Well – I really don't
know if I'll have it ready by tonight, boy. There's a lot of, well,
quite complicated things to work out – things that can't be
hurried. I mean, perhaps you'd give me a few days."

"Look, Hughie, you can see for yourself that it's a job which
needs to be done urgently – so Louise and me need to have an
idea of just how much it's going to cost. I mean, if it's too much,
then we'll have to look elsewhere. We don't want to, but like

everybody these days, we've got to keep an eye on the pennies."

"Well – yes I see what you mean; it certainly does need doing." He shrugged his shoulders, and said, with an air of resignation, "I'll go right home now and make a start on working out a fair price."

"That's great, boy, thank you – I'll ring you this evening, say, about nine?"

The builder appeared horror stricken: "It'll be hard to work it out by then – but, but, well I suppose I could have a go."

The implacable expression upon Don's face told the builder, as well as any words, that this potential customer would accept no prevarication.

Hughie turned to go – "I'll be away then, Don – and see what I can work out."

"Thanks, boy," replied the customer about to return to the house. However, a thought came to him, and he called after the builder.

"Hughie, if we do accept your quote, how long before you can start?" No sooner had he asked the question than he regretted it, the fellow giving the kind of answer which was well in line with the kind of reply standard from a man who was a terminal prevaricator – and one which Don should have anticipated.

For Hughie stopped in his tracks, turned to face the homeowner, then went through the well honed ritual of blowing out his cheeks, shaking – then scratching – his head, finishing with a classic pursing of the lips. "Well, it's hard to say, boy, to be honest – I've a fair bit on at present, and one or two rush jobs amongst them. No, it's not easy to answer that one. All I can say is that I'd get around to it as soon as I could."

Fed up with the convoluted negotiations always involved when trying to get the jobbing builder to commit to a price and a starting time, Don was about to shrug his own shoulders, and abandon all attempts at getting the information. Before he did, though, a memory flashed into his mind; one which brought forth a puzzled expression and a sharp retort and question: "Hang on, Hughie – where's all this work come from suddenly? I remember in the pub only last week you telling the landlord, when he asked

177

you if you had much work on, that things were slow but you were hopeful it would all pick up soon as summer was almost here. Now you say you've a fair bit on – or words to that effect. Which is it – do you have plenty of work, or very little? If it's plenty, then things have certainly improved for you in just a few days."

"Well – well – well, I don't have many jobs on, true; and that's what I was meaning in the pub. I do have a few smallish jobs to do though – you know, the kind of urgent ones that folk want done yesterday – you know what I mean."

"Yes – like mine." Don fixed the builder with an 'old fashioned' look. "Ever since I've known you, Hughie – a very long time now – you've always prevaricated on both estimates and time of starting jobs," said he. "To be honest, it never fails to amaze me; I mean you've been in the building business your entire working life, yet you never seem able to give a price, and you rarely give a commitment regarding a starting date – why?" The question was put reasonably politely, but, nonetheless, with a touch of annoyance.

The builder looked so embarrassed that Don wished he'd not asked the question – and was about to say so. Hughie, though, stuttered out a response before he could do so. "Well, Don, well, you know, I don't mean to prevaricate but – but – but I've always been nervous about giving quotes, even though I've been in the business so long, as you said. It's just that it's easy to get it wrong in terms of both materials and the time needed to do the job – how long I'll take is especially hard to forecast; you just don't know what problems you're going to find once you start a job. And when it comes to starting dates, I never like to promise a certain day 'cause, well, you know, anything can happen – the job I'm doing can take longer than expected, or I could be home with the flu or something. You know how it is, Don – you never know what's coming, do you?"

The potential customer smiled briefly, then nodded. "True enough, boy, you never know what's going to happen in the future. Still, if we look on the bright side and assume that the job – or jobs – you're doing take no longer than you expect and you are able to avoid the flu, and any other illness – and accidents, of course – then when can you start the work, assuming we accept your quote?" Immediately following the question, Don made a mental bet with himself, one which he was destined to lose, but only just.

He watched patiently as Hughie again went through his full repertoire of pursing lips, blowing out cheeks, scratching and shaking his head. After a couple of minutes – a seeming eternity to Don Briggs – the builder answered his question by posing one of his own.

"What day is it today?"

To the homeowner it wasn't a reassuring enquiry – after all, if he didn't know what day of the week it was, then chances of getting a firm starting date from him were not great. In this, though, he was to be proved wrong. "Tuesday," said he.

Dixon nodded, pondered once again – for no more than twenty seconds this time – then stated, "Thursday, boy – yes, Thursday morning, first thing – or thereabouts," he added hastily, as the term implied a very early start, something which he was not sure he'd be able to manage because he had a darts match down at the pub on the Wednesday evening so could well have a bit of a hangover the following day.

Briggs nodded with some alacrity: "Fine, Hughie, excellent in fact," he replied, trying to suppress the surprise that was within him. He had anticipated a date far earlier than could reasonably be expected when considering the builder's habitual prevarication, for he had dealt with the man enough times over the years to be well aware that if he was pressed, with some firmness, for an early starting date, he would virtually always deliver one, the other 'urgent jobs', taking so called priority, disappearing like snow before the sun. However, he had pencilled in, mentally, Friday or the following Monday as being the most likely days for the work to be put in hand; Thursday, though, was unexpected.

Briskly, he agreed the day – no time for prevarication on his part. "Excellent, Hughie – if we accept your quote, then Thursday will be ideal, thank you. Anyway, I'll let you get away and phone you tonight."

The builder nodded. "Right, boy, I'm off then." He pulled his coat quite tightly around him as the rain began to fall quite heavily. "It's certainly going to be dirty, just as they said – and the wind's rising. Well, speak to you tonight then, boy."

With that, the builder turned away and moved briskly around the side of the house towards his battered old pick up parked at the front, Don's, "Bye, boy," being lost in the breeze that was fast moving towards being a gale.

The rest of the afternoon and the evening, also, saw a nasty storm sweeping up the Tamar, lashing land already waterlogged, and as Don sat down by the phone a few minutes after nine o'clock to contact the builder, there was no sign of the storm abating, rain hitting the southerly facing windows like pebbles. As the phone rang, Don began to wonder what sort of tale awaited him from the builder. For certain, he did not expect accuracy – or even clarity – from Hughie regarding his quote to build the retaining wall. His reading of the situation was, unfortunately, all too close to that which ensued. The basic courtesies observed, Don got to the nitty-gritty. "How much, then boy – how much is it going to cost us for you to build the wall?"

There was a pause of several seconds before the builder gave his response – one true to form. "Well, boy. It's not that easy to give a hard and fast price, as I said this afternoon. You know, when building anything there are always, sort of, things that can't be foreseen; things go wrong, problems come along which you don't expect, if you see what I mean."

"I don't doubt that's true, Hughie," the potential customer retorted, "but I see no reason why you cannot give us, at least, some estimate as to how much it will cost. I mean, even if it's only to the nearest hundred quid, it will be a guide and be of some help."

The silence from the other end of the phone was profound, and as Don waited, with rare patience, for a response from the builder, images of the fellow's facial contortions came to him as the builder pondered the, to him, complex mental task he was given. This hopeless inability to come up with a price was something which Briggs had always found most surprising in Hughie; for the man was no fool, always having a good knowledge of life and the world around him. Basic arithmetic, also, was no great problem to him, he being able to calculate in his head at a merry pace numbers needed to win darts matches, even though he might have had a bellyful of beer and cider.

At last, Hughie spoke, "Well, boy, it isn't going to be less than five hundred quid," said he, his tone betraying a measure of stress.

"So you're telling me it's going to be five hundred pounds, Hughie," came the reply in a tone which suggested that the potential customer saw that figure as a firm price. It was certainly one Louise and he would be happy with as they had anticipated a figure somewhat higher.

"Well – well – no – no – not really," spluttered the hapless Hughie. "What I mean is, there's no way it'll be less than that. To be honest, it's more likely it'll be more; could be a brave bit more, too."

"Well, how much more?" rasped Briggs. Never a patient man, despite his essentially easy going nature, he was getting – rapidly – very tired of a conversation which already appeared as if it would take a long time to reach a conclusion. "Are you saying it'll be six hundred quid – is that what you're saying, Hughie?"

"No – no – no – not necessarily; but I can't see it being less than that, boy. I mean – well, it could be – to be honest – it could be when everything's added in – well, it could be as much as a thousand pounds."

"How much? Did you say a thousand?" The words were spoken in a tone which betrayed total shock.

"Well – yes – yes; I mean, I don't say it will be, but it could be. I was thinking earlier – I built a wall similar to this back last year; other side of Tavistock it was – close to the moors. I remember that was up around a thousand – and it wasn't much bigger than this one; perhaps no bigger at all. Yes, round about a thousand, boy, I fancy. Although I must admit I can't remember the exact amount, to be honest; but I do know it was a brave bit, Don, and materials will have gone up since then; mind you, at the same time I've got to say that I had to build that on some boggy old ground so it needed a deeper foundation – that's as I remember it, anyway. Your place is much firmer, so it'll not need as deep a one, I wouldn't think, so it'll not need the same materials or labour. That could bring it back a hundred or so – perhaps even more; it's hard to say really."

The prospective customer had reached the end of his limited patience. Here he was going round in ever widening circles with the most annoying man the construction industry had ever produced, when he could be in his front room with Louise, drinking the contents of the freshly opened bottle of red wine perched upon the coffee table, and watching a fresh episode of *Foyles War*, one of his favourites.

"Hughie, look, I've got things to do – so I can't stand here at this phone beating around the bush any longer. I really can't." He stopped talking briefly, then put forward an idea which had just occurred to him. "Tell you what, boy – lets agree a figure here and now, which will be fair and acceptable to us both. You said to begin with that it would be more than five hundred and could even be as high as a thousand, and, well, to be honest, five hundred quid would have been less than I would have expected, with a grand far more. So let's split the difference; what if we settle for seven hundred and fifty. That would seem to be fair to us both, boy, don't you think?"

The alacrity with which the builder agreed the price astonished Don Briggs. All the prevarication had evaporated, it being replaced with a surprising, and exceedingly rare, positivity. "Yes, Don, yes – that's fair enough. I've got no problem with that, none at all. We've got a deal then, have we?"

It was the customer's turn to prevaricate – albeit only briefly: "Well, yes, we have in theory, Hughie. The only thing is, that Louise and me always talk things over when it comes to spending money on the house, garden and suchlike; so I'd like to mention it to her and see if she's happy with it. I'd be very surprised if she wasn't, but it's only right to check with her first. Tell you what, Hughie, I'll have a chat with her before we go to bed and then phone you first thing in the morning – say, about eight o'clock – if that's all right with you."

"Yes, yes – that'll be all right, boy. I'll still be about – I don't usually get going 'til quarter past, or so."

"And if we agree the seven fifty – and I don't doubt that we will – then you can start Thursday morning, Hughie; that's what you said, isn't it?" He knew only too well that such was what the man had stated, but, where the somewhat unreliable and erratic builder was concerned, such things needed to be checked – and re-checked.

"Yes, boy, that's right – I'll be there first thing, don't you worry about that." The reply was upbeat and brimming with confidence.

After wishing the fellow 'good night' and reminding him that his phone would ring early the following morning, Don replaced the receiver and went belatedly into the front room to watch what little remained of *Foyles War*, obtaining Louise's agreement to the £750 sum regarding the building of the wall, during one of the numerous commercial breaks.

A wild, stormy, exceedingly wet night followed a tempestuous day – one which, whilst it did not delay Don's phone call to the builder the following morning, changed the conversation radically: Simply – the retaining wall was no longer needed, as there was nothing to retain. For the collapse of the bank was clearly far more imminent than anybody could have predicted, the high winds and almost two inches of rain which had fallen during the previous afternoon and night, being the ultimate force of destruction. Thus what was a bank was now a scree of soft, rich, brown and exceedingly wet earth which had slid some seven or eight feet into the garden. Thus did Don impart this somewhat dramatic news to the builder, informing him that, obviously, though reluctantly, he did not need his services regarding building a wall.

Hughie saw the situation and accepted it with aplomb: "Well, if there isn't anything to retain, boy, then there's no need for a wall," said he, chuckling. "Mind you, there must be a brave bit of earth slid into the bottom of your garden, Don."

"Mountains of it, boy – damned nuisance it is, and no mistake. We'll have to move out a lot of it, I would think."

"Tell you what, Don, whilst I can't help you there – I've not got the gear to move a lot of earth, unless a wheelbarrow will do the job," said he with a loud guffaw, "I know a man who has. My brother, Frank's the man you want. He's got a small lorry and a small digger to carry out the earth from the back of your house to the road. Tell you what, boy, why don't I give him a ring and get him to come round and give you a price. I'm sure he'll be delighted to – he told me only last week he's not got a lot on at present. You know Frank, don't you? Mind you, he's not lived local for years now; he moved up Okehampton way twenty odd years back – but you'll remember him for certain."

Hughie was assuredly correct there – Don remembered Frank Dixon, all right; just about everybody in the parish would have remembered him, if they'd lived there a while; and they would recall a man in a class of his own as a builder and contractor, one who regularly reached levels of unreliability, incompetence and all round ineptitude beside which the building efforts of the hapless Hughie were creations of magnificence. Also, Frank lacked the friendly, affable nature of his brother and could be unscrupulous – possibly even dishonest. He had moved out of the parish because nobody would give him work and now it looked as if he had arrived at the same state of play in the northern part of the district.

The situation called for quick thinking. He liked Hughie, and didn't wish to offend him by making any disparaging remarks about a brother to whom, it would appear, he remained quite close, 'blood being thicker than water'. His thought processes, however, were not as sharp as they once were, so he floundered around for several seconds wittering a few 'oh's and 'ah's and a couple of 'well, boys' before inspiration, suddenly, was his. "Yes, yes, thanks Hughie – thanks, I appreciate it. Still it's best if you don't contact Frank just yet, 'cause we might not want any of the earth moved – no, we may keep it as it is and make a feature of it; landscape it in fact."

Whether or not Louise and he would go in such a direction, he knew not (although it did strike him that such an idea was not the worst he'd ever had) but he was more than pleased with himself having come up with a feasible plan of belated action on the spur of the moment. Such self satisfaction was to be exceedingly brief. Indeed, within seconds his will to live was under savage attack. For the voice on the other end of the phone purred with delight.

"That's even better, Don – that's Frank's main work these days, landscaping; he enjoys that, and there seems to be more work available in that direction than in the building trade, or so he finds. Not that he's busy at the moment, as I said, a bit earlier. What I'll do is I'll phone him and tell him what's happened to your bank and get him to get hold of you, then come along and have a look at the job. That sound all right, boy?" It sounded anything but all right to Don Briggs, but before he could articulate that fact in terms which would mollify the amiable builder on the other end of the line, that fellow – master of procrastination and prevarication though he assuredly was – brought the conversation to a brisk conclusion by saying, "You just leave it with me, Don – I'll get hold of Frank right away. If I phone now I'll catch him having his breakfast. Knowing him he'll be in touch right away. Anyway, you take care, boy – not many of us left." With that – one of the man's favourite forms of adieu – the builder was gone, leaving a bemused potential customer in his wake.

For several seconds Don Briggs sat by the phone gazing aimlessly at nothing in particular. Had it not been as early in the day, he would have poured himself a Scotch of shameful proportions but, with some considerable effort, resisted, calling to mind his own long held belief that whilst the fellow who drank whisky in the evening had excellent judgement, he that did so in the morning had a problem. He got up from the chair and shuffled slowly towards the kitchen to join Louise, who was engrossed in the local paper at the breakfast table. He tried to think of a way in which, when he phoned, he could tell Frank Dixon, politely and without in any way giving offence (being essentially a very easy going, courteous fellow, he always sought ways of dispatching bad or disagreeable news as gently as possible) that his services regarding landscaping the collapsed bank assuredly were not required.

He sat down opposite his wife then proceeded to pour tea into his large beaker; suddenly, inspiration engulfed him. He would leave Louise to deal with Frank Dixon – yes, that was it. For she and the incompetent builder had 'history'. More than twenty years earlier, the fellow had come along and erected a secondhand garden shed which they had purchased at a farm sale. He had been paid instantly in cash as he requested which, Don was to say later, was on their part a lesson learned (never be too quick in paying bills). For within forty-eight hours, a strong south westerly had sprung up and, in consequence, the sloppily erected shed had fallen down. Despite all their efforts, they were unable to either get the man to come back and erect it again, or to repay the money despite concerted efforts on his part and a magnificent verbal attack by his lovely, feisty wife. She had declared then and there, however, that never again would Frank Dixon set foot on their property. Now, Louise was essentially a charming, courteous lady, but when roused, she took no prisoners – and she rarely forgot past blows and injustices.

When Frank Dixon phoned, as assuredly he would do – being a man with a hide as thick as an elephant, no conscience and a convenient memory loss when it came to former sins – then he would let her answer. And he would not warn her – Louise acting spontaneously was Louise at her best. Smiling to himself, he quickly quaffed his tea, poured himself another, leant back into his hard kitchen chair and waited for events to transpire. It had not been a bad morning he mused to himself; he was about to see his dear wife demolish a builder and contractor who was a disgrace to his profession and – every bit as important – they were going to save seven hundred and fifty precious pounds.

XV

The Character

Jason stood near the lychgate, turned up the collar of his overcoat against the bitter wind blowing off Dartmoor, and eyed the steady stream of folk passing through the gateway en route up to the church. He felt a touch apprehensive; clearly he looked it also, for he was confronted by a tall, burly man, probably in his late sixties. "Don't mind me saying so, boy, but you look a bit lost."

Jason smiled. "No – no – not really. It's just that I don't know whether or not I should go on into the church or wait a little – I am a touch early."

"Go on in – if you don't you'll end up standing at the back, perhaps outside even – Cuffie was a very well known man. I'm Harry Carter, by the way."

The younger man took the proffered hand in his – "Jason Marlow. My wife and I moved into the house next door to Mr Bray – Cuffie – just a couple of months back. Clearly we did not know him very well, but he and Mrs Bray have been very kind to us in that short time, so I thought the least I could do was to attend his funeral. Unfortunately, my wife is unable to come – she's visiting her mother in London who has not been well lately."

They passed through the lychgate and walked up the path. "They'll turn out for Cuffie – a very, very popular man, and certainly well known. A total shock, his death. Just sixty-six – only recently retired. Dropped dead – literally – down the pub. Heart attack."

Harry's prediction was accurate, the church overflowing with mourners; some forty or more remaining outside. From the vicar's address, and a eulogy delivered by Billy Walton, Landlord of 'The Spirit of Drake', Jason was able to get an idea of the sort of fellow his neighbour had been. A man of many parts, who had been born in the village and lived there all his life, it seemed he was friendly, generous, a good sportsman in his youth, a chap who liked his liquor and one who had lived a somewhat erratic and chequered life in terms of employment. "A man," as Billy put it "whose leaving of this world could never go unnoticed."

At the end of the service, the vicar announced that Cuffie's widow, Martha, and her family invited everybody to 'The Spirit of Drake' for refreshments, following the interment in the local cemetery.

Once outside the church, Jason bade farewell to Harry and was about to move off when the older man grabbed his arm: "No, don't go yet boy; come down to the 'Drake'. If I know Martha, and those two boys of hers, they'll make sure that poor old Cuffie has a good send off; there'll be plenty of good grub, and liquor by the bucketful – and all of it free. You say your wife is away, so she'll not be missing you – so come on down. You'll be able to meet several other local folk as well."

Jason shrugged his shoulders. "Why not," said he, and walked down the hill with Harry and, at least, a hundred others (although it was clear that many mourners had not responded to the invitation) towards 'The Spirit of Drake' at the bottom. The pub filled rapidly with mourners. Harry, who was an old hand at village 'wakes', ushered his companion towards a table near the roaring log fire. "Let's grab a couple of seats here boy – warm and not too far from the food," said he, indicating a feast of pasties, sandwiches, pies, gateaux, trifles and so forth, arrayed upon a couple of long tables just a few feet from where they were going to sit. No sooner had they sat down than they were joined by a trio of others, all about Harry's age – mid to late sixties – who grabbed the remaining empty chairs around their table.

Promptly, Jason was introduced to them. "This is Lou – he's got the barber shop down beside the war memorial. And this is

Roger – just retired from County Highways – and Alec, who learnt his trade as a farrier and blacksmith just in time to see the back of the last working shires in the parish."

"Yes, great timing that was," agreed the tall gaunt 'Smith', a wry grin playing around his mouth as he shook the newcomer's hand. "So, I spent most of my working life making iron gates, garden furniture and such like. I retired last year."

Conversation became somewhat sporadic for a brief period as plates were handed round, then filled rapidly from the large, heaped platters being carried around by the pub staff. Jason had no sooner filled his – though modestly compared with those around him – than he found an empty glass thrust into his hands, which, promptly, was more than half filled by scotch, a large bottle of which had appeared, seemingly miraculously, in Harry's hands. "Here's to Cuffie," cried he, "one of the best."

"Well, I'm not too sure about that," retorted the retired road man, after downing most of his whisky. "He was a right beauty, really – but life was never dull when he was around, that's for sure."

Jason sipped his whisky, but within a few seconds more, his comrades had drunk theirs, and had them replenished instantly by Harry. Further conversation ceased temporarily, as the five of them (although Jason was not in the same league as the others) emptied their plates, and then replenished them (although, once again, the newcomer's efforts were puny beside those of his older companions), the only words uttered being the likes of "first class pasty this" and "lovely bit of ham" and "best bit of trifle I've had in many a day" and so forth.

Eating was interrupted, temporarily, when the frustrated farrier took delivery of a tray from a waiter, upon which stood five pints of best bitter; he handed them round. Jason, however, declined the pint offered him. "Not for me, thanks – I fancy I've had enough already."

"But you've only had a drop of scotch," rasped the barber.

"I'm not really a drinking man if I'm honest," replied the younger man, a touch guiltily.

"You could never have said that about Cuffie," snorted Harry.

"He could drink for England; and when he'd had a few, he was game for anything."

"Yes – like that night he knocked out the professional at Goose Fair. Remember that lads?" Roger was being most generous in using the term 'lads'.

"Remember it?" retorted Alec. "How could anybody ever forget it?"

"The professional? Goose Fair?" puzzled Jason.

"Yes – yes, in the boxing." Alec drained the remains of his pint, then explained himself. "It was probably about forty-five years back – Tavistock Goose Fair Day. Well, we used to go around together in those days – several others as well, who don't live in the parish any more; nor in the area for that matter."

"They could be dead," interjected Roger, with a sombre portion of reality.

"Well – yes, I suppose they could," agreed the teller of the tale, none too pleased at being interrupted. "Whatever, there were often as many as ten of us – we had all gone to school together. Well, we'd had some liquor that day – and Cuffie more than any of us, which was par for the course. After we'd turned out of the pub – the old Newmarket in the Square – "

"Been thrown out, if truth be told," – an honest but, in the eyes of Alec, unnecessary interruption from Lou.

"Well – well, yes, that's about it," he agreed grudgingly. "Anyway, we all went down the fair – in the car park and the wharf, just as it is now. In those days there was always a boxing booth, where local lads could challenge the pro boxer, who took on all comers, and usually hammered them. Well, the showman asked for a challenger and before we knew what was happening, Cuffie was stood up on the stage confronting the pro. So we all packed into the booth to see him take the fellow on. He was given a pair of gloves, and to win a fiver, he had to go the three rounds – which few ever did. And if he knocked the pro out, he won a tenner – and it had been donkey's years since anybody had ever seen that happen. Well, for the first couple of rounds, Cuffie never laid a glove on him and took a fair thumping himself – although he never went down. Then in the third round, he came out of his corner, did Cuffie, somehow caught the pro with a fantastic right hook, and laid him out. It took a couple of minutes to bring him around – and the showman was not pleased. Still, Cuffie won a tenner – a week's wages in those days."

"That wasn't the only fight he had either," added Harry. "He had a few punch ups in this pub over the years and outside – usually over a woman."

"Shocker for the women was Cuffie. He led poor Martha a dog's life in many ways – she could never trust him. Yet for some reason she always thought the world of him." Alec shook his head in bewilderment. "Baffling really."

Revelations regarding the deceased's eventful and, at times, disreputable past ceased – albeit temporarily – when his elder son, Steve, rose to thank the gathered throng on behalf of his mother and all the family, for their attendance at the funeral in such numbers and for their kind messages of sympathy and support. Also, he pointed out that a goodly amount of food remained and, in consequence, the waiters would continue to circulate with platters – and trays bearing drinks.

Conversation was somewhat desultory whilst plates and glasses were refilled – then emptied – then filled again. Jason, who was feeling a touch the worse for wear, felt that the only way to avoid further imbibing was to restore conversation.

"Why – why was he called Cuffie?" He enquired, stumbling a little over his words. "That wasn't his real name, was it?"

"No – his name was Cuthbert," replied Harry. "He was always known as Cuffie, though, even at primary school."

"And what did he do for a living?"

"All sorts over the years. He worked on a farm when he left school, but left that and for some years went salmon fishing in the Tamar; he made a good living there, but part of the reason for that was the fact that he took a lot of fish out of the river when, legally his licence did not permit. He ended up in court several times for it, and even did a month in Exeter Prison about thirty odd years ago. When the river got 'fished out' he packed it in, and did several different things: He was a bin man for the council for a while, but got the sack because of his shocking timekeeping.

Then he went taxi driving but had to give it up when he lost his licence because of drink driving. Then he worked as a builder's labourer for a spell, but when he got his licence back, he set up as a builder himself."

"Hopeless, he was," chuckled Roger. "He had no trade, precious little common sense, was as unreliable in this as he was in everything else, and couldn't read a plan to save his life. And his work was poor – shocking, at times."

" 'Good enough Cuff' was what everybody called him," said Alec, with a raucous laugh. "That's 'cause no matter how bad a job he did, he would always say – 'That's good enough'."

"How did he ever get any work?" asked an incredulous Jason.

"Because he was cheap," retorted the retired 'Smith'. "And the fact he could usually talk his way out of trouble helped as well."

The throng about them was thinning rapidly, whilst empty plates and glasses were being collected – clearly the 'wake' was drawing to a close. Harry looked about him. "It seems we're about to be thrown out, lads," said he, "but before we are, I think we should raise our glasses one last time to the man. To Cuffie – rest in peace." The rest muttered the words in tolerable union, then drained their glasses.

Espying a bottle of Scotch with roughly a quarter of its contents remaining, ignored on a nearby table, Alec promptly grabbed it, divided the contents three ways (Jason still having some remaining in his glass), raised his into the air and rasped, "To Martha and her family – long life to them all," and in unison with his two comrades, emptied the amber, fiery liquid in little more than a gulp. With that, their glasses were returned to the table top, and the trio of old friends prepared to leave.

Whilst the others stood up and put on their coats, Jason still sat, seemingly lost in thought. Harry noticed the reverie and promptly broke into it. "What's up, Jason. You look as if you've the troubles of the world on your shoulders."

The newcomer smiled, wanly, got to his feet and reached for his coat. "No – no troubles," he replied. "It's just that I don't understand after listening to you all, why Cuffie was so highly thought of – so popular. I mean he was often aggressive – violent, in fact; he was a serial womaniser and often cheated on his wife; he drank far too much, was a poacher, had been to prison – and as a builder he was incompetent, yet was quite happy to take people's money even though he'd done a poor job, and knew it. Frankly, he seemed to have few qualities – yet the church overflowed for his funeral. I find it baffling."

Harry smiled. "Yes, he had his faults – as we all do. But he was a one off, was Cuffie – not one of the common herd, as the saying goes. He was the sort of bloke who, in his erratic, eccentric, sometimes outrageous way, added colour to village life. He was always good company and, in his way, a good pal." He paused briefly, then shrugged his shoulders. "He was a character, Jason, and wherever he is now, up there with Saint Peter or down with 'Old Nick', he will be amongst friends."

j

XVI
Don't Do as I Do

It was Alfie Turner's fault, all of it; so mused Will Black as he gazed at the ceiling.

He was in such a state that death would have been a happy release, having suffered a highly unpleasant night when the only times he did not feel that the bedroom was spinning around his bed, was during his many stumbling staggers to the bathroom to stick a throbbing head into the lavatory pan. He had once read that the fine crooner, Dean Martin, had said that a man wasn't drunk if he could lie on the floor without holding on. If that was a fair test, then he had failed it miserably as it was only by gripping the bedclothes in his version of a vice like grip, that he had stopped spinning around the room. And none of it would have happened if Alfie had behaved just a little more responsibly.

After all, until the last hour or so, it had been a delightful day. The marriage of Lizzie – daughter of their mutual friend, haulage contractor, Ray Jordan – to a journalist from London, had been the occasion. The ceremony had been held in a small church on the edge of Dartmoor, with the reception at a nearby country hotel, amongst the best in Devon. The weather had been superb – June at its best – and everyone had sat in the balmy open air, surrounded by the hotel's immaculately kept garden with stunning views of the moor in the distance. Not that they had much time to gaze at it, as the seemingly never-ending supply of delicious food required constant attention, whilst the filling and

194

refilling of glasses by hardworking and attentive waiters did wonders for the aura of goodwill and bonhomie which permeated the celebration. And how the wine flowed – red, white, champagne, all washed over the assembled guests (at least a hundred) like the River Tavy in spate. It was after Will had consumed his fifth glass of champagne (he had lost count of the number of glasses of red and white wine with which he fortified himself), that Alfie had played the 'joker' which was responsible for the dreadful night – and morning – which had come his way.

Like producing a rabbit from a hat, his old, heavy drinking friend had placed on the table a pristine bottle of single malt Scotch. "Bought this back last October," said he, "when we were on holiday up in the Western Isles. We visited this distillery, and I couldn't resist a bottle of this brew – twelve years old, it is. No better way to send a young couple on the road to matrimony than to toast them in good 'Scottish wine'."

"I'll give you no argument there, Alfie," enthused Will. "A dram of highland water will finish the day off nicely."

His wife, Stella, however, was in strong disagreement. "You've had quite enough already, Will," she rasped. "More than enough, in fact. Any more you will be ill."

Alfie's wife Angela, who rarely drank at all, was in full agreement, and extended the admonition to include her husband, whose intake had even outstripped Will's.

The pleading for abstinence, however, fell upon deaf ears, although Will did make some effort to placate his disapproving spouse. "Just one, maid," he slurred. "Just one to show willing – and to make sure I do not upset Alfie here," he ended, lamely. He was, though, a man of his word, for he did have just the single glass of whisky. The trouble was, though, that Alfie emptied almost two thirds of the bottle into a brace of large wine glasses, filling them almost to the brim. Will remembered his first sip of the magnificent brew (followed by a contented sigh and the comment – "Lovely; like mothers' milk,") and was to remember little further of the day, including the journey home. This service had been provided by Angela Turner, who had fulfilled the eternal role of the habitual non-drinker and delivered Will and Stella back to their abode, doing so with the same courteous efficiency with which she had collected them that morning and taken them to both church and reception. She then drove the mile or so to their own house, her inebriated husband, virtually asleep, beside her in the front of the car.

There might well have been occasions in Will's fifty, or so, years on this earth, when he had felt worse than he did this sunny June morning, but he could not remember any. He lay in his bed trying to summon the willpower – and strength – to rise when suddenly his befuddled brain was lanced by a shrill, insistent order – "Will, get out of bed. I called you more than half an hour ago, yet you're still there. If you don't get a real move on you'll be late. In fact, I fancy you'll be late now whatever you do."

Stella – who invariably stopped drinking whilst still in full command of her faculties – was feeling as fresh as a rose, and had no sympathy for a husband who had important commitments that day, yet had continued, against her advice, to drink an absurd amount of whisky; truly a self-inflicted wound. Her normally easy going, tolerant demeanour was submerged beneath the anger she felt towards the man who, at times, seemed incapable of exerting any self-discipline. During the next twenty minutes or so, that man somehow managed to wash, shave (partially) and dress, before stumbling down the stairs to the kitchen.

"You've no time for breakfast," said Stella tersely. "You had better go immediately – you're very late already."

"I'd kill for a coffee," he muttered.

"You don't have time, Will – off you go. Don't you realise, it's almost a quarter to ten."

He nodded, appreciating the strength of her argument, went out the back door, trudged in leaden fashion to the garage, opened the up-and-over door – then stopped in his tracks, as a realisation washed over him, a simple but vital one; there was no way that he was fit to drive that car, or any other, at that moment. For the bright blue of his Vauxhall Fiesta seemed to dance before his eyes, the car itself apparently swaying from side to side. He stood there for a few seconds, then turned and walked back to the kitchen. He opened the back door, saw Stella glance his way in surprise, and said wearily, "There's no way I'm in any fit state to drive, maid. Perhaps you'd phone them and tell them I'll not be in this morning – tell them I'm ill."

"But you're not ill, Will," retorted his spouse, fiercely. "You're hungover – which is a very different thing. You cannot let them down, not at this late hour – it would be most unfair." She removed the apron she was wearing, threw it down onto a worktop, and moved towards the door. "Come on," she snapped. "Lock the door behind you – I'll drive you there. It'll only take a few minutes. You can walk back when you've finished – it'll help you clear your head. I don't know how I didn't think just now about the fact you're clearly in no fit state to drive; I should have. If the police breathalysed you now the contraption would explode, you've so much alcohol within you. You should be ashamed of yourself, Will – you really should."

Stella in this mood (very rare, it had to be said) was not a woman to argue with, so her suffering husband did as he was bid.

It was five minutes later he alighted in the large square of the old town, waved goodbye to his wife as he did so, then scurried off towards the old building some fifty yards away. He glanced at his watch as he entered a side door of the early Victorian structure – three minutes to ten; he had never been so late in all the fifteen odd years he had been involved. In fact, more often than not he would be the first to arrive, rarely failing to get there later than half-past nine. As fast as his rubbery legs, aching head and churning stomach would allow, he climbed the steep, spiral granite stairway until it terminated at an ancient door. Noisily, he lifted the latch and entered the large, beamed room beyond. A woman and a man, standing close to a similar door on the far side of the room, were gazing in his direction.

"Will – you're here," cried Janet Holman (who was in the chair that day), relief sounding in her voice. "We had given you up – I mean you're usually the first to arrive."

"I'm so sorry Janet – Mike," he stuttered. "I've never been so late before – a bit under the weather to tell you the truth. Stella feels I should be in bed but I said to her that I couldn't let you down." To his shame, the blatant lies were spoken with heroic conviction.

"You certainly look rough, Will," opined Mike Travis. "It's above and beyond duty you turning out at all."

"No – no – no; I couldn't let you down – that's not my way," said he, piously. "It's probably just a stomach upset – something I ate, no doubt."

"Well, you're here – that's the main thing," said Janet in businesslike fashion. She glanced at her watch and noted the hands were indicating a minute to ten. "Not a great amount on this morning. An assault, a couple of speedings, one no insurance – and the Carter brothers are going to plead 'not guilty' to poaching salmon out of the Tavy."

"As they always do," muttered Mike.

"Oh, and we've got an excess alcohol," Janet added. "Name of Adam Barlow. I don't know who he is – he's not local as far as I am aware."

"He drank too much at a wedding reception yesterday. Lizzie, Ray Jordan's maid – it was her wedding apparently. He was done driving away from the hotel," explained Travis.

"Drink again," snapped the teetotal Janet, severely. "Criminal irresponsibility – that's what it is. I've no patience with it. Three times over the limit, he was – three times." Such behaviour, clearly, had shocked her.

Will Black nodded his agreement with all the enthusiasm his throbbing head would allow. "Quite so, Janet; shocking it is – absolutely shocking. Some people, at times, seem to have no sense of right or wrong. To be honest, I cannot understand anybody drinking that much to start with, let alone driving afterwards." With that, he followed his magisterial colleagues into court to bestow judgement and justice upon their peers, aware that even his dormant conscience would probably be awakened by the utterance of such blatant hypocritical nonsense – someday.

XVII

If Only

Doctor Jack Watson, cradling a glass of single malt in his hands, sat gazing somewhat forlornly at the flickering flames, crackling away in the large open fireplace. Despite the presence in the house of gas central heating, he loved open fires and duly lit one every day through the winter months. His expression gave evidence of the dismal, worrying thoughts which dominated his mind. This was a time when, as so often in life, he could reasonably ponder the syndrome known as 'If only'; indeed, there were several of them. If only the ground that day had been soft; the reality, though, was that the 'Point-to-Point' had only gone ahead because in the view of the stewards, following a very late inspection, the turf had thawed out sufficiently – just – to allow the event to start. If only the mist which rolled down off Dartmoor had not been sufficiently thick to prevent the air ambulance flying to the rescue. If only the nearby Tavistock ambulances had not been busy answering other emergency calls. If only the ambulance despatched from Derriford Hospital, Plymouth, had not been caught up in traffic jams thus causing a delay of almost an hour and a half before it arrived. If only the bottle of Scotch they had placed beside him in the hospitality tent had not been nearly full and, most crucial of all, if only the accident had happened during the first race, when just a smidgen of the 'Scottish wine' had passed his lips, rather than the last when virtually the entire bottle had been tipped down his throat.

He drained his glass, poured himself another liberal portion from the bottle on the low table at his elbow and gazed again into the fire. He shook his head sadly – if only his Helen, the love of his life, was still here to listen to his troubles and, usually, to minimise them as she had so often been able to do in the past. She, though, was dead these five years – a heart attack had taken her well before her time. There were his children, of course, Harry and Melanie, with whom he had an excellent relationship – a deep, loving friendship – and his four grandchildren. They, though, in pursuit of career and prospects, had many years before done that which so many Devonians had over the decades – moved north in search of good work and success, living in London and Reading respectively. Thus, whilst they were in touch on a regular basis, he only actually saw them half a dozen times a year – if that.

He emptied the glass, tipped in another generous measure, then leant back in his chair and shook his head in a mixture of frustration and perhaps even despair; for he knew very well that there was another issue regarding his downfall which needed to be added to the list, one which, if it had come to pass, would have made all the others irrelevant – if only he had possessed sufficient self control that afternoon to have imbibed only very modestly, if at all. It was far too late now, though – the damage had been done and before this cold evening had passed he would surely pay a high and humiliating price for his love, increasingly so, of malt whisky.

To think he had been connected to the local 'Point-to-Point' for virtually his entire lifetime. He remembered as a very small boy being introduced to such events by his father, Andrew Watson, also a doctor, and for decades the official medical presence at these events – and many other local sporting occasions, also. His son rapidly developed a love of horses and racing and when a little older, Jack, being of a slightish build, had often ridden in races in the four annual events (to some success) right up until the age of eighteen when he went off to Medical School in Bristol.

After qualifying, then doing his two years statutory National Service, he returned to West Devon and joined his father in the practice, taking it over when Andrew retired; and upon that good man's death, just three years later, he took upon himself the duties the old doctor had performed, as medical man to these racing events held close to Dartmoor. That was over forty years back, and he had been Doctor to the Point-to-Points, plus many local gymkhanas, ever since, remaining so even though he was now in his seventy-ninth year, and had retired from general practice some ten years previously. It was now, though, almost certainly about to end – and it upset him greatly to even think of it.

He poured again from the fast emptying bottle at his side, then leant back into his chair and again gazed into the fire. To be fair to all concerned, he could understand the furore over the accident and his lack of ability to be able to do anything to alleviate the lad's suffering and injuries.

Young Danny Mason, a slightly built lad, not yet seventeen, had been in the saddle of his uncle's mare – very well fancied with much money resting on her – when the chestnut, stumbling badly following a highish fence, had thrown her jockey with considerable force onto the only partially thawed turf. Those standing close by knew instantly that Danny had broken his leg – there was a staccato crack almost like a muffled pistol shot the instant he had hit the ground. Stewards and spectators had run to aid the poor lad the instant the race had passed on – and, immediately, the doctor was sent for. Unfortunately – indeed shamefully – he had been unable to respond as he was by then marooned legless in the hospitality tent, after consuming copious quantities of Glenfiddich.

So poor Danny Mason, after being stretchered off, was left to wait in agony until the arrival, belatedly, of the ambulance from Plymouth, no other local doctor being available.

Jack Watson afterwards pointed out that there was very little he could have done as the lad clearly needed hospital treatment; the race secretary, though, pointed out most forcibly that had not the former GP been so deep 'in his cups', he would at least have been able to inject some morphine, or whatever was appropriate, to alleviate the jockey's agony. This, of course, was absolute truth, and the elderly doctor was all too well aware of it – and felt guilt to a degree he had never before experienced.

All this had happened a month before, a period during which the only positive news had been that the jockey was making steady progress, his injury – a nasty fracture – not expected to cause any lasting effects. This, though, for the veteran former GP was of little comfort and in his shame he was imbibing ever more heavily. All his life he had enjoyed his liquor – especially whisky – but it was not until his Helen had died that it had gone on an upward spiral, which now was almost out of control. Now, assuredly, it would have cost him his post as Medical Officer to the Point-to-Points and Gymkhanas which the Committee organised throughout the year, something which brought him a modest retainer but which, more importantly, he had always greatly enjoyed – and ever more so since his retirement.

To him it was a social occasion rather than a duty, meeting up with folk he had known for years, some all of his life; in fact, Dougie Phillips, the long serving chairman had been a friend since they had met up in the first form at Tavistock Grammar School during the Second World War. It was Dougie to whom he tendered his resignation the day following the accident, seeing it as his only honourable course of action. His old comrade, however, had refused it saying that it was premature and that it was better to allow some time to pass and await the outcome of the next meeting of the Events Committee. This was taking place that very evening and the doctor was awaiting news of it, the chairman having promised to call in on him with such as soon as the meeting had ended.

His hand shaking a little, he poured another copious portion of liquor into his glass, and took a large swig from it. The news, he was certain, was going to be bad – the worst. Indeed, he wished increasingly that his initial resignation had been accepted, for had it been then at least he would have been seen to have done the honourable thing and walked away by his own volition. Now he would be sacked and his reputation sullied permanently – that's if it was not already.

Other clouds, also, were darkening the horizon. For Danny Mason's Parents – especially his mother, Jennie – had been vociferous in stating their intention to sue the Events Committee and, even worse, himself. The veteran medical man had not the slightest doubt, even though he had not sought any legal opinion, that the Masons had the strongest of cases. It could cost him thousands and, to him even worse, totally destroy a reputation and good name it had taken a lifetime to establish.

He had always been a kind, caring, conscientious man in both his private and professional lives. He had rendered to his patients – and such were the vast majority of the local community – a service, a dedication and an understanding which had never been particularly common in general practice, and which was now virtually extinct. He looked upon patients locally as friends who put their trust in him, and thus whom he would never knowingly let down. If it was in his power to cure, he did so, if not then he ensured the patient was seen by someone who possibly could, as soon as possible. When he had retired a decade earlier, the despondency – almost grief – within local folk was virtually akin to that which would have prevailed at news of his death. Instinctively they knew that an era had ended, and doctors the like of Jack Watson would not be seen again; and they were right, the new breed being practitioners of skill and professionalism, but to whom medicine was the vehicle conveying them towards a good living – not a calling.

Upon retirement he had been respected by all, loved by many – and it was that he valued more than anything material. Indeed, it had been a great source of comfort to him during the lonely years since Helen's untimely death. Now that would be destroyed; he would be remembered as a drunk – a man who put the imbibing of a free bottle of Scotch before his duty as a healer. Continuing to gaze into the fire, he shook his head wearily – and again raised the glass to his lips, swallowing the remainder of its contents.

His reverie was shattered by a loud banging on the front door; he put his glass down onto the low table by his side, then got slowly – and rather shakily – to his feet. That would be Dougie Phillips – for some reason, the Events Chairman always ignored the bell, preferring to batter the big front door with the heavy knocker. Watson opened it, exchanged perfunctory greetings with his old friend, invited him in, led him through to the sitting room, and watched his visitor make immediately for the fireplace, then extend his hands to within six inches of the flames.

"We met in the ante room of the Village Hall," rasped the chairman. "The back room of the Bull and Bear was booked unfortunately, that's where we usually meet as you know. So we couldn't get a drink, and the place was cold as charity – heating clearly on the blink. Wait till I see that Parish Clerk. It costs a silly amount to hire the damned place – and you almost freeze to death."

"Then you'll need a drink, Dougie," said the doctor, lethargically.

"Yes, I will, Jack, thank you. I see you've a bottle of Scotch there," said he, casting a searching glance at his host after noting the meagre amount which remained – little more than 10%. "You'd better make it a smallish one as I'm driving." The 'smallish' one requested manifested itself into a generous double, the doctor then pouring the remains into his own glass. He motioned his guest to sit down in the chair at the farside of the fireplace, then slumped down into his own. He glanced at Phillips – then eyed him keenly. "Well, Dougie, which is it to be – am I going to be sacked, or permitted to resign?"

The visitor sipped his whisky, nodded approvingly at its silky texture, then eyed his host. "Neither," he replied tersely.

"Neither? But it's got to be one or the other; there isn't a third option – is there?"

"Of course, there is, and the committee have decided to take it – they want you to remain as Medical Officer to the Point-to-Points and the Gymkhanas. A unanimous decision, Jack." The news bearer allowed his normally somewhat inanimate features to register a broad smile. "So nothing's going to change, old friend, and I cannot convey to you just how happy I am to be able to tell you that."

Several seconds passed before the doctor could fully assimilate the dramatic – and wonderful – news he had just been given. Finally, he managed to splutter, "But Doug – that's – that's marvellous"; he shook his head, then pulling a somewhat tired looking handkerchief from his pocket, mopped the tears which were running down his cheeks. "I don't understand though – what about the Masons? What about the law suits they threatened against myself and the committee? I've been lying awake at night worrying about that, Dougie, I can tell you."

"There'll be no law suits against anybody, boy – and no threat of them, either. There was this morning, mind you, but it all turned on a phone call I had at lunchtime. It was from Jennie Mason – and it was as welcome as it was unexpected. She started off by asking me if it was true that you were the Duty Doctor at the race when her son broke his leg. I was somewhat amazed at the question – I thought everybody knew you were always our medical man. But it seems that whilst she knew you always had been in the past, for some reason she had assumed you had given it up when you retired as a GP. Also neither she nor her husband, Vince, were there that afternoon – they would almost certainly have heard your name mentioned if they had been. All they heard subsequently was that the doctor was dr.... er, had been drinking and was not in a sufficiently good state to attend their son. When she heard it was you, though, Jack, she said – and I give her exact words, or thereabouts, 'As it was Doctor Watson, I cannot believe for once minute that he had been drinking – he wouldn't do that. He's a wonderful man. It was probably that he was feeling a touch poorly – he's elderly and it was a bitterly cold afternoon.' It transpires, also, that you delivered young Danny – I didn't know that."

Jack nodded. "And Jennie herself, for that matter; a snowy, bitter day in the winter of 1963 – I well remember it."

The chairman smiled. "I didn't know that. She did tell me though that you were very caring and kind when her mother had a cancer scare some years back, and managed to get her husband, Vince, booked in to see a specialist almost immediately when he had a hernia problem some fifteen years ago. So, all in all, you're a hero in the eyes of Jennie Mason – the whole family in fact. There's no way they'll ever think badly of you, Jack – and certainly they'll never sue you. And we, the committee, are also absolved in their eyes, thanks to our association with you."

The old doctor again had to resort to using his handkerchief – "I find I spend half my life crying these days, Dougie," said he, in somewhat exaggerated fashion. "I'm stunned – absolutely. These good people are so kind to me."

"I only cry on Saturday afternoons at Home Park," grunted his friend, a long suffering supporter of Plymouth Argyle. "And folk aren't being kind to you, Jack; you've served the people of this community for a lifetime with dedication, devotion and compassion. Some forget, of course, but most don't. You've given them your loyalty – now they're giving you theirs. Anyway, there it is. The Honorary Medical Officer for all our events remains your good self – and hopefully for years to come."

"Thank you, Dougie – and the committee, as well of course. This is the best news I've heard for a very long time and I make this promise here and now – there'll be no more drinking when I'm on duty."

"Too right there won't," rasped Phillips. "You'll be very, very sober. Still, having said that, we wouldn't expect you to sit about all afternoon without a drink to hand. There'll still be a bottle there for your use."

"A bottle?" There was a touch of incredulity in the doctor's voice.

Dougie grinned. "Yes, Jack, a bottle. Wine this time, though, but not of the Scottish kind – non alcoholic, I'm afraid."